W9-BPM-564

THE MARIO BALZIC NOVELS

BOTTOM LINER BLUES
SUNSHINE ENEMIES
JOEY'S CASE
UPON SOME MIDNIGHTS CLEAR
ALWAYS A BODY TO TRADE
THE MAN WHO LIKED SLOW TOMATOES
A FIX LIKE THIS
THE BLANK PAGE
THE MAN WHO LIKED TO LOOK AT HIMSELF
THE ROCKSBURG RAILROAD MURDERS

BOTTOM
LINER
BLUES

BOTTOM LINER BLUES

207226

Balzic had a lot of trouble with summer: the older he got the more he relished the weather, but the longer he stayed a cop the more he was irritated by the idea. Summer was when people with children took vacations, as though most people were still farmers, which as far as he was concerned was true only because the people who ran the schools still believed children were needed by their families to work the fields and harvest the crops. If the people who ran the schools didn't believe that, there wouldn't be any logical reason to close the schools for the summer.

As if Balzic needed other reasons to be irritated about summer, tourist promoters in Conemaugh County seemed more convinced with each passing day that the Pennsylvania Turnpike was backed up for miles with cars jammed full of people panting to find the two exits into the county and to know that farming was the largest single industry in the county, which it was if all you had in mind was the number of dollars circulated. But if you were thinking about the number of people who once had been employed in the industries that used to dominate the landscape, mining and making coke and steel, you were working on memories, and not very good ones. In the whole county, not one mill was making steel, and the only deep mines still open were the ones somebody had neglected to seal.

But tourist promoters and politicians didn't want to talk about closed-up factories and sealed-up mines; no, that was negative, that just made people feel bad. What they wanted to talk about was what was thriving, what was flourishing, what was big and getting bigger, what was making large dollars; that was positive, that made people feel good. And so they scavenged around in the United States Census Bureau data until they discovered that large dollars in Conemaugh County were being made on big farms getting bigger. It didn't matter that most of the farms in the county were owned by corporations formed by local doctors and lawyers and tax accountants, or by other corporations whose boards of directors met in Chicago or Kansas City or St. Louis. What mattered to the promoters and politicians was that farming was Conemaugh County's biggest industry—the Census Bureau had said so—and the people ought to be told about it because it was positive, it was something they could feel good about, and because once they were told, why you'd have to build a fence to keep them from wanting to rush right into the county to spend their money. Feeling positive and good about somebody else's commercial good fortune naturally made people want to leave their own homes and go to where this good fortune was happening, and to spend some of their own money just to see how positive it made you feel about spending your money in the same county where some people were making lots of money. This was as natural as the day follows the night.

2

If that kind of logic wasn't enough to set Balzic's teeth on edge, the next surest thing to do it was that these same promoters and politicians were making noises about forming ad hoc committees "to brainstorm the possibilities of building museums or theme parks to preserve the heritage of mining coal and making steel—to preserve their memory—"to get some of the tourist dollars that are going to Sea World and Disneyland"—that's what some tourist group proclaimed in the flyer that landed on Balzic's desk around the Fourth of July.

Politicians and promoters alike seemed to be in love with the water amusement park that had been built along the Monongahela River in Allegheny County very close to where U.S. Steel's Homestead Works once made steel. Balzic was sick of hearing about it. Twenty-some water slides had been built against the hillside overlooking the Mon River, every one of them demonstrating repeatedly that gravity was still a force in nature: if you got onto one of those slides at the top, very soon you would be at the bottom. You would feel cooler. You would feel good. You might even feel positive. The only thing Balzic could feel positive about the water slides was that nobody who was cooling off going down them had ever broken a sweat in the Homestead Works of U.S. Steel.

In one of Balzic's blacker moods, he thought that the surest way you know something's dead was when somebody started talking about preserving its memory. There wasn't a coffin around that could match a museum for saying something was croaked. Coal-mining museums and steel-making museums to match Sea World or Disneyland or a bunch of water slides? Given a choice on a hot day between being splashed by Shamu the killer whale or zipping down long wet slides into cool water, what family wouldn't positively choose to take their kids to look at a building full of miner's lamps and lunch buckets? Balzic had gotten roped into going to a railroad museum in Johnstown once. From his point of view, the pathology lab in Conemaugh General Hospital was cheer-

3

ier. Wandering around in a dingy building in bad light, looking at rails and spikes and gandy dancers' hammers was about as much fun for him as looking at a corpse with no ID.

What really irritated Balzic about summer was that most of the young male officers in the Rocksburg Police Department had children and those children wanted to go down water slides as much as any other children which forced Balzic to spend an inordinate amount of time trying to find enough bodies to patrol the town. Every time he did that he was reminded of how many people he was supposed to have and how many people he actually did have. He did not feel good. He did not feel positive. It wasn't as though Rocksburg was like some of the other towns around western Pennsylvania, like Aliquippa and Ambridge and Braddock and Clairton and Wilkinsburg and Rankin, cities so busted out they had earned the official title "Financially Distressed," which meant they had pretty much been taken over by the state of Pennsylvania. A Financially Distressed city didn't have enough of a tax base to pay for any of the services people normally associated with civilization: no police department, no street department, no sanitation department, no health department, and their volunteer fire and ambulance departments were hanging on with fewer and fewer members and aging, cannibalized equipment. What was truly distressing in a Financially Distressed city was that commercial life was as tantalizingly close as the pictures on a TV set but as far away as the boarded-up storefronts on the main street. If you looked at TV, you knew it was out there somewhere, but if you walked downtown, you knew it was somewhere else.

Rocksburg had not sunk that low yet, but every time Balzic had to scramble to find enough bodies to put in the cruisers, he had to ask himself why he was still making the effort. He frequently found himself staring out his office window at the parking lot beside city hall, jingling change in his pocket and fretting that on any given day in June, July, and August, it would be an accident if he could find two officers to put in the five black-and-whites sitting there. Some days he considered himself lucky if one of the black-and-whites was on the streets for more than eight hours.

To make matters worse, Councilman Egidio Figulli, the chairman of the safety committee, wanted his daughter to begin her career in law enforcement by taking over the job of School Crossing Guard Mary Haremchek, who had to quit because her husband's employer had moved his replacement window factory to a right-to-work state in the South.

Balzic had only a few things against Councilman Figulli, one of them being that he was always in a hurry because he was one of those skinny runts who could eat all day and whose metabolism was such that even when he was sitting still he looked like he was doing the tarantella. That wasn't exactly what Balzic had against Figulli. It was that Figulli thought he had personally had something to do with his metabolism, as though he'd ordered it from God, and that was why he was so energetic and everybody else was so slow to get things done for the city. It wasn't that Figulli didn't get things done for the city. The city's finances being what they were, there wasn't a whole lot anybody—including Figulli—could do for the city, but Figulli seemed to be doing so much more because if he did one thing, his metabolism allowed him to light on the Sons of Italy, the Ukrainian Club, the Moose, the VFW, and one of the fire department social clubs all in the same night to tell everybody about it, after he'd called the *Rocksburg Gazette* and shredded some reporter's ear for fifteen minutes. Even that in itself didn't bother Balzic.

What bothered him was that Figulli took something not of his own doing or making, his metabolism, and turned it into an attribute, a quality of his character, and made himself obnoxious by talking constantly about how slow and stupid everybody else was who moved at more or less normal speed. It wasn't any different in Balzic's mind than any other bigot's attitude: "I'm a white man (and energetic) because God wanted me to be a white man (and a go-getter) and I made sure of that because while I was in my daddy's scrotum, I ordered myself from his menu—and from my momma's eggs too, of course. I coulda picked anything to be—fat, stupid, black, spic, faggoty, even a woman for cryin' out loud, you name it—but God wanted me to be a white man (and a real hustler) with brains in America, and what kind of guy would I be to argue with God?" Not that Councilman Figulli could even conceive of that kind of logic; he just never ceased trying to collect political debts because of his quick walk and quicker talk.

Balzic was cruising the streets himself, thanking somebody for knowing how to make air-conditioning work in automobiles. It was July and it was one of the hottest Julys in the history of Rocksburg—at least that's what the *Rocksburg Gazette* kept announcing on its weather page. Every day, the paper said, the city was tying or setting high temperature records, and that had been going on since the Fourth of July, which itself tied a record at ninety-six. Since then it seemed every day was in the nineties and every night was only ten degrees cooler. To make everything worse for everybody, farmers included, it also hadn't rained since the second week of June. The governor had named a drought task force, and county and city pols and bureaucrats were going around saying they ought to do the same thing. All of which made Balzic wonder, if the pols and bureaucrats in Harrisburg couldn't make it rain by forming a task force, why the local bureaucrats thought they could, since neither bunch seemed to have had a whole lot of success with it before.

Balzic was creeping through the alleys, barely going ten miles an hour, when he got the call from 911, the county dispatching service.

"Chief, Troop A state police got a major traffic problem on 119 south, they've got every unit they can spare out there and they wanna know if somebody can go talk to this woman in Kennedy Township. You available?"

"What's her problem?"

"I'm not real clear about that, but it's not any big deal, that's for sure. Troop A said she wants somebody to explain a PFA to her I think, or something. They told her she oughta call a lawyer but she said she wanted to talk to a police officer 'cause she already did talk to a lawyer and didn't get any satisfaction, so if you could do that, Troop A said they'd owe you one."

Balzic snorted. "Troop A owes me about a thousand. I can't cover Rocksburg with the people I got, I'm out here drivin' around myself for crissake. State pays them to cover the townships, where the hell they think I'm supposed to get gas money to drive around out there, huh? What kind of problem they got on 119?"

"Uh, they got a rig full of cows flipped across both lanes and they got injuries and entrapment, plus some of the cows got loose and they had to shoot one and some lady freaked out on 'em, I guess. It's not real clear, except it's one of those things I'm glad I'm in here and they're out there."

"Must be some fun. So, uh, where's this lady live wants to talk to a cop?"

"Uh, that's a Missus Valery or Valeriana Cochoran or Cork-orian, Troop A was not real sure about anything except the address, which was off the main street, uh, in the old Edna Number Three, off the Rocksburg Road behind the mall—"

"I know where it is, the road I mean. Hell, I didn't know anybody lived back in there. I thought that was abandoned years ago. Hell, decades."

"Well, she's maybe a squatter or something. Anyway, apparently that's where she is. They didn't give me any other address, so I guess you're gonna have to go back there and holler or something."

"She lives there and she wants to talk to a cop because she didn't get any satisfaction from a lawyer?"

7

"That's what Troop A said. Uh, gotta go, Chief, thanks a lot."

Six minutes later Balzic pulled off Rocksburg Road onto what had once been the back road into the mining town surrounding the portal to the deep mine known as Edna No. 3 when it had been working. Not much of the macadam was left, and the potholes, gullies, and ruts were such that Balzic had to slow to between five and ten miles an hour, and even at that speed he was being jostled against the seatbelt and the back of the seat and the door.

He drove about a quarter of a mile over these bumps and through a long stand of sumac, locust, crabapple, and brush so crowded against the road on both sides that at times he could barely see more than twenty yards ahead. Finally, he broke into a clearing where the main street of Edna No. 3 started. It ran ahead for perhaps another hundred yards or so, houses on both sides, if it was possible to think of these deserted messes as houses. Some of their roofs had already developed a swayback, windows were shattered, doors hung open, ragweed and Queen Anne's lace were growing through the porches. There had been two other streets that ran parallel to the main street and two streets that crossed those three, making at one time twelve blocks of houses. Most of those had been abandoned in the late 1950s after three events, related or not, depending on who was talking. First there had been an explosion and fire in the mine. Ten miners were killed immediately, a half-dozen or so died later from burns, and many others were injured too badly to ever work again and so became wards of the state. When the mine reopened, the miners insisted that nothing had changed, that the poor ventilation which had caused the buildup of methane that exploded was the same as before. They struck the mine, and struck it so violently that even the United Mine Workers field reps had trouble supporting it in private to the police. The Rocksburg PD was called by the state police half-a-dozen

8

times to assist them, and it caused Balzic no end of problems trying to justify his behavior and the behavior of his fellow officers to bring the appearance of order among all those men and women who seemed perfectly willing to die by gunfire to keep from dying under ground. Then, when it looked like some sense was being made by federal and state mediators, somebody—it was never discovered who—dynamited the portal and the tipple and set fire to the company store. The mine owners blamed the union, the union blamed the owners, and the only conclusion police and fire investigators could come to was that whoever did it knew what they were doing because every piece of evidence they found led nowhere. The company store and three whole blocks of houses burned to the ground. The mine never reopened, and the miners left in the night, hours ahead of bill collectors and sheriff's deputies if they were lucky, in the backs of school buses rented by the sheriff's office if they were not.

Every word that came to Balzic's mind when he thought about Edna No. 3 in the late fifties, with the exception of remorse and regret, seemed to start with the letter *d:* disheartening, discouraging, disgusting, depressing, dismal. It was not anybody's shining hour, not the miners, not the mine owners, not the police, not the courts. They'd all had an equal hand in the misery, as far as Balzic was concerned. It was one of his worst times as a police officer, worse than his disagreement with his mother about the rightness of his doing a job most miners despised in principle as well as in the particular. Balzic's father was buried in a mine, and Balzic had had to talk long and hard to convince his mother that being a cop was not an insult to everything his father had stood for, worked for, lived for.

Driving down the main street of Edna No. 3 was unsettling and unnerving because it brought it all back, all those things that had never gotten settled, never come to any better conclusion than sullen, grudging agreement not to bring them up anymore. His mother's death had only made it worse. Sometimes he thought he spent half his waking hours trying to find ways to explain things to people who were no longer alive. More likely he was trying to explain them to himself. Either way, he wasn't making much progress.

With the cruiser bumping and lurching along the decaying main street of Edna No. 3 and his mind filled with the chatter and clash of ugly memories and unresolved disputes, he was trying hard to stay alert. Despite his trying, he still almost drove right into the woman in grubby T-shirt, shorts, and sneakers standing in the middle of the street with her hands folded tightly across her chest, a child sucking all the fingers of its left hand and hanging behind her left leg with its right arm wrapped around her knee.

He wasn't going fast enough to skid when he hit the brakes, but he was startled enough about not seeing her and whether she was going to move that he tromped on the brake pedal and started the cruiser swaying back and forth after it stopped. He made a mental note to see if he could squeeze some money out of council to get new shock absorbers for the front end. The next thing that came to his mind was where she'd called from; there wasn't a wire he could see that was connected to more than two poles, and none of those went to a house in his sight.

He shut the engine off, undid the seatbelt, and got out slowly. "You call for a police officer?"

"Yeah. Are you one?"

Balzic nodded and produced his ID case and held it out at arm's length as he walked slowly toward her. The child shuffled its feet to get closer to her leg.

"Uh, if you wanna take this ID and make a call to check it out with 911 or the state police or anybody, feel free."

She took the ID case and looked at it for a moment and looked at his face a couple of times. "Nah, that's okay. Ain't no phone anyhow."

"How'd you call the state police?"

"Up the mall there," she said, nodding in the direction behind Balzic, handing his ID case back to him.

"So, Missus . . . uh, what's your last name again?"

"Again?" She gave a twisted, smirky smile. "I ain't said it even once yet."

"Well, ma'am, my name as you could see from my ID is Balzic. I'm chief of the Rocksburg PD, which you could also see. So tell me your name for the first time."

"Well, I ain't sure I want to jus' right now."

"Is it Corchoran? Are you Valery Corchoran?"

"Who tol' you that?"

"Dispatcher from 911."

She rocked from one foot to the other and made some sound, no words, just noises that Balzic couldn't decipher.

"You're not from around here, are you? I mean, you don't sound from here at all."

"No? Jus' how do I sound?"

"You sound West Virginia or Virginia or Maryland or where all those states come together, somethin' like that."

"Is that important? I mean, y'all goin' tell me what I wanna know only if I tell you my last name and where I used to be from?" She stopped rocking and shifted weight to her other foot, and the child shuffled around to that leg, switching hands in his mouth, as well as arms from one leg to the other. Balzic was thinking of the masculine pronoun as he observed the child, but he wouldn't have bet much on which gender it was.

"I always like to know who I'm talkin' to, in case I have to talk to 'em again, that's all. It helps when lawyers start askin' me where I got my information from."

She said nothing, leaning her head first to the right, then to the left, and also tapping the toe of the foot she was not leaning on. "Lawyers," she said.

"Uh, lawyers what?"

11

"Nothin'. Jus' thinkin' out loud."

"Uh, ma'am, can we, I mean, is it all right with you if we find some shade? I mean, the sweat is just rollin' off me. We can sit in my car, it's air-conditioned, you know?"

"Y'all can get in your car if you want, but I'm stayin' right here."

Balzic turned around and looked at the street behind him. "You expectin' somebody, ma'am?"

She said nothing. She screwed up her mouth and squinted as though trying to decide how to proceed. After a long moment she said, "You married?"

"Yes."

Another long moment. "You ever fight with your wife?"

"Fight how? Physically? Or just argue?"

"Both."

"Well, I've never touched her in anger and she's never touched me that way, but we've had some hellacious arguments over the years, yeah. Then too, we've been in some pretty long sulks, uh, I have anyway, and I'm sure there've been times when she wanted to belt me and I know there were some times I wanted to belt her, but we never did."

She mulled that over. Balzic took off his coat and walked back to the cruiser and opened the door and put one foot inside. "Really, I'm gonna have to get in the car here, ma'am. I'm too old to be standin' out here in this sun without a hat."

She shrugged. "Fine with me," she said.

"You're welcome to sit in the back if you'd feel more comfortable back there."

"Fine right where I am."

Balzic tossed his suit coat across the seat ahead of him and flopped inside, closing his eyes as he directed the cold rush from the air-conditioning vents onto his face and chest. When he opened his eyes she was standing right where she'd been before. She'd made no attempt to get closer to the cruiser, so Balzic put it in gear and eased it forward alongside her. He hated to roll down the window to allow any of the wonderful coolness to escape, but he could see that was the only way she was going to carry on this conversation, so he rolled it down and looked up at her. He didn't have to look very high; she was only a couple of inches over five feet. Couldn't have weighed much more than a hundred pounds. He studied her face, looking for bruises or cuts, but saw none. Her arms were bare and there were no bruises there either. No needle tracks either, but of course that meant nothing. Hypes found all kinds of strange places to put needles, under their tongues, at the tops of their thighs under the cheeks of the butts. The child was practically hidden from his view so he couldn't see anything there.

"You have any kids?" she said after nearly a minute had passed.

"Yes. Two daughters. Both grown, both out on their own. Both still not married, workin', havin' a good time I guess. I don't see 'em too much anymore, so I figure they must be havin' a good time."

"You ever fight with them?"

"Did I ever hit them? Is that what you're askin' me?"

She nodded.

"No. It wasn't because I was anything special, I mean it sure wasn't because I was any model of patience and understanding. Mostly I think it was because they never pushed me that way. But if I was to tell you the truth, I guess I would say it's 'cause mostly my wife and my mother raised them, so you'd have to ask them, not my mother, she's dead, but my wife, uh, you'd have to ask her if she ever had to hit 'em. But I seriously doubt that she did. And again, it wasn't 'cause we were anything special, it's, uh, the kids just weren't like that. They were really good kids. I mean, even when they were in the terrible twos they weren't really very terrible." Balzic wondered how long he was going to have to keep this up, taking her test to find out whether he was the cop she wanted to talk to.

13

Since she seemed content for the moment to stare at him as he talked, he figured he might as well keep talking. "I mean, uh, even when they were goin' through puberty, you know, their hormones just firin' away, they never got real crazy. I mean, I always felt they were pushin' us, testin' us to see how far they could go, but, hell, not even when they started to develop, you know, when they started into adolescence, they never gave us a whole lot of trouble. 'Course, on the other hand, maybe they were real good actors, you know? Maybe they just knew how to con us, I don't know. And then too, I'm sure if my wife was sittin' here, she'd have a whole different story to tell, you know what I mean? Uh, you sure you don't wanna get in here?"

"Uh-uh," she said. "I'm fine."

Well, the hell with this, Balzic thought, I'll be here all day at this rate. "So the dispatcher said you said you'd already talked to a lawyer and you didn't get any satisfaction, is that right? Said you wanted to know about a PFA."

She pursed her lips and looked off for a moment. "Um, what I'm doin' here is, uh, lemme start over. What did you say—PF what? What's that?"

"PFA you mean? Protection From Abuse order? You don't know about that?"

She shook her head no. "Did this ol' dispatcher say that's what I wanted to know about? Like I was lookin' for protection or somethin'?"

"So you're not, is that it?"

"Shoot, I don't need no protection. Don't know where he got that idea."

"Uh-huh. Well. Never mind about that," Balzic said. "Just tell me what's goin' on, okay?"

"Well, what's goin' on is, umm, or what I think I'm doin' here is, lessee, how do I wanna put this? Okay. Okay, what I am doin' here is, uh, I'm tryin' to prevent a crime here is what I'm doin' and I gotta be real careful how I do it 'cause

14

if I don't there's gonna be another crime and the victim is gonna be me, does that make any sense to you?"

"Yeah. Yeah, it does. So what kind of crime are you tryin' to prevent?"

"Well, see, I gotta tell you about my ol' man first. Okay?"

"Okay with me."

"No, that's not what I mean by *okay*. What I mean by *okay* is, is it okay, I mean can I trust you not to go jumpin' his body 'cause of what I tell you, that's what I mean by *okay*, okay? Will y'all just sorta listen first, I mean, and not go off and jump his body or somethin', that's what I mean by *okay*."

"Well, two things. First, you haven't told me anything yet, and second, I never make promises about things I don't know. I mean if you tell me this guy is gettin' ready to shoot me, I mean, that's not okay with me, understand? If you tell me he's got a rap sheet half a yard long, I'll just file that information away. I deal with people with rap sheets all the time. You tell me he habitually carries a folding knife, that's one thing. You tell me he's drivin' around with a loaded sawed-off shotgun under the front seat, that's somethin' else again. You tell me he has a short fuse, that's one thing. You tell me he has two convictions for aggravated assault, that's another thing. So whatta you wanna tell me?"

"Well . . . lemme see, the first thing I wanna say is, if he finds out I've been talkin' to you, it'll all depend how soon he wants to call the ambulance how fast I get to the emergency room. 'Cause my ol' man don't like nobody talks to cops. He'd sooner kiss a hooker with AIDS than deal with a snitch, and far as he's concerned, anybody talks to a cop is a snitch, don't matter if you're jus' askin' directions, so that's why we're here, if y'all was curious or anything."

"Does that mean you don't live here?"

"Live here? My gawd, you think anybody lives here? I mean, an-y-bod-y? Sweet Jesus, I know times is tough, but gawd, y'all really think people live here?"

"So what you're sayin' is, you don't, is that it?"

"Ho lordy, no. Double no. Y'all think I would have a cop drive up to where I live and be out in the street talkin' to him like we're doin' here after what I jus' tol' you about my ol' man? Y'all sure you're the chief?"

"Uh, you don't have to be real smart to get to be chief. Really what it takes more than anything is, uh, about all it takes is the brains of a bulldog. You get a good bite and you hang on long enough, pretty soon they give you your own office." Balzic squirmed around to get a handkerchief out of his suit coat and wiped his forehead and upper lip. "So this crime you wanna prevent, you wanna tell me about that?"

She looked away for just a second, then looked down at the child still sucking its fingers by the leg opposite from Balzic. "My ol' man," she said slowly, "my ol' man . . ." She stopped to chew the inside of her lower lip. She also unfolded her arms and reached down and smoothed the child's hair. "My ol' man has another ol' lady and she has a new ol' man and they got my ol' man's other three kids . . . and, um, my ol' man has been thinkin' for a long time now somethin' funny's been goin' on between this new ol' man and the kids, and if somebody don't, um, if somebody don't check it out? You know? If somebody don't check it out, my ol' man's goin' do somethin' and I ain't smart enough to predict what that somethin's goin' be, y'all understand what I'm tryin' to say?"

"You're not smart enough to predict what your old man's gonna do? But you're standing here tellin' me about it? How'd you get here?"

"What difference does that make?"

"You didn't ride in here, right? You walked? From where? The mall? That child doesn't have any shoes on. You carry him?"

"Him's a her. She walked some. I didn't have to carry her much, did I, Coo?" She rubbed the child's head again. Coo said nothing, her eyes unblinkingly fixed on Balzic.

16

"You called from the mall, you walked down here from up there, that's at least a mile, in this heat, with your child, and what're you tryin' to tell me—your old man is gettin' ready to arm-wrestle this guy? C'mon, cut it out. It's too hot, let's just get to it. What's the problem? This guy abusin' the kids, huh? Physical? Sexual? Both?"

"See, the thing is, we ain't got no proof, I mean, we really don't. I mean the kids don't say nothin' about it. It's jus' they're different than they used to be, but that ain't enough reason for me to think somethin's goin' on, I mean I think somethin's goin' on but I don't necessarily think it's the same thing goin' on that my ol' man thinks is goin' on, but, um, my ol' man don't see it that way. And he ain't the greatest guy in the world, I mean he's got his faults and he sure wouldn't be over to dinner at your house, but the man purely loves his kids and he thinks somethin's up 'cause of the way they're actin' when he's around 'em, and I can't make no sense with him 'bout it no more. And I don't want him goin' inside again. He says that's real selfish on my part, but, I mean, he's it for me. For this'n too. I mean, without him, it's back to West-by-God-Virginia for us, and sweet Jesus I can't do that again. I mean, I jus' can't. I can-not."

"Well, I'm hearin' what you're sayin', but have either of you called the Children's Bureau? Do you know what the Children's Bureau is?"

"I done called them suckers already! Three weeks ago. They're jus' a bunch of politicians' daughters if you ask me. They go up to people and ask 'em really smart questions, like, 'Have you ever abused your child?' They was askin' me that! I'm the one goes in there to talk 'bout somebody else and they take one look at me and all of a sudden they think it's me blowin' on Boomah. Like what in sweet Jesus' name they think them real perverts goin' say when they ask 'em that? 'Yeah, sure, we screw our kids once every day and twice on holidays? We got a box fulla videotapes, you wanna see

17

'em?' For-git them. They ain't no help at'all. 'Sides, Boomah wants to do somethin' yesterday! I been holdin' him down for three weeks now, I can't hold him down no more, and if you let on I done tol' you this, shoot. . . . Shoot me, 'cause I'll be a busted-leg pony."

"Well, listen, ma'am, I don't know as many of the caseworkers as I used to, but the people who do the legwork in the Children's Bureau, believe me, I don't know one of them who got the job because of who their parents were. That's not really the kind of job you'd pick for your kid. I can see from your face you don't believe me, but the fact is they're all overworked and underpaid and it's an ugly job 'cause if they make a mistake about not removin' a kid from some pervert, believe me, the whole world's gonna know about it after the coroner's hearing. I've been through a lot more of those things than I want to think about, and when that happens, the kid is not the only victim."

"Well, I guess I talked to the exception to the rule."

"Maybe you did, I don't know. I'm sure they've got some lemons workin' there too. You know a place where everybody knows what they're doin'? And where everybody does it—all the time? Where do you work?"

"Me? You mean a job work, like that?"

Balzic nodded.

"Shoot. Boomah don't let me work. Not at any ol' job, like flippin' Big Macs you mean? No sir. I watch this'n and I try to keep my ol' man. . . . Ain't we gettin' off the subject here?"

"This Boomah, is it? Your old man? Does he have a job? Or is he strictly cash only?"

"Boomah works. He does."

"Where? You want me to go talk to him or what? I can't talk to him if I can't find him."

"You talk to Boomah?" She pointed her index finger at Balzic and laughed in spite of herself. Her index finger curled up. "Not hardly. Y'all sure you're the chief?"

18

"Aghhh, listen, I really have other things to do. You want me to help you, you have to help me. I've already told you I'm not the smartest guy in the world, but if you want me to do something, you have to let me in on it. I'm not a mind-reader. Exactly why do you want to talk to a cop? Any cop, not just me. That's what you asked for, correct? You wanted to talk to a cop. Okay, why?"

She thought that over for what was barely a minute, but in the heat and silence it seemed much longer. The sound of traffic coming and going to the mall was hardly distinguishable from the slight rustling of the grass and weeds and the few trees up and down the street. Mostly the trees and weeds were not moving.

Balzic lost his patience. He put the car in gear and was about to release the footbrake when she focused on him suddenly and said sharply, "Hey. Where y'all goin'? I'm still thinkin'!"

He put the gearshift in park again and waited.

"Shoot. I don't know why, okay? I mean, I know why but I don't know why. I mean what am I gonna do? Boomah's goin' kill that sucker. And Boomah . . . I love him like nobody ever loved anybody, but, gawd, it ain't like Boomah's got a plan or nothin'. I mean he's jus' goin' go over there and beat that man to death with a brick or a ball bat, he won't even know what till he gets there. . . . And you know what's goin' happen . . . doncha?"

"If that's what happens, yes, I know what's gonna happen."

"Right. And I know it too. Y'alls goin' catch Boomah in about two days, 'bout the third time we run outta gas. I mean, what am I gonna do? Boomah don't understand that if he goes and does that he ain't never goin' see his kids again. Not those three. Never never never never. And I can't make him understand that. I tol' him, I said, 'You do that and them three kids is goin' wind up in three different foster homes and you know what they're like.' I mean I thought that was

19

what would get to him, 'cause that's how he was raised up, in foster homes all over the place and you know he got punked in some of 'em, I mean he tol' me he did, but you think that would get to him when I said it? Noooo. All he sees—all he wants to see is that man's brains on the floor or the street or someplace. Gawd, what am I gonna do? I don't even know how to cook. Boomah cooks. I can't even make cornbread out of a box."

"Well, ma'am, I'll say again what I've said already. I can't do a thing for either one of you if you don't tell me where I can find Boomer. That's what you're sayin', isn't it? Boomer. B-o-o-m-e-r? Sounds like you're sayin' Boom-AH."

"That's jus' how I talk. It's the way you spelled it."

"Well if you don't wanna tell me where I can find him, then tell me where the other guy lives. Maybe I can do some good there. Maybe I can get the Children's Bureau to put him on top of their list." Balzic was lying through his teeth. It didn't work like this at all, but he wasn't going to get anything out of her by telling her how it worked. "It's been done before, and Lord knows, I've done it."

"Oh gawd, would you do that? Would y'all really go and do that? I mean if you could get somethin' on that sucker, gawd I'd . . . I don't know what I'd do, but I'd do somethin' right, I promise I would 'cause you don't know what a mess I'd be if I lost Boomah and I know what he's goin' go and do. Could you do it today? Now, like right away I mean?"

Balzic shrugged. "Just give me the name and address. I got nothin' else goin' on. I'll figure out something. After that, I'll see what I can see. What's the name?"

"Uh, it's Farley, you know like Harley bikes? Only with an *F.* Farley, and his last name is Gruenwald. G-r-u-e-n-w-a-l-d. And they live in that there Straford Acres, you know where you turn off Main Street when you go north outta town where it turns into 66? You know where I'm talkin' about? In that Straford Acres?"

20

"Stratford."

"Stratford Straford, I get mixed up sometimes. You really goin' do it? You really goin' do it now?"

Balzic nodded. "Unless something more important happens, yeah I'm gonna do it. You want a lift back to your car?"

"Huh? Oh no, that's okay. I don't mind walkin'. I like walkin'. Gives me a chance to talk to Coo here. I can't talk and drive at the same time. I wreck. You're really goin' do it? Honest?"

"I'm really goin' do it," Balzic said, hearing himself starting to talk like her. "I really would like to have your name, though. I mean, how am I gonna let you know what's happening?"

"Oh I'll call you, yes sir, I will. You can believe that. You won't have to find me."

Isn't she the sly one, Balzic thought. She's been over this road before, probably more than once. "Well, have it your way," he said. "So long."

"So long. Gawd I hope it works. Really I do."

"I'll do my best," he said, and put the cruiser in gear and turned around in what had been somebody's front yard years ago. He was starting to drive away when he stepped on the brakes and said aloud, "What the hell am I doin' here? Must be losin' my mind."

He backed the cruiser up until it was alongside her once again. "Listen. This is not the way it works. I'm not gonna go chasin' a name through the Children's Bureau 'cause your old man's got it in his head he wants to beat somebody up and you got it in your head you're not gonna give me your name. I don't know what the hell I was thinkin' about, but believe me, ma'am, it would take me days to figure this thing out goin' at it from that direction. And no way in hell am I gonna drive away from you without gettin' your name and address. That's just not gonna happen. Heat must be cookin' my brains or somethin'."

21

She looked at him, her mouth open, brushing wisps of hair away from her face. "Y'all mean you ain't gonna do it?"

"I'm not gonna do anything until you give me your full name and address and Boomer's full name and address and occupation and the address of his place of employment, that's what I'm tellin' you. How would you like it if somebody said something about you, accused you of something and just disappeared—"

"Y'all mean you ain't never done nothin' about somethin' when y'all got a phone call? What about all them TV ads say call this hotline or that hotline or some such and you don't have to give your name, what about that?"

"Those things scare the hell outta me, ma'am. 'Cause anybody got a beef with you, they can turn your life upside down in about half a minute. I don't know what I was thinkin' about when I started to drive away from you, I guess I been behind a desk too long, I don't know, but if one of my officers had come back in with a report like you've just given me and they didn't have your name? Hell, I would've chewed them a new behind. Might even have suspended 'em. Not now I wouldn't. Never mind that. So what's it gonna be, ma'am? You gonna give me your name and address or not? Boomer's full name? 'Cause without that, everything stops right here."

She bent over farther and held her hair away from her eyes and peered in at him. "You're crazy in the head, Mister Chief of Police, if y'all think I'm goin' give you Boomah's full name and where he works at. I may not be the smartest person ever lived, but I'm a long way from stupid. Boomah ain't never laid a hand or a fist on me, but I seen what he did to a snitch once and that was only over a couple rusted-up dirt bikes somebody stole. That ol' boy ain't walkin' right, he ain't talkin' right, he ain't breathin' right to this day. I love Boomah, but I ain't lookin' to wind up like that ol' boy snitched on him, nossir."

Balzic shrugged. "Well, then I guess it'll have to play out

the way you said. Remember? About the third time you run out of gas, Boomer can start gettin' his good-byes ready? Is that the way you want it?"

"Well hell no that's not the way I want it! That's what I'm tryin' not to happen. But I'm not goin' put myself in the middle of hell 'cause you want a name. I mean, this'n's mine. Whatta y'all think's goin' happen to her if Boomah does to me what he done to that snitch? I ain't got no family. My family put me out when I was fifteen. Y'all goin' take care of this little girl for me? Huh? While I spend 'bout six months in some hospital I ain't got the money to pay for?"

"I understand you got a problem, ma'am. What you gotta understand is I got a problem too. Just because you say somethin' about somebody, about somethin' might happen—I don't know you. Never seen you before. Don't know anything about you. How do I know you haven't stolen this child?"

"Huh? What? Stolen what?"

"You heard me. Stolen this child."

"You . . . you, y'all's crazy in the head. This chil' is mine."

"See how fast you get on the edge when I say somethin' bad about you?"

"Get on the edge? Well hell. What you said is crazier'n'hell."

"What you said is your old man's gettin' ready to kill some-body, but you won't identify anybody except the guy you say is the target." Balzic threw up his hands. "Your old man's gettin' ready to kill somebody, or so you say. How do I know you don't want to bury an ax in your old man's back and you think you can use me to do it? Or the same for this Farley guy? I mean, you could have all kinds of reasons for turnin' me loose on either one of them, and what do I have from you? Nothin'. Ma'am, what you're talkin' about, no matter how you look at it, is at the very least sendin' me off on a paper chase that would take me days, weeks maybe. And I just don't have the time for that. I'm tryin' to take you at your word, but if you don't give me some names, I just can't do it. It goes against everything I know about gettin' admissible evidence. I'm sorry, but there are rules about this kind of stuff and they don't make exceptions for me. Or you. If this is on the square, if you want my help, either you give me some names or I'm leavin'. Up to you, ma'am."

Her eyes were filling up and her lower lip was starting to quiver, but that didn't stop her from saying, "Well I got one thing to say to you, Mister Chief of Police. Fuck you and the car you're ridin' in, is all I got to say. C,mon, Coo." She reached down and swept up the child and placed it on her right hip.

Balzic shrugged and said he was sorry and he drove back out as he had come in, lurching and bumping along at ten miles an hour, glancing in the rearview mirror to see her staring after him and walking in that staggery way small women do when they've got a heavy child on their hip.

Well, Balzic thought, these goddamn family things, custody crap and abuse crap and sex crap and god knows what this is about and all the talking I did and I let her get away with one last name. I'm slipping, I really am. Too old for this crap by about ten years. Get the Children's Bureau to put them on the top of their list, is that what I said? One day I'm gonna pay for these lies. . . .

*   *   *

Balzic drove up to the Rocksburg Mall and parked on the lower level near the Montgomery Ward auto repair and tire shop and went inside to the pay phone near the fountain at the end of the court where, depending on the commercial season of the year, the train rides and putt-putt golf and puppet shows were set up. As Balzic reached in his pocket for change, he watched workmen dismantling a stage near the fountain while another was vacuuming the floor and getting ready to put down the putt-putt golf course.

Balzic called the phone company and asked for Jack Whit-low. In a moment, Whitlow's silky voice came on. "John Whitlow. May I be of service?"

" 'May I be of service,' " Balzic mimicked him. "You damn well better be of service. Can you think of anybody who'd wanna talk to you if you weren't?"

"Balzic," Whitlow said, sighing. "And I was just sitting here thinking what a wonderful day it was, here in the air-conditioning, surrounded by soft music and with a secretary who actually calls me mister and thinks it's part of her job to bring me coffee. You still writing parking tickets, Mario?"

"Naw, I'm goin' to the community college and studyin' criminal investigation so I can retire and get a cushy job with Ma Bell."

"Mario, you don't often say funny things, but that was one. Really. The idea of you working with electronic communications equipment, that is funny. How many times has the FCC cited you for befouling the airwaves now? Twice, three times?"

"You know what FCC stands for, Jack?"

"Uh, let me think, in your mind, FCC would stand for, uh, sexual-intercoursing penis-sucking communists."

Balzic grunted. "Close. First two are right. The last one's cockroaches."

"Well now that we've exchanged pleasantries, Mario, what is it you want today?"

"Just a name, number, and address check. Farley Gruenwald in Stratford Acres off 66 north in Kennedy Township."

"Farley? Farley Gruenwald? You making this up?"

"C'mon, Jack, just run it through your pinball machines, okay?"

"Pinball machines? Oh, Mario, that was crude. Truly. But memorable. Yessir, crude but memorable. Hold on."

Balzic barely had time to turn around and get a decent daydream going before Whitlow was back on the line.

"Can't make your day, Mario. The phone is unlisted."

"Aw c'mon, Jack."

"Mario, are you asking me—let me be quite clear about this—are you asking me to violate federal and state law regarding the publication, dissemination, and/or verification of unlisted phone numbers, is that what you're asking me to do?"

Oh what a ballbuster, Balzic thought. "Jack, I coulda saved myself a quarter, you know? I coulda gone straight to the courthouse and got a subpoena and I'd still have my quarter—"

"I love to hear you complain, Mario. It's like music. Bad music, but still music."

Balzic sighed away from the mouthpiece. "Next time I call I'll have my harp with me and I'll play you—never mind. Just gimme the number, okay? Don't make me run down the courthouse, it's too goddamn hot, and half the time their AC don't work."

"You play a harp? Is that what you said? A harp you carry with you? You? You play a musical instrument? What are you talking about? A harp's almost as big as a piano. What are you talking about?"

"Never mind, Jack, okay? Just gimme the number, c'mon, I'll owe you one."

"Well, you want to owe me one, I want to collect one right now. The one I want is an explanation about this harp stuff. It's your turn to come on. This is fascinating. A whole new side of your, uh, it's hard for me to say the word, but, uh, character? Not the word that springs to mind when I think of you, Mario. It's too easily confused, I mean, when some people talk about a person's character, the implication is that the person has one. Which is not what I think of when I use the word as it relates to you? You following me on this? I know it's complicated."

"Hey, Jack, gimme a break, okay?"

"Ah ah ah," he sang in three ascending notes. "The explanation, please."

Balzic again sighed away from the mouthpiece and made yet another promise to himself to find some brakes for his mouth. "Uh, Jack, uh, a harp is what some people call a harmonica. Mouth harp? Ever hear that? Then it just got shortened to harp. I guess. I don't really know why it's called that."

"And you play one of these? A harmonica? Or harp? You? What do you play? 'Oh Susannah'?"

"As a matter of fact, yeah."

"And 'Row, Row, Row Your Boat'? And 'Three Blind Mice'?"

"Uh, yeah."

There was silence for a while. Balzic thought he could hear laughter, but he wasn't sure. On the other hand, knowing how much Whitlow enjoyed making people shuffle their feet and look at their shoes, Balzic was sure.

"Mario, the number is—" Whitlow had to cover the mouthpiece again to regain his composure. When he came back on, he gave Balzic the phone number and house number of Farley Gruenwald, pausing often to clear his throat after every second or third sound he made. Balzic took it without interruption. He even said thank you before he hung up.

He put another quarter into the phone and dialed the Children's Bureau in the courthouse. This was going to be a wasted quarter for sure, because every good contact he'd ever made in the CB had either retired or died, except for Louie Gilpirin, and Louie was as close to retirement as Balzic was, so it was not likely Louie was going to do anything as foolish as jeopardizing his retirement benefits by rooting around in the CB's computer to chase this wild goose. But it was cool in the mall and he didn't have anything else to do. That was a lie. He knew it was a lie almost as soon as the thought formed. The truth was he was bored stiff riding

27

around playing beat cop. He was practically screaming for something to do, something to chew on, something to think about besides what he would do after he retired.

He was put on hold immediately after someone picked up the phone. He turned and absently watched the workmen taking the stage apart and putting the sections of flooring onto a cart. He looked up at the large clock on the wall above the stairwell on the second floor and saw its minute hand advance almost five minutes before he heard the line open again.

He identified himself and asked for Caseworker Gilpirin.

"Mister Gilpirin is not at his desk at the moment. He just stepped out. Would you like to hold?"

"Sure. I'll hold. Tell him it's Mario Balzic. Maybe that'll get him back faster."

"I beg your pardon?"

"Never mind. It's an old joke. I'm holdin'."

Five minutes later, Louie Gilpirin picked up his extension and the person who had answered hung up.

"Mario, how goes it? Long time no hear nothing. What's up?"

"Uh, you busy, Louie?"

"Don't know who my family is, can't remember what my wife looks like. 'Course I'm busy."

"No, I mean right now you busy? You got somebody with you or something?"

"Uh-ha. Mario, every time you ask me that question, do I have somebody with me, am I busy right now, the next question's gonna be, have I ever heard the name such and such. Hmmm? Is that the next question?"

"Sort of. How's the name Gruenwald strike you. Farley Gruenwald. That ring any bells?"

"Not in my steeple it doesn't."

"Well how about—"

"Mario, I'm gonna stop you right there. In two months,

28

fifty-nine days exactly, I walk. I walk into the sunset, and I take with me a state pension of nearly two thousand dollars a month, plus Social Security, plus a life insurance policy. I am not, repeat, I am not gonna screw that up now looking for some Farley whoever. You know how the computers work here as well as I do—"

"Yeah yeah yeah, I hear you, Louie. I know the rules, I know what you told me about the computers, Jesus, you been tellin' me that ever since you guys got computers—"

"And I'm telling you again about our computers and I'm telling you now the answer is no, as in capital N, capital O. You remember Frank Moskowicz? Huh? Remember what happened to him? You know what his legal bills are right now? Huh? Try seventy-eight thousand dollars and rising— that's about March, which was the last time I talked to him— and he's no closer to his pension now than he was four years ago. For a favor to a cop, for one favor, he has lost his job, his pension, his house, and his wife, in that order."

"Hey, Louie, I hear you, I hear you. I just thought I'd give it a shot. One shot, you know."

"Right. You took your shot, you missed. Put your gun away."

"Well, listen, Louie, I appreciate your talkin' to me, you know? But, listen, if you should be over at the water cooler or by the coffee pot or in the john and you should hear anybody talkin' about a Farley Gruenwald? Huh? From Stratford Acres, 108 Avon Drive, Stratford Acres, in Kennedy Township, you know? Like if you should overhear something, you know, that you wouldn't have to have your computer code on the files or anything, you know, just strictly eavesdroppin', sort of, would you give me a call, huh?"

Louie sighed. "You're relentless, you sonofabitch, you know that?"

"Hey, Louie, in my old age, I do not like that word anymore. I'm suddenly real sensitive about that word."

"Huh? Beg your pardon?"

"Ever since my mother died, I don't appreciate that word anymore is what I'm sayin'. I know it's supposed to be, you know, just among friends and that's the way friends talk, but I don't want my friends to talk like that to me anymore is what I'm sayin'. That all right with you? And while I'm at it here, it's not as though I haven't kicked in a few doors for you, my friend. Over the years, you know? It's not as though you never called me to, uh, violate the fucking Fourth Amendment, huh? Huh? It's not as though I never sent one of my men around the back door to come back out front in two minutes, with, uh, with this sudden corroborating information that child abuse was goin' on at that very instant inside the house where you guys could never find any corroborating evidence. Huh? Hey, Louie, we ain't a couple of cherries here, my friend. We've played this game a few times. And your buddy Moskowicz didn't take the gas because his entry code showed up in the computer once too often, you know? There was something else goin' on there with him, you know? Like that kid old Moskowicz got this sudden yearning for? Huh?"

"Oh, Mario, that's unworthy of you, really, that is—"

"Hey, just 'cause you didn't know about it, that didn't mean I didn't know about it. Just 'cause the CB, just 'cause the conventional wisdom there was all phonied up, that didn't mean it was phonied up. Trust me on this one, Louie, it wasn't phonied up. There was photographic evidence. Plenty of it, and not just with that one kid."

"Mario, . . . Mario, I've known you for a lot of years, but really, this is outrageous, this, you, you're talking about a very old friend of mine . . . Frank Moskowicz would not, I mean, I don't know what to say. Those charges were total and complete fabrications and they were dismissed here, he was exonerated here, and, and—"

"Hey, Louie, I hate to be the guy to tell you this, but he was exonerated, he was given the old whitewash 'cause nobody at the CB, and especially none of the county commissioners wanted to deal with that kind of shit. The charge that was phonied up, my friend, was that his entry codes were on files they weren't supposed to be on. That's what was phonied up, not the stuff about him dorkin' the kids. Cause he *was* dorkin' the kids. The DA used the computer stuff to dump him, that was strictly ass-coverin' time, and anybody who tells you otherwise is lyin' or doesn't know what's goin' on. So, uh, since it seems this conversation is pretty much over, Louie, how about transferrin' me over to the prothonotary's office, okay?"

"Uh, what? I didn't hear you. What did you say?"

"I said, how about transferrin' me over to the prothonotary's office. I'm kinda runnin' short on quarters here and I'm at a pay phone."

"You'd be safer going through the operator again. Our phones aren't working real well these days. They don't work any better than the air-conditioning around here."

"Well switch me back to the main operator, okay? Can you do that?"

"It'd be safer to call her yourself."

"Okay, Louie, I get you. Thanks anyway," Balzic said, hanging up.

Balzic pulled down the coin return absently and stuck his finger in it. You never knew, pay phones were just as subject to screwups as everything else these days, and people were always in a hurry and forgetful and . . . shit, he thought, I shouldn't have done that to Louie. But he should've known about Moskowicz, hell, Louie's not stupid. Maybe he did know and he just thought I was trying to jerk him around, maybe that's what he thought I was doin'. What did he say? "Unworthy?" Nah, he really didn't know about Moskowicz. Jeez-oh-man, I never learn. Never.

Balzic walked over to the fountain and looked at all the pennies on the bottom and thought about all the people who every day made the rounds of all the pay phones, doing just what he had done, cruisin' the coin returns, trying to make a quarter. That made him think of the police chief in another town about half the size of Rocksburg who played the state lottery out of his pocket three times a week on the one-in-seven-plus-million odds that he could save his town, or that's what he said. Or that's what a reporter who wrote the story for the Associated Press said he said. Balzic wondered what the guy would do if he won. Would he really turn it over to the town? Hell, after that story in the paper, what choice would he have. He burned his bridges talkin' to that reporter, he'd have to turn it over to the town. Christ, what've we come to? I'm looking at pennies in a fountain and that schmuck is playing the lotto. Law-and-order politicians, the bastards. Lock everybody up but don't give anybody any money to hire the cops or build the jails. What somebody ought to do is put a razor-wire fence around Utah and make all the cons live with the Mormons, no booze, no dope, no nicotine, no caffeine, and every morning two guys show up in their suits and ties and the cons can't shut the door in their faces, they got to stand there and take it, every word those two missionaries say. Nah, that's too cruel and unusual for cons. Nah, it's exactly cruel and unusual enough, except it's the wrong cons. The cons it ought to happen to are the cons who never get convicted—Congress. The whole time they're in session.

Balzic was feeling almost jaunty about that private little joke. He thought of the congressmen he'd seen on TV, those smug, pompous, self-righteous, boozy-woozy word machines who could turn the most complicated human actions into good and bad, black and white, right and wrong, yes and no, this is good and that's bad, whenever it applied to the saps and stiffs who didn't have money to contribute to their campaigns. But they made sure every law they passed did not apply to them or to the people who gave them the money to keep them there. Then, suddenly everything that applied to them or their patrons was extremely complicated, with so many loops, nicks, and crannies nobody but lawyers could find their way through without stepping on a landmine.

He was cackling to himself about what should happen to Congress and he knew this cackling was one of the surest signs he was getting old. More and more he was taking pleasure in pointing fingers at somebody else for what was wrong, and laughing about it. Adolescents did that, blaming everybody else for what was keeping them from taking their rightful place in the universe, but lots of old people did it too, blaming everybody else for the mistakes they had made themselves and for their present discomfort. But it wasn't all old people. It was the ones who were always going to be fifteen even when they were seventy. If he didn't start watching himself more closely, he was going to turn into one of them, a sixty-four-year-old teenager with solutions for everybody else's problems except his own.

He was walking extra slow to linger in the wonderful fake weather and postpone for as long as possible going outside into the real midafternoon stew when he remembered that he was carrying a stack of envelopes, bills Ruth had written the checks for two days ago and that he'd been carrying ever since and had forgotten to mail. So when he finally pushed through the exit to the lot where he'd parked his cruiser, he was trying to remember if there was a mailbox on this level or if he had to drive around to the other end of the mall by Kaufmann's Department Store, where he knew there was a mailbox.

He stepped off the concrete onto the macadam, intending to turn around and put his back to the sun and look back into the shade to try to spot a mailbox. The heat had already hit him as soon as he'd come through the door, but the sunlight momentarily dazzled him and he felt the slightest vertigo. The cruiser was going to be sweltering, but the sooner he got the bills posted the sooner he could get the AC cranked up in the cruiser. He thought about going to start the cruiser first and then coming back and dropping the mail, but right in the middle of that little debate a horn blared at him at the same instant he felt something brush against his pants and heard the squeal of the tires.

He heaved himself toward the sidewalk and turned in time to hear "Asshole!" and to be blinded by the sun as the car that had brushed his pants pulled around a double row of cars and disappeared in the lot. All he could see was that it was glistening black and that it was a Honda—he had seen the logo on the trunk. The vertigo rolled over him again and his breath started to come in shallow gulps.

He threw up his hands and let them drop to his side, and cursing and muttering under his breath, he walked gingerly toward what he thought was a mailbox. It had the right size and shape, but in the blinding sun he couldn't tell. He kept walking toward it, trying to shield his eyes with his arm, and when he was about five or six paces away from it, he saw that it was a bright green garbage receptacle and didn't look anything at all like a mailbox. The vertigo came back again, a short wave of it, not even half a second, then it was gone. Beyond the garbage receptacle, there was a tree, and in the brilliant light its leaves were a silvery grayish green, the color of something he knew well but couldn't at that moment recall. He started to turn around and the vertigo came back, up and down, wavy and circular, and his breathing was getting shallower and shallower and he could feel his heart picking up the pace. The words, *green* and *black* and *Japanese,* and what was behind them, what was deep in his memory, were working on him, and his stomach was on the verge of turning, and Mary mother of god was he not in an amtrac covered with everything that used to be in his body, heaving up and down, round and round in smaller and smaller circles waiting for the assault wave to form, his stomach and bowels and bladder making the same wild motions as the amtrac on the

34

water, and overhead the fire from the ships ripping the air, tearing his senses to shreds, rockets and machine guns and antiaircraft cannon and three-inchers and five-inchers on the converted landing craft and destroyers, only hundreds of yards offshore firing point-blank into the black beaches, sixteen-inchers on the battleships three or four miles offshore, and everything else the Navy had in between, and then the planes from the carriers making their last runs over the beaches, strafing and dropping bombs, the napalm billowing white orange black, their engines howling as they pulled up around Mt. Suribachi and now, here in the middle of July 1990, Balzic was nearly frantic with fear that two colors, green and black, and a Japanese car had let loose in him. He was nineteen again in the Twenty-eighth Regiment, Fifth Marine Division, heading for Green Beach at the base of Mt. Suribachi, Iwo Jima, and he was swallowing hard to keep down the saliva that kept filling his mouth.

He pinched the flesh on his jaw and whispered aloud, "C'mon c'mon, wake up. You're here, man. Rocksburg. It's Rocksburg for crissake, get it together. . . ." His eyes were filling with tears, his nose was stuffing up, his throat was tightening, and he was fighting not to sob. Jesus Christ, man, he thought, is that all it takes, two fucking colors, green for the Green Beach and black for that black shit you stepped into when you jumped out of the amtrac, and that goddamn Honda, is that all it takes to set you off? Is that all? Is that where you are now? Forty-five years after the fact, what do you need to tell you it's time to quit? What the hell are you waiting for? You're sixty-four goddamn years old, you need a telegram? Sixty-four goddamn years old and you're in worse shape now than you were when you got off Iwo-fuck-ing-Jima . . . that cathole of black ash and red blood and guys calling on the beaches for the medics, in voices that had no word for them, there was never a word anybody could imagine for what their noises ought to be called, the ones strong

35

enough to feel their lives dripping and spurting away, their blood mixing with the ash that stunk of sulphur, and noise like no noise Balzic had ever heard or would ever hear again . . . except when something brought it back like now and he heard it all over again and he could not make his ears stop. . . . What the hell is so magical about the age of sixty-five that I think I have to keep this goddamn job for? Should've quit fourteen years ago, the first chance they ever gave me to quit, stupid bastard, fourteen more years on the pension, for what, for what, for some goddamn politician to get his daughter-in-law a job to give me a special headache?

He exhaled hard through his mouth and tried to make his stomach touch his spine and held it there until he had to inhale and he did that slowly, slowly, counting to eight, and then exhaled hard again, pushing his diaphragm back and up and holding it until he couldn't and then inhaled again slowly, slowly, looking at the silvery grayish-green leaves on the tree just a few feet on the other side of the bright green of the garbage receptacle. He suddenly recalled what it was about them. The leaves were the color of Marine utilities, the grayish-green trousers and jacket they wore to kill in, to die in, to scream in, to cry in . . . and he could smell himself, sweat, vomit, and excrement, and that stinking black ash from the volcano, the black beach that ate his feet up past his ankles with every step and filled his nose and almost tricked his nose into forgetting what he smelled like all the while he was sloughing his way fifty yards off the beach, lurch and sink, lurch and sink, stumble to the knees, get up, get moving, get off the beach, those fuckin' bastard Japs, where'd they go? Maybe they're all dead, why don't they shoot, where the fuck's the artillery, what the fuck are they waiting for, they ain't dead, they ain't I don't give a shit what the swabbies said about nobody survivin' that barrage, the swabbies lie, everybody lies, they're still here they didn't all die no way they all died, they're here they're here they're here, they got lots more than just rifles left, they just don't have rifles left, oh god look at the beach Jesus Christ look at the beach, where the hell's everybody gonna go, get that tank moving get that tank moving they're dead they're all dead . . . god god god listen to this they're here they ain't dead Jesus Jesus what the fuck is that, the whole fuckin' mountain is shootin' the mountain's on fire dig dig can't dig this fuckin' shit you can't dig I got to dig dig dig you sonofabitch you're dead if you don't dig . . . dig or die dig or die dig or die. . . .

Balzic slumped against a brick pillar and peered into the shadows of the canopy over the doors he'd just come out of. He heard himself breathing, deep and raspy, tears were rolling down his cheeks, his nose was dripping, his face was burning, he was shivering. Anybody wants to know, this is the flu, I got the goddamn flu. Listen me, listen to me, who cares, who's gonna ask me what's wrong, I got the flu, Jesus, making up stories for people who ain't here. God I'm thirsty, Jesus, is my mouth dry. . . .

He forced himself to walk to his cruiser, but he had to think about it, about making the steps, first one, then another. He was lead heavy, pressed, oppressed, depressed, his feet scraping across the concrete and then the macadam. His cruiser wasn't thirty steps from where he was and up only a slight grade, but it looked like it was up a mountain and he was in the flat below, listening to the mountain explode, the thunder up there and the rain of bullets and shells down here, and Jesus, there I go again, forty-five years later and I'm still hearing it, still seeing it, rows and rows of crosses, two stone columns with the sign, FIFTH MARINE DIVISION and crosses, crosses, crosses, hundreds and hundreds of crosses, Marines all dead, and now the fucking Japs were buying everything, here comes Sony buying up the Volkswagen plant, getting ready to make TVs where the Germans made VWs for ten years . . . . Jesus, I gotta get a drink, my tongue's stickin' to the roof of my mouth, come on, legs, work, god, that's what I was sayin' then, come on, legs, don't let me die here. . . .

Come on, man, it's just the Iwo Fever, that's all, the old Iwo Fever, nothing new, same old crap. You know what it is, man, some people call it panic attacks and some call it anxiety attacks, and those booky farts, they call it existential dread, love that one, that existential dread, love to see the booky fart who came up with that one, that existential dread. Maybe that was a real good name for what some people got, but it don't have nothing to do with what I got. What I got here is the ol' Iwo Fever, sneakin' up on me like a Jap car brushing against my pants on a summer day, nothing at all to worry about one second and the next second all I can do is tie my ass to the planet 'cause that little breeze from a car turned into a tornado and I'm hanging on by my fingernails. . . .

Balzic's thirst was overwhelming him. His lips were sticking together at the corners and his throat was so raw he was starting to think maybe it wasn't Iwo Fever at all, maybe he was getting a strep throat or something. He couldn't help laughing at himself, at the way his mind was working. One second he was lost among the silvery grayish-green trees and black Japanese cars, being swept back nearly half a century to sensations and emotions that weren't *there* but were as real as the trees and the Japanese car, and the next second he was arguing about the accuracy of his self-diagnosis.

He made it to his cruiser finally, after plodding up the macadam for what seemed an hour. He slumped inside, turned the ignition on, and as soon as the engine turned over, switched on the AC. He got back out, closed the door, and waited for the AC to work, wiping his face with his hanky and remembering the time he'd gone to the Veterans Administration Hospital in Oakland, Pittsburgh, to see if he could make sense with somebody about his Iwo Fever. The only thing that had come out of that excursion was he'd learned a new name for it: post-traumatic stress disorder. If "existential dread" had sprouted out of some booky fart's brain, then "post-traumatic stress disorder" had to have sprouted out of some bureaucrat's brain. Balzic couldn't think of that cluster of words without seeing a desert of desks, computer terminals on every one, gray somber faces staring at the screens, typing only the words that fit into the spaces on the forms.

He had to get some water. His throat was raw, and standing beside his cruiser wasn't making anything better, so he clambered back in, turning his face to the AC vent for a long moment, then drove off, winding his way through and around the mall traffic until he was back on the road into Rocksburg. In about ten minutes, he was walking through the back door of Muscotti's, hoping that for once Dom Muscotti had relented and turned the air conditioner on. As Muscotti had said, often enough to irritate all his customers, "I like air just the way it is, without no conditions."

Vinnie was behind the bar talking to Mo Valcanas and somebody Balzic recognized but couldn't identify. Farther down the bar sat three of the regulars, each staring moodily into their beer or at their cigarettes.

Balzic slumped onto a stool beside Valcanas and asked for water.

"Water?" Vinnie's eyebrows shot up. "I ain't gonna make no money humpin' no goddamn water. You're gonna make me walk all the way down the end of the bar and I ain't gonna get a chance to make a dime?"

"You okay?" Valcanas said. "You don't look too good."

"Don't feel real good either."

"What's the matter?"

"He's drinkin' water, that's what's the matter," Vinnie said, filling the glass, then sidling back up the bar and sliding the tumbler in front Balzic, who took it and drained the glass.

"Another, okay? Never mind, I'll get it myself." He lurched off the stool and went to the end of the bar where the water pipe was. He filled and drank two more glasses and then filled another and brought it back to the stool next to Valcanas.

"Jesus Christ," Vinnie said, his arms folded across his chest. "You know there's a drought warnin' on, you know that? I ain't even supposed to ask nobody if they want water, and you just drank about half-a-buck's worth right there."

Balzic took another long drink, about half the glass. "Why don't you turn the air conditioner on, huh?"

"Here we go again, another guy can't stand the heat. You know that air conditioner's broke."

"Aw stop it. That goddamn thing's never on, how can it be broke? I can't remember the last time that thing was on."

"It's broke I'm tellin' ya. Whatta you want from me. Go talk to Dom. You oughta be happy the fans are on and I got the doors open. Tell him, Greek."

"You don't look too good, Mario."

"That's the second time you said that, Panagios."

"Well I'm saying it because you don't."

"And I'm tellin' you, it's probably because I don't feel real good, okay?"

"Well what's the matter?"

"He's drinkin' fuckin' water, that's what's the matter."

"Will you get outta here, huh? Really pisses you off 'cause I'm drinkin' water."

"Water's for makin' ice cubes, makin' whiskey and water, washin' your car, makin' the tomatoes grow, washin' your dick after you get laid, it ain't for drinkin'."

"I say again, what's the matter?"

Balzic looked at Valcanas and shrugged and sighed. "Aw I just scared the hell outta myself. Wasn't payin' attention, got the sun in my face and turned around and almost backed into a car in the mall, just brushed against my pants, you know, never saw it comin'—didn't hear it either, come to think of it—no big deal, but it rattled me and, uh, so here I am, drinkin' water and makin' Vinnie all disgusted."

"Well nothing to worry about there," the man on the other side of Valcanas said. "That's Vinnie's natural state. Disgusted."

"You remember this guy?" Valcanas said, pointing with his thumb over his shoulder.

Balzic shook his head. "I don't remember his name, but the face I remember. Don't know from where."

"From here," Vinnie said. "Used to be part of the furniture for crissake. Used to be you couldn't get him outta here with a crane, with dynamite."

"Myushkin," Valcanas said. "Nick Myushkin. Remember now?"

"Oh yeah, yeah, I gotcha now. The Mad Russian."

"That's me. Maddest Russian there ever was. Gettin' madder too." He laughed hard while speaking, his broad, round face turning red from the combination. He was short, thick, wide, with large, veiny hands, wrists, and forearms. He was wearing a white T-shirt and gray shorts and running shoes with no socks.

"He just found out you can't get welfare if you own your house," Vinnie said. "Like he's been asleep for the last twenty years or somethin', like that Rip Van what's-his-face."

"Winkle. But it's not just that," Myushkin said. "They've got this thing they call 'workfare'—"

"Whatta ya mean, they got it? They had it since Thornburgh was governor, where you been?"

"Yeah, okay, right, since Thornburgh, but the thing is if you don't agree to work the kind of jobs they want you to work, they won't give you anything, but the fuckin' jobs they want you to work only pay minimum wage, and I'm trying to figure out how to tell these goddamn bureaucrats the money's not for me, it's for my wife, 'cause I don't want their goddamn money. My wife wants their money, not me. I'm a fugitive from capitalism."

"A what?"

"A fugitive from capitalism, an economic outlaw, you know, one of those people all the news magazines write about, the ones that spend most of their time apologizin' for the Fortune 500 companies? You know? *Time* and *Newsweek* and *Business Week* and *Forbes* and all them. You know, whenever somebody bitches about the thousand richest Americans and how they've got it rigged so they don't pay taxes, you know, those magazines send their snoops out to dig up guys like me, economic outlaws, guys that work for cash. You can relax, Chief, I'm not on one of your posters." He turned to Valcanas and said, "I can see, uh, with the chief I'm goin' over like a fart at communion, so, uh, so to get back to me, how'm I gonna explain to my wife why this isn't gonna work, c'mon, Mo, help me out here."

"I've told you. Welfare law, labor law, they're not something I've done a lot with in the last five or six years. Before I can even think about talking about it, I'd have to spend about a day with the statutes, and I know you don't have that kind of money."

"How about a little pro bono?"

"Forget it. I'm pro bonoed out."

"Well, hell, we can work something out. You need your office painted? I'm gettin' real good at paintin'. Inside, not outside. Four steps on the ladder's my limit, unless it's a barn and I can use extenders."

"I don't need my office painted. Besides, you could paint my office in about one day and we haven't talked about how much you want an hour. Then there's what I'd have to dream up to make it fit on my taxes."

Myushkin's eyebrows shot up. "Hell if that's a problem, maybe I should be talkin' to another lawyer."

"Oh Jeezus, that was cold-blooded," Vinnie said, nearly doubling over with laughter.

"Don't hurt yourself," Valcanas said.

"Well c'mon, Mo, what am I supposed to tell my wife?"

"Tell her to come in and talk to them herself. If she's the one who needs it—look, this much I know: she's not going to get anything while you're living with her, I don't have to read the statutes for that. Is the deed in your name?"

"Yeah. I think. Come to think of it, I'm not sure whether it's in both our names or just mine. Don't know why we wouldn't have both our names on it."

"Well check it out. But no matter whose name is on it, you're gonna have to disappear or she's not going to get anything. And they'll still put a lien on it no matter whose name is on it. If I were you, I'd sell it, move into an apartment. But if they put a lien on it because you're getting welfare, when you sell it you have to settle with them first. Sell it now, is my advice, before your wife starts getting the checks."

Myushkin shook with laughter. "I've been tryin' to sell it ever since Volkswagen said bye-bye. So's everybody else. What the hell you mean, sell it? Nobody's sellin' houses 'cause ain't nobody buyin' 'em, you know?"

"Well maybe now that Sony's movin' in, the market'll open up."

"How? Why? It's gonna be another couple years before Sony gets two shifts goin'. Hell, the Chinese commies are still takin' the VW stuff out of there, all the car tools. From what I hear they've got at least two months' work to get all of that out, and I don't care what Sony's PR guys say, it's gonna be a long time before Sony hires more than one shift, and they've already said that's not gonna be more than seven, eight hundred people. And that includes all the white-necks. So who's gonna buy my house? Besides, it ain't like it's gonna be featured in *Architectural Digest,* you know?"

Valcanas shrugged. "It's livable, isn't it? I mean, you live in it? It's not infested with vermin, the roof's sound, right?"

"Oh yeah, sure sure, it's livable, but man, it's just four little rooms and a bath and a basement, that's all. The attic's not

43

finished. But when people put a For Sale sign up out there, the neighbors just start laughin'. Well, they don't even laugh anymore, they just shake their heads. 'Cause everybody's tryin' to sell their fuckin' house, you know? I mean, most of the people where I live are just like me, too old to find another job, too young for Social Security, and we ran outta unemployment, Christ, years ago. I mean we're back in the barterin' and poachin' stage, it's like we're back at the end of feudalism, when all of a sudden the lords and ladies found out they could make more money with the factories than they could with the farms, so there were all these serfs walkin' around with their thumbs up their asses, sayin', uh, you know, 'Hey, Stashu, what the fuck happened?' "

Vinnie, the corners of his mouth turned down in a mocking smile, looked at Balzic and nodded toward Myushkin. "Same old Mad Russian, still makin' speeches. You oughta run for Congress, you know that? You'd be perfect."

"Watch your mouth, I ain't no goddamn thief. I may be a fugitive from American capitalism, but I ain't no whore for the Fortune 500," Myushkin said, laughing hard.

"You wished you was a whore for somebody," Vinnie said, laughing just as hard, " 'cause then maybe you'd have some money, honey, whatta you think, Mario, huh?"

"The way it's goin'," Balzic said, thinking of how few men he had in his department and how many he was supposed to have and how he was spending more and more time doing a patrolman's job, "the way it's goin', I'm afraid we're all gonna be wishin' we were somebody's whores."

"You sure you're all right?" Valcanas said, peering down at Balzic.

"Yeah. I told you, I just scared the crap outta myself is all. Got a little flashback on somethin', you know? What do the bureaucrats call it now? Post-traumatic stress disorder? You know, the stuff during Big Two they called 'battle fatigue,' remember?"

"And before that, in World War One, it was 'shell shock,' " Myushkin said.

"What? You gonna tell us you were in World War One now, for crissake?" Vinnie said, laughing hard again. "I knew you was old, but I didn't know you was that old. And you only look about sixty."

"Fifty-five, my friend, fifty-five. Younger than you. I only read about Big Two. You were in it."

" 'At's right, goddamn right I was in it. The whole fuckin' shootin' match."

"I thought you were in the motor pool," Valcanas said. "I thought you drove a truck."

"Yeah, sometimes I drove a truck," Vinnie said. "You had to do a lotta stuff, whatever. But I was in Europe the whole time."

"Yeah? Doin' what? If you were in Europe the whole time it's 'cause you were among the seventeen or eighteen thousand guys that went over the hill—"

"Oh bullshit, you just wait a minute now, you're talkin' about my war record here—"

"Now listen who oughta be runnin' for Congress," Myushkin said, howling with laughter at Vinnie. "Listen to him, c'mon, c'mon, I wanna hear this, c'mon, tell us how you won the Battle of the Bulge."

"I was there, I was there, right in the fuckin' middle of it. I got the fuckin' papers at home to prove it."

"Forgeries," Valcanas said dryly.

"Why you sonofabitch Greek, what the fuck was you in, the goddamn Coast Guard, huh? Tell us about the time you built a still, huh, that's your fuckin' war story, the time you built a still down in the engine room of that tub you was on."

"It was not a 'tub,' it was a cutter—which for the uninitiated," Valcanas said, leaning down to Balzic and winking, "is what every ship in the Coast Guard is called, two hundred feet long or fifty feet long—"

"Yeah yeah," Vinnie said, "come on, let's hear how you

45

won the war off the coast of Maine or wherever the fuck you was—"

"For a time, yes, it's true, I defended my county's New England coastline from the threat of Nazi wolfpacks, the terror of the Atlantic, the infamous U-boats—"

Balzic glanced up at Valcanas. " 'The terror of the Atlantic'? 'Infamous U-boats'? What the hell're you drinkin'?"

"Let him go, let him go," Vinnie said, laughing, but not too friendly. "I wanna hear this."

"Oh what is this you want to hear about this?" Valcanas said, leaning across the bar and scowling at Vinnie. "Remember me? I'm the attorney who called the Veterans Administration on behalf of a certain bartender who shall remain nameless but who is standing in the immediate vicinity, any of this ringing any bells? I have a copy of that certain bartender's military record in my office. You want to continue this discussion, hmm? About who was doing what during the Glorious War, the Just War, hmm? Or you wanna pour us all another drink here."

"You got it," Vinnie said. "Comin' right up."

"Christ almighty," Myushkin said, grinning wide-eyed at Valcanas, "what do you have on him? I never saw anybody shut him up that quick before."

Valcanas said nothing. He just sniffed a few times. Then he turned back to Balzic and winked again.

When Vinnie returned with Valcanas' drink, he filled the draft beer glass in front of Myushkin and looked at Balzic. "You gonna do somethin' here or you still gonna do that?"

"This," Balzic said, holding up his glass of water.

Vinnie took the money from a stack of bills and change in front of Valcanas, made change, set it carefully on the same pile, and said, "Thanks, Greek."

Myushkin snorted a laugh. "Holeeeee hell, service with courtesy, man, I'll tell ya, charcoal mail'll do it every time, won't it. Huh? Boyoboy, I don't know what the Greek's holdin', but I'd sure like to have a couple pounds. Got-damn, Vinnie, I never saw you close down that fast long as I've known you."

"That's all right, I'm okay, you just worry about you, Russian."

"I am, I am. I'm just tryin' to get some bullets for my financial guns here, you know. Any little thing you can turn into a quid pro quo, I figure, take it, stick it under your mattress and run, hell." He was laughing all the while he was talking so that his words came in bursts between the snorts and haws and howls.

"You're havin' too much fun, Russian," Vinnie said.

"Can't be," Myushkin said, howling even louder. "It's against the fuckin' law for Russians to have fun, don't you know that? Russians get thirty days just for goin' to a wedding for crissake—unless they go to a funeral in the same month. The funeral cancels the wedding out, that's how come Russians love funerals. It's genetic. If a fuckin' Russian ain't laughin'—or drinkin'—he's cryin', it was decreed the first time the czar got blessed by a bishop, no shit."

"Hold on to your hats, here it comes," Vinnie said, his mouth turned down in that faint mocking smile of his.

"It's true, it's true," Myushkin said, stabbing the bar with his index finger. "The first czar said to the first bishop, 'Hey, you can have their souls, all I want's their backs,' and the bishop, in the true style of the Orthodox Church, said, 'Put her there, pardner, we got us a deal that oughta last for a thousand years.' And he was right. And no fuckin' capitalist ever bitched about that deal until the commies came along in 1917 and said, 'Hey, gang, party's over, it's our turn to party now.' And you didn't know why politicians called 'em parties, didya, Vinnie, huh?"

"What?"

"Parties. You know? Democrats, Republicans, Communists, Fascists, ya know—parties? You don't know why they call 'em that?"

47

"Christ that's old, that's crippled, that's senile. Come up with somethin' new here, if you're gonna put on a show."

"No, man, the joke's still goin' on. You can't stop laughin' at the joke. That's what's wrong with America. They think 'cause they heard the joke before, it's old, which means, therefore, the reason for the joke is old, so they don't laugh and they don't pay attention, but that don't get it, man. That doesn't make it. I'm liv-in', fuck-in' proof the joke's not old. It oughta be told a thousand times a day, that joke about who's having a party 'cause those fuckers in Washington and Harrisburg are havin' a party on us, man, it don't matter what they call themselves, man, Democrats, Republicans, Liberals, Conservatives, the bastards are all gettin' fat on us—them and the rich pricks that keep puttin' 'em in office."

"Easy easy," Vinnie said, holding up his hands. "I think maybe you oughta go home for a while, take a little snooz-eroo, you know, you'll be okay."

"Whatta you talkin' about, go home. I'm not drunk. Whatta you think, 'cause I'm talkin' loud here, you think I'm outta line or somethin'?"

"Hey, you're makin' speeches again, same fuckin' thing you used to do all the time when you was in here before—"

"Before what? When I was in here before what?"

"When you was in here before you moved to go to work at Volkswagen, that before what, that's what I'm talkin' about."

"So what? So what was I, uh, so I was a pain in your ass or somethin' when I was in here spendin' my money?"

"No, nah, it's just you're makin' a speech again, that's all I'm tellin' ya. Don't make no big deal out of it, all right?"

"Well so what was it, Vinnie, I wanna know. You mean all those years I put money on the bar in here, I mean I thought we were friends, you know, and now what you're tellin' me is all I was was a customer, a goddamn speechifier, huh, is that it?"

"Now see? There you go, makin' a big fuckin' deal out of

48

it, and I'm tellin' ya, don't do that. See, you don't have to do that. Just go home, sleep it off, you'll be better, that's all I'm sayin'."

"And I'm sayin' I'm not drunk, so what do I have to sleep off, that's all I'm sayin'. What the fuck, I had three beers, Jesus Christ, this is the third one, I ain't drunk half of it yet, that means I'm drunk?"

"No I ain't sayin' you're drunk," Vinnie said, his hands splayed by his hips, "what I'm sayin' is you're startin' to make speeches which is what you used to do before and we used to have some trouble with that, that's what I'm sayin'. Hey, Greek, help me out here for crissake, guy looks like he's gettin' ready to fight me for crissake, you know, hey, I'm just tryin' to make everybody happy for crissake."

Valcanas drained his glass and said, "I just remembered. I have urgent business back in my office. You all have a nice day, hear?" He gave a sardonically jaunty salute and left.

Vinnie turned to Balzic. "Straighten this guy out, willya, huh? He thinks I'm sayin' things I'm not."

"The whole world thinks everybody's sayin' somethin' they're not, why should you be any different?"

"No, nah, come on, look at him. Look at his face. All of a sudden he's pissed off. Coupla minutes ago, he was tellin' jokes for crissake, now he thinks I said somethin'. I didn't say nothin', tell him."

"Your mouth's still workin', you tell him," Balzic said, sliding off the stool and going to get more water.

"So there you are, Vinnie," Myushkin said, laughing again. "You dug the well and you forgot to bring the ladder. Pretty scary huh?"

"What well? What ladder? What're you talkin' about, Christ. Holes, ladders. Speak English for crissake. I don't know which is worse, fuckin' Russian or fuckin' writin'."

"Fuckin' what?" Myushkin said, his voice rising instantly.

"You heard me," Vinnie said. "I said I don't know which is

worse, far as you're concerned. I said, far as you're concerned, I don't know if it's worse 'cause you're fuckin' Russian or 'cause you're fuckin' writin', that's what I said, you heard me."

"Hey, don't talk about that in here, I asked you before about a dozen times, that's private, and I don't want you talkin' about it in here, that's my business."

Balzic couldn't help himself. He saw where this was going and he thought he'd better get into it despite his better judgment. As he hiked his rump onto the stool, he said, "Talkin' about what don't you want him talkin' about?"

"That's none of your business either—"

"Ah he's a goddamn writer, you know? I only met two writers in my whole life, this one and another one used to come in here, that what's-his-name, big goofy fucker, and this one and they're, the both of them, they're both nuts. Can't make no sense with neither one of 'em. Like this one. Go home, I'm tellin' ya. You come back tomorrow, everything'll be sweet, but today, better you go home 'cause you're startin' to get fucked up and I don't want no shit with you."

Myushkin shifted around on his stool and squared his shoulders. "I'm not fucked up even a little bit and as long as you stay out of my business I'm not gonna give you any shit but you tell me I'm drunk when I'm not and you start puttin' my business in the street I'm gonna give you a whole lot of shit—"

"Hey, that's it. You're shut off, you're done, get outta here," Vinnie said, reaching for the glass of beer in front of Myushkin at the same instant Myushkin saw that reach coming and tried to grab the glass himself. Vinnie got there first and had the glass almost across the bar when Myushkin's hand caught up and jerked it away, but in snatching the glass out of Vinnie's hand, he pulled his hand back into the beer tap on something sharp. He let out a howl and dropped the glass which sloshed beer all over Vinnie's shirt and pants but somehow didn't break when it clattered to the bar.

"Aw now look at this for crissake. What the fuck. Why don't you wise up, goddamn Russian, get outta here, get the fuck outta here, I'm tellin' ya. Look at my shirt for crissake. You know how this is gonna stink?"

"Won't stink any worse now than it stunk before," Myushkin said, sucking the back of his left hand. "Gimme some ice."

"Fuck you, get your own ice. Get outta here—"

"Okay okay okay, that's enough, you two are givin' me a headache. Knock it off."

"Tell this asshole!" Vinnie said. "Don't tell me knock it off, tell him, I work here for crissake. He's drunk—"

"You call me an asshole?" Myushkin said his eyes wide in disbelief and anger. "What d'you call me?"

"That's enough I said. Knock it off the both of ya."

"Asshole is what I called ya 'cause that's what you are. And don't *you* tell me knock anything off, I work here god-damnit—"

"Hey you. You! Myushkin," Balzic said, pointing behind him in the general direction of the tables. "Go sit over there."

"What for? Me sit where, what the fuck, what am I supposed to sit there for, all I was tryin' to do was get my beer back, he's the one actin' the fool here—"

"Would you look at my pants? Huh? Look like I pissed my pants for crissake—"

"Just keep quiet a minute huh, Vinnie? Huh? Okay. Just shut up a minute. People wonder why there ain't ever gonna be peace in the Middle East, peace in Ireland, peace anywhere, all they gotta do is come in here, Jesus, Mary, and Joseph, I'm tellin' ya. You, Myushkin, please go over and take a seat, okay, otherwise I'm gonna have to arrest you, okay?"

"Arrest me! For what? What the fuck did I do you're gonna threaten me, you gotta threaten me like that—"

"What you did is what you're doin'—you're disturbin' my

peace. Go over there and sit down and keep quiet for a while, we'll get this straightened out just go sit down, okay?" Balzic was standing and nodding with his head toward the tables when he saw the blood dripping onto Myushkin's shorts. "Hey, you cut or what? Lemme see that."

"I'm fine, I'm fine, you just tell this guy he ain't talkin' to any asshole."

"Vinnie, get some ice, okay, put it in a clean rag, huh?"

"What, is he cut? Huh? Hope to fuck he bleeds to death, look at my pants, I just got these outta the cleaners yesterday for crissake—"

"Aw will you shut up and get some ice, okay? He'll pay for cleanin' your pants, okay? Just get some ice."

"I ain't payin' for nobody's pants—"

"This ain't the fuckin' emergency room. He's bleedin', fuck'm, I ain't no nurse. Take him up the fuckin' hospital, Keerist, gotta mop the goddamn floor again, look at this—"

"When he gives me the money back for that beer I'll think about payin' for his pants—"

"Come on, outside, let's go," Balzic said, putting his hand on Myushkin's arm.

Myushkin jerked his arm away. "Go outside for what? Go where outside? You arrestin' me? Huh? What the fuck'd I do?"

"I wanna talk to you, c'mon c'mon, let's just go take a little walk outside."

"Better get him the fuck outta here," Vinnie said, nodding his head many times and hitching up his pants.

"Or what?" Myushkin said. "Or what? Huh? What's gonna happen if—"

"Come on," Balzic said. "Just put one foot in front of the other and walk, hear?"

"You never mind what's gonna happen, just get the fuck out, that's all you got to know about, just get goin', that's all."

"Yeah? Or what? Come on, I wanna hear what." Myushkin

tried to shuffle around Balzic to get closer to the bar, but Balzic wasn't having any of that.

He waited another second until Myushkin was glaring at Vinnie and doing little side steps to see around Balzic, the better to show his menace, then Balzic reached across with his left hand and lifted Myushkin's left arm and slipped his right up under Myushkin's left elbow until he had Myushkin's left arm hyperextended over his own right arm, and then he closed the fingers of his right hand around the back of Myushkin's neck. He led Myushkin to the front door, kicked open the screen door, and took him out on the sidewalk where he said, "I'm gonna let you go now, but first I want your word you're not gonna do anything stupid." He added a little emphasis by pulling Myushkin's hand down, hyperextending his elbow farther and bringing him up on his toes. "Whatta ya say, do I have your word? Huh? You're not gonna do anything dumb? Okay?"

"Okay okay okay, yeah, I'm not gonna do anything dumb."

When Balzic let go, Myushkin immediately began to stretch and rub his left arm. "You're the one did somethin' stupid."

"What?"

"You got blood all over your suit, look, it's on your sleeve, your tie, look. Go 'head and look, what, you think I'm tryin' to trick you or somethin'? This ain't no trick. Look."

Balzic searched Myushkin's face for a couple of seconds and then stepped back and looked down at himself. It was true, there was blood smeared on his right sleeve, right lapel, tie, and shirt.

"So now I guess I'm gonna get the bill for that too, huh? Man, I don't know how I got to be so lucky. This is just my lucky day I guess. May I leave now, or you really gonna arrest me?"

"Nah I'm not gonna arrest you. Come on, I'll take you up the emergency room."

"What for?"

"What for? Christ, you're drippin' blood on the sidewalk here. You cut yourself on the beer tap, I don't care how many times it's been cleaned, that tap's been in there forever. When was the last time you had a tetanus shot?"

"I'm not goin' to the hospital, thanks but no thanks."

"You got to get the bleedin' stopped, you probably need stitches, you need a tetanus shot for sure, let's go."

"I'm not goin' to the hospital. You arrestin' me or not?"

"I told ya, no I'm not arrestin' you—"

"Then good-bye," Myushkin said and started back into the bar.

"Hey, where you think you're goin'?" Balzic said, catching hold of Myushkin's arm, but this time he'd been expecting it and there was no holding him. He spun away. "I'm goin' back in to get my change—if it ain't already in Vinnie's pocket, that okay with you?"

"No it is definitely not okay with me. You go back in and I will arrest ya. You can bet all the money you got on that."

"Yeah, well all the money I got happens to be on the bar— if he didn't cop it already, which would be a first."

"Okay, okay, you stay here I'll go get it. How much? And don't lie."

"Oh it's a real goddamn fortune. Twenty bucks less three beers—half of one I didn't even get to drink. I can't believe this. I'm standin' in the middle of Rocksburg, I got a hole in my hand, I got blood all over a cop, I got nine books translated in eight languages, and I got seventeen dollars to my name—if a bartender didn't steal *that*." Myushkin threw back his head and shook it and laughed and sighed.

"Yeah, right," Balzic said. "Stick around, I'll be right back."

Myushkin started after him, but Balzic stopped him. "Where you goin'? Stay here."

"Oh man, I gotta hear this, you kiddin'? I gotta hear what

he's gonna say. There are some things you just cannot make up, man, you know? Some things you have to hear, come on, I won't say anything, not a word, I promise. Honest."

"Okay, okay, but the first word outta you and you're goin' to jail, you hear that? Huh?"

"Okay, all right, I heard ya. Just go 'head, I'll be right behind ya."

Balzic led the way in and Vinnie stopped mopping the floor behind the bar and started groaning and moaning as soon as they came in.

"Now what?" he said. "I thought you was takin' him to jail, whatta you bringin' him back in here for?"

"He wants his change."

"Oh is that what he wants, oh he wants his change," Vinnie sang. "He wants his change. It's right there, right where he left it. Only there's five dollars short."

"Short?" Myushkin said, then caught himself and covered his mouth. "What short?" he whispered behind his hand.

"Whatta you mean five dollars short?" Balzic said.

Vinnie pointed at his pants. "Hey, it cost me four dollars and seventy cents to get these outta the cleaners yesterday, it's gonna cost me the same to get 'em out again, and I'm takin' it now. You think I'm gonna wait for that chudrule to pay for it, then you think I'm the dumbest dago that ever come outta Italy—and the dumbest dago in Italy ain't made it over here yet, he's still there, he's too fuckin' dumb to find out where they sell the tickets."

Balzic put his hands over his ears. "Jee-zus Kee-rist, enough, enough, enough—"

"See," Myushkin whispered, "some things you have to hear, you can't make 'em up, no way, you can't."

Balzic counted the change. "What, it's a dollar a draft now?"

"Whatta you think, huh? You think more?"

"Yesterday it was ninety cents."

"You got it right. Yesterday," Vinnie said, continuing to mop and nodding many times.

"Today it's a dollar," Balzic said, shaking his head.

"Hey, lemme tell ya, it's still the cheapest draft in town, everybody else been chargin' a buck ten, buck fifteen, buck and a quarter since New Year's. You got a problem with that, take it up with management." That settled it as far as Vinnie was concerned. He wrung out his mop in the rollers on the bucket and pushed it back into the kitchen.

Balzic handed the twelve dollars to Myushkin and started to lead him by the arm out the front door again.

Vinnie stuck his head out of the kitchen to holler, "And if youns're wonderin' what the other thirty cents is for, it's for my pain and sufferin', four seventy to get my pants clean, thirty cents for pain and sufferin', punitive damages, ya fuck."

Balzic held up a finger in front of Myushkin's face and told him to stay put. Then he went down the steps to the men's room, got a handful of paper towels and brought them back up and told Myushkin to wrap them around his hand. "I don't want you bleedin' all over my car," he said.

Myushkin followed him out on the sidewalk, protesting all the way that Balzic had no reason to arrest him, he wasn't drunk, he hadn't assaulted anybody, he'd just spilled the beer because he was trying to get what was his, he was being cooperative, and so on.

"Just get in the car," Balzic said. "And don't bleed on any-thing."

Balzic drove to Conemaugh General Hospital and parked in the lot closest to the door of the trauma center. Every time Balzic looked at the sign over the door, he wondered if there was anybody who called it anything but *the emergency room.*

He was out of the car and walking toward the door beside the dock where the ambulances parked when they brought

56

patients in—the dock had been built so it was even with the floor of the ambulances—when he realized that Myushkin was not beside him. He turned around in time to see Myushkin slipping out of the cruiser without closing the door and trying to tiptoe away.

"Hey!" Balzic snarled. "Where the hell you think you're goin'?"

Myushkin turned and shrugged. "Oh I thought I'd hitch-hike out to the Rollin' Rock Club, play eighteen holes, have a little dinner, you know, some trout maybe, you know trout in, uh, little wine, little lemon juice, maybe some asparagus with hollandaise, maybe a little broccoli with just a whisper of garlic and extra virgin olive oil. I told ya, I wasn't goin' to the hospital. I thought you were gettin' ready to arrest me, I didn't know we were comin' up here, I mean, you didn't exactly discuss it with me, you know?"

"What *is* your problem?" Balzic said, squinting and hunching forward as though that would help him see more clearly what was ailing this guy.

"Hey, it's real simple. I don't have insurance, that plain enough for you?"

"Yeah, so?"

Now it was Myushkin's turn to squint and hunch forward. "Whatta ya mean, so? You ever go in—no, you never did. Lemme tell ya what you should try some time, just for your own information, you know? Some time, when you got nothin' else to do, put your scruffy clothes on and walk in there and tell 'em you got a pain somewhere and your doctor's out of town and let him take all your information down until they get to that part about where they wanna see your insurance card—"

Balzic put his hands up and waved them from side to side. "That's an old story, c'mon, let's go. Come on."

"Hey, I'm sorry, but I'm not goin' in there and have some bitchy bureaucrat with a bouffant practice her patronizin' act

57

on me, no thank you, I had enough grief for one day." He was backing up slowly as he talked.

Balzic shook his head, and held up his index finger. "You need a tetanus shot."

"So? I'll get one."

"Where? With no insurance, where?"

"What the hell're you, the conscience of Conemaugh County? What the hell do you care where I get one? I know a doctor."

Balzic laughed. "You got no insurance for the hospital but you know a doctor, and, uh, oh man, what am I talkin' to you for. Go on, get outta here. No, wait a minute."

Myushkin turned away, then turned back and waited, suddenly amused.

"You said somethin' before, somethin' about you wrote some books and you had 'em in how many languages?"

Myushkin's amusement was growing. He shuffled forward a few steps. He spoke in a very low voice. "I don't usually talk about this in public. In fact when my brain bone is actually connected to my tongue bone, I never talk about it at all, so I was runnin' my mouth without thinkin', which is somethin' my wife says I been doin' a lot lately, which is neither here nor there, but tell me, 'cause I'm in a real dangerous position here—I'm curious, and when I get curious I'm subject to doin' the dumbest thing in the world, which is what I'm doin' right now, which is askin' people why they wanna know somethin'."

"Askin' people why they wanna know something is dumb?"

"Yeah," Myushkin said, wide-eyed and nodding many times with his wry smile growing. " 'Cause the older I get, the more I ask that question, the more dumb shit I hear, the more the dumb shit clogs up my brain. And every time I need for some good shit to come out of my brain, the harder it has to work to get over and around all the dumb shit that's in there. But I'm hooked. Why you wanna know about this?"

Balzic shrugged. "I'm just tryin' to figure out how somebody who wrote all those books in all those languages only has, uh, seventeen bucks to his name."

"Twelve bucks. Twelve. Five less than seventeen. Four-seventy compensatory, thirty cents punitive, remember?"

Balzic nodded. "So how come?"

Myushkin canted his head. "Ohhhhhh I get it. You been readin' *People* magazine, haven't ya, huh? Yeah. You been readin' about all the rich and famous authors, haven't ya? The Tom Clancys and the Louie L'Amours and the Danielle Steels and the Jackie Collinses and all those Sidney guys and the Irving guys, yeah. And you can't understand what—exactly? That I'm on foot? That I only got twelve bucks? Or not only that I ain't drivin' a Mercedes or a Rolls, but I also ain't on 'Runaway with the Rich and Famous,' right?"

Balzic shook his head and shrugged. "Sort of, you know. Not that exactly, but I mean, no health insurance? No car?"

"Oh I got a car all right, except my wife's drivin' it. Toyota. Good car, still runs good after eight years. Japs know how to make cars. Better'n those fuckin' thieves in Detroit. But they don't make cars there anyway. They're like those fucks in Hollywood. They don't make movies, they make deals. In Detroit, they don't make cars, they make rebates. The whole goddamn country's run by accountants and lawyers, you gonna stand there and tell me you don't know that? Huh? You're the chief of police in Rocksburg, P-A, the industrial asshole of the U.S.A., and you haven't figured that out yet?"

"You're not gonna tell me how come, uh. . . ."

"How come what? I'm broke? No insurance? Huh?" Myushkin shook his head and laughed. "Man, the first thing you gotta do is stop readin' those magazines, man, or you'll never know anything. All those goddamn magazines are is capitalist propaganda, man, they're nothin' but fuckin' mind control, man."

"Uh, you sayin' those writers you named, uh, you sayin'

they don't make the kind of money everybody thinks they make or what're you sayin'?"

"Hey, unless I sat down with their contracts, I have no way of knowin' what those writers make, but I do know somethin' about the publishing hustle, and, man, I'm here to tell ya, don't ever believe anything a reporter says about how much a publisher's payin' a writer. I mean, when you read in one of those magazines about how much a writer got from a publisher, it's like when you cops bust somebody for drugs and you tell the reporters how much the drugs are worth, you know? Maybe not *you* necessarily, but when most narcs are talkin' to reporters, they're always talkin' street value, am I right? Retail, man, and it's always about twenty times what they want everybody to think they, uh, intercepted. Well, narcs and publishers got that in common, man, 'cause whenever a reporter's around, the fish just gets bigger and bigger. I mean, when it comes to how much money writers make, man, there ain't nobody in the world more gullible than reporters. 'Course, there ain't anybody more gullible than reporters about anything, man. Most reporters, not all of 'em. Some of 'em are pretty sharp."

Balzic nodded and grunted several times while listening, but then said, "Come on, let's go, you're drippin' blood all over the parkin' lot here."

Myushkin stared at Balzic and shook his head incredulously. "Man, why are you such a hardhead? I'm way past the psychology in my life when I need to take abuse from people just to prove how Russian I am. I've been up to my eyebrows in abuse for a long time, you know?"

"No, I don't know, but I do know you better get somebody to look at that. And we're right here. I'll just tell 'em you're my prisoner, they won't give you any static. I do it all the time."

Myushkin screwed up his face. "I, uh, I don't understand,

what, you bored? Your heart bleeds for me, you, uh, you got a quota for parkin' tickets, you got a quota for good deeds, what?"

"Maybe Vinnie was right, maybe you do make a big deal outta everything."

"Hey, man, I don't make a big deal out of *everything*. I write books. I make a big deal out of *some things*. Writin' books *is* makin' a big deal out of some couple of things, that's what it is. I mean if you're gonna come up with seventy-five, eighty, ninety thousand words, man, you're makin' a big deal out of *some* things, that's what writin' books is, man. It's takin' some things that everybody walks by every day of their lives and never sees and tryin' to tell those same people what they've been missin', that's what it is. So what, right? So the what is, I spend most of my time alone, so when I get around other people I get a little carried away and think I gotta run my mouth to make up for all the times I wasn't around, so it sounds to other people, people like Vinnie, you know, he spends his whole day makin' small talk, so every time big teeth me walks in and starts chewin' the words, Vinnie thinks I'm makin' a big deal, but it ain't nearly as big a deal as he thinks. I mean, Christ, if I ever tried to tell Vinnie what I was really thinkin'? Man, he'd be callin' people to come put me over there with the Thorazine zombies." Myushkin nodded over his shoulder to the mental health clinic across the street.

"Well," Balzic said, sighing. "That may be so, I don't know, but you're still drippin' blood and we're still here."

"Look, I hit a vein, that's all. I keep the pressure on for a couple more minutes it'll stop. Hell, once I had a doctor stop an artery in my leg from spurtin' in about twenty-five minutes, just put a bandage on it and held his fingers and thumbs on it, it stopped. It just takes a little while, that's all. Who's the one makin' a big deal now?"

"Okay okay," Balzic said, holding up his hands. "I give, I give. At least let me go inside and get you some gauze and some tape."

Myushkin threw back his head and laughed. "Oh god, go 'head, who am I to spoil your fun. A guy told me once, never prevent somebody from feelin' noble, they'll never forgive you. Just remember there's a corollary to that, you know? About never lettin' a good deed go unpunished? See, that's the kind of stuff you can't tell Vinnie. Little subtleties like that really piss him off."

Balzic turned and went inside, shaking his head, and found a nurse he knew, and when he'd finished telling her about Myushkin, she gave him some gauze bandages and a pressure bandage and the end of a roll of tape. He wasn't inside more than three or four minutes, but when he brought them back out, Myushkin was gone.

Balzic snorted quizzically, shrugged, and went over to his cruiser. When he slumped behind the wheel, he found a note on the dashboard on a small piece of notebook paper. It said, "Thanks but no thanks. It's not the first aid I don't want. It's the company. Some times the worst thing in the world for a writer is good company. It makes him try to say what he ought to be trying to write. S/M.N. Matthews."

Balzic snorted again. And again. Then he folded the note up and put it in his own notebook and looked at his watch. It was time for supper, time to see his wife, time to watch the blue jays and grackles and sparrows on his deck, time to go home.

*   *   *

Ruth was cutting up cucumbers and tomatoes and onions for a salad when Balzic walked into the kitchen. He kissed her on the side of her head when she signaled with the knife and half a tomato that she couldn't hug him just then. She seemed somber to him, though maybe it was because she had no makeup on. She didn't wear much makeup generally, mostly just some powder on her nose and cheeks and chin, and lipstick. In the summer when she liked to lie in the sun and read, her face turned considerably darker because she never seemed to burn from the sun, just grow darker and darker until at times she could look almost black.

Balzic's mother used to kid Ruth about not staying in the sun too long or people would start to think she was Sicilian. Even though Ruth was descended from Italians, it had taken her a long time to understand that to some Italians, Sicilians were not Italians, but Africans. The first time she actually heard it expressed happened on a night when she took Mrs. Balzic to see some friends and "The Untouchables" was on the TV. The woman they had gone to visit, Mrs. Dipretto, a woman from a village in Abruzzi not far from Mrs. Balzic's childhood home, was fussing with her husband about turning the volume down so they could talk, but he said he wouldn't be able to hear it if he turned it down. Mrs. Dipretto said to her husband finally, "I don't know why you watch that show anyway, it gives Italians a bad name. Makes the people here think all we are is the Black Hand." Mr. Dipretto gave his wife a withering look. "What the hell you talking about? These people ain't Italians, everybody knows that. They're Sicilians, they're from Africa. Go in the kitchen if you want to talk."

Every Italian man Ruth had ever known in her life thought there was something special about the province he or his ancestors had come from, so this business about the Sicilians wasn't anything out of the ordinary, not once she'd found out about it, though after she'd found out, she wondered what else she hadn't been paying attention to while she was growing up. The thing she remembered most about growing up, some of the best fun she'd ever had, was listening to the men and women at the weddings and parties arguing about why everything was better where they'd come from in Italy, the wine was better, the sauce, ohmygod the sauce was better, as though there was only one kind of sauce anybody was allowed to put on pasta, which, of course, was better because the wheat was better because the farmers were better because their ground was sweeter because their animals made better manure.

"You're lookin' real thoughtful," Balzic said.

"Well, maybe it's 'cause I was thinking."

"About what?"

"Oh, just how the old dag's used to argue and fuss and fight about how where they came from everything was better, but what made me think about that was how Ma used to tell me not to lay in the sun too much because people were going to think I was Sicilian."

"Jesus, this must be incest, what we got here, 'cause that's what I was thinkin' about. I was thinkin' about how dark you get in the summer. Like now, when it's real bright outside and you don't have the light on in here, man, you really look dark. Black almost."

"Hey, who knows, maybe I am African." She continued to chop the tomatoes.

"Is that really what you were thinkin' about?"

"Oh, Mario, god, I've been thinking about lots lately, you know that."

"Uh, Ruth, you're not gonna start about that again."

"Did you read what I wrote to you?"

"Yeah I read it of course I read it. You gave it to me I said I was gonna read it I read it."

"Listen to you, already you're starting to talk like a machine gun, already you're mad."

"I am not mad. Why do you do that, why do you tell me I'm mad when all—"

"I tell you you're mad 'cause most of the time I've known you you're mad, angry—"

"And I keep telling you, I couldn't be mad all the time

64

'cause nobody can stay mad all the time, it's too goddamn time consuming. Too goddamn exhausting."

"See, that's another thing you do when you're mad. You start to put the *g*'s on the ends of your words. When you're not mad, you don't do that."

"Well then that proves it, right? I mean, if when I get mad I put the *g*'s on the ends of the words, then that mush mean—"

" 'Mush mean?' "

"—must mean, don't make fun, I get tangled up sometimes. That mush mean, oh shit, hold it, that must mean, there goddammit I got it right, that must mean that there's a time when I don't, right? Don't put the *g*'s on the ends of my words? And so that must mean there are times when I'm not mad, I mean that's what you said—"

"But you're a machine gun again, listen to yourself, my god, Mario, and your voice goes up—"

"Listen, Ruth, listen a minute—"

"I listen all the time, Mar. Listening to you is what I've been doing since I was eighteen. I listen real good. It's you who doesn't want to listen to me, you know? Why do we have all this mail? Huh? Sometimes it's like the post office around here. Look at the fridge. Look, go 'head."

"I don't have to look I know what's on the fridge, come on, cut me some slack here, Ruth, for crissake—"

"Mar, cutting you slack is what I do. Cutting you slack is what I've been doing since I was eighteen. But I never complained about it. Never. Did I ever complain about it?"

Balzic grumbled something under his breath.

"What? What did you say, I didn't hear you."

"I said . . . I said it sounds like all you're doing is complaining."

"Oh god here we go with the *g*'s again." Ruth sighed and leaned on the table and arched her back. "Sometimes I get a headache, Mar. Sometimes it lasts for three, four days.

65

Sometimes I take so many Pamprin I scare myself, but I never tell you about it. I never told you about it, and I've been getting them since I was in high school."

"I don't understand. Why didn't you ever tell me? Why're you tellin' me now?"

"Because I used to tell Ma, you know?" Ruth's eyes filled up. "I miss her so much . . . and I hate it, I honest to god hate it, because everything I told her, it was because I wasn't telling you. And now here you are, your eyes are big as cups, you're lookin' at me like you always did when I got the least little bit sick, you get scared first, and then . . . then you get mad."

"Oh come on."

"No, Mario, no, it's true. You get mad at me when I get sick."

"Ruth, that doesn't make any sense. Why would I get mad at somebody for gettin' sick, Christ, that doesn't . . . hell, I was just up the hospital tryin' to take care of some guy I hardly know."

"That's your job, that's what you do out there, outside, that's not what I'm talkin' about at all. I'm talkin' about me. In here. You get, honest to god, I know you're not gonna believe this, but you got mad at your mother when she died. I mean, a week after, she wasn't in the ground five days and you were pissed off at her for dyin'. You got drunk, boy, you don't even remember, Mario, you were so pissed off at her for dyin' I couldn't believe it. And then I said, to me I said this, not to you, I said, what's not to believe—that's exactly what he does with me. First, he gets scared, which is what you did with Ma, then you get pissed, furious."

"I got furious because she died, I didn't get furious with her. For dying, not with her, that's ridiculous."

"But that's what I'm saying, exactly. You got furious. That was what came up in you. I mean of all the things you have inside, of all the emotions in you, of all the things that might

66

come up, no. Fury, rage, that's what comes up. And when I tell you about it, you look at me the way you're lookin' now, like I have three heads and you don't know what the hell you're doin' here."

"Is this . . . is this all . . . is this all about how you wanna go to work, is that what this is about?"

"Mario, no, listen to me, please, I want to get a job because I'm getting crazy in here. I don't want to get a job because you get mad at me when I get sick. I get lonely. Lonely . . . god. I told you, I don't know how many times I told you, she was your mother, but she was my friend, and now, Jesus, Mario, you're sixty-four and you're working more hours now than you ever worked when you were a patrolman—"

"Nobody knows that better than me—"

"Well you're the chief!"

"So?"

"So if you're the chief and you can't change it so you don't have to ride around like a patrolman, who can? If you can't, who can, that's what I'm saying. But that's not what I'm sayin' either, that's not any of my business."

"You're right, it isn't."

"Oh my god, you should see your face. Tropical storm Mario, a couple more miles an hour and you turn into a hurricane—"

"Hey, just skip the jokes, okay, huh? Whatta we talkin' here."

"We're talkin' here that, wait, let me think. Oh. Right. What we're talkin' here is you're confusing two things. Really. You're confusin' why I want to go to work with what you do when I get sick and why I never told you I got sick because I didn't have to tell you because I always had Ma to talk to and now she's gone and I'm crazy lonely, that's what we're talkin' here."

"And you're tellin' me these things ain't related, is that it?"

"Well sure they are. And sure they're not. I mean, when I

tell you that I never had to tell you when I was sick it was because I knew how you were gonna react, like I said already, first you'd get scared and then you'd get pissed. But it was okay that I knew that about you because when I talked to Ma about it, the first thing she'd do was laugh and tell me that's men for you, her husband, your father, was the same way, but then we could talk about it, she would listen to me and I had somebody to learn from, so I guess you could say I got spoiled. I got so I didn't say the things I should've been sayin' to you because I knew I didn't have to, I could always say them to her—god, you should see your face, Mar, really."

"My face is the way it is—whatever it is—because I keep thinkin' about all the times you told me how much you loved me 'cause of the way I was around people when they needed help and now all I'm hearin' is—"

"Mario, I wasn't lying to you when I said that, I'm not lyin' to you when I say that now. You're lookin' at me like you think I'm such a hypocrite when it comes to you. I know how you are. I know who you are. But what I'm tryin' to tell you is there's a part of you you don't know anything about, that's all. It's the part that gets mad at me when I need help, that's all. I don't know—"

"You sayin' I'm never around to help you? Or I was never around? Or I never help you even when I'm around? Which?"

"Mario, please don't look at me like that, you scare me."

"I'm not lookin' at you any way, how'm I lookin' at you?"

"Mario, you could pick me up and shake me now, that's how you look—"

"Oh what, I'm a wife beater now too? What the hell is this? Are we talkin' about the same two people here? Huh? You and me?"

"Of course we are. Certainly, Mario. . . . Mar, listen to yourself." Ruth heaved a great sigh, her shoulders rising and dropping. She arched her back again, then rolled her head from side to side. "God, my neck hurts, my head hurts—"

"Then maybe you should see a doctor if you're havin' headaches that last for, for how long? Three days? Christ if I had a headache that lasted three days I'd be climbin' the walls."

"I don't want to see a doctor. My neck's tied in knots, you know, I'm tyin' myself in knots trying to think how I can make you understand why I want to get a job, I'm tryin' to save my life here, 'cause it's important to me to have you understand me. You have to. You're the only one who makes any difference to me. I can't ask the girls to help me, I can't ask them to come and hold my hand while I try to figure out what to do. Mario, since your mother died . . . I am so . . . lonely. And when I try to tell you about it, every time I've tried to tell you about it, you look at me as though I'm sick, you act the way you do when I'm sick, it's like you think being lonely is like havin' the flu or something, measles, you can't wait to get away, get out of here, get someplace away from me . . . and I know what it is, it's because you can't stand to see me weak. I know that now, I never knew it before, because when I get weak, you get scared. You think I'm going to leave you. That's what you did with your mother, and I'm beginnin' to think that's what you did all your life with your father, when he died, it scared you so bad, didn't it?"

Balzic shook his head many times and started to pace around the kitchen, pausing at the screen door to the deck to look at the birds taking a bath.

He turned around and looked at her intently for a long time. "I don't know, maybe you're right. But I don't think it was 'cause of my father, though maybe it was, I don't know. All I know is I can't remember any of their names, none of 'em, not a one."

Ruth frowned and squinted up at him. "Can't remember whose names?"

"Nobody I was at Iwo with, not a one. Maybe that's what you're talkin' about now, I don't know."

"Did you get scared again today, did it come back again?"

"Yeah, it was real bright and I was lookin' for a mailbox out at the mall and I turned around and walked out into the goddamn parkin' lot and almost got hit by a car, a goddamn Japanese car, and the whole goddamn thing came flyin' back at me. I'm tryin' to think now, I mean, hell, those are the only two emotions I can remember. I remember bein' scared, Jesus, the words for what you feel then, those words are so goddamn puny for what you feel, but I guess if you're gonna put 'em in a sequence, that's the way it goes, first fear, then fury. 'Cause I think fury's the only thing that gets you through the fear, or over it or whatever."

"Oh, Mar, I'm sorry. I didn't mean to pick on you today. The last thing you need is somebody pickin' on you after that—"

"No no no, it's okay, I'm not lookin' for any pity here. I'm not lookin' to take a waltz around what you're talkin' about either. I mean, I just can't figure out why I can't remember their names. Not a goddamn one. Remember that time I ran into that Jew who made it through Auschwitz? He told me the only way he could deal with bein' alive was God gave him a purpose savin' him, so he remembered all their names, that was the purpose God gave him, or so he said. And he told their names to everybody, everybody he met he'd just keep repeating these names, and when I told him how I couldn't remember anybody's names from Iwo he called me a liar, he said I couldn't have been there, that was why God let me live, to remember their names, and I almost punched the fucker, remember that?"

Ruth nodded and came and stood beside him and hooked her arm through his. "Maybe that's why you can't remember, maybe you're still so mad at all of them for dying—"

"Yeah but they didn't all die, that's what I can't understand.

Lots of 'em made it out. I knew them too. I wasn't the only one who walked back onto a ship, there were lots of 'em. How come I can't remember *their* names either?"

"It was probably just the whole thing. Not probably. It was."

"Maybe. But sometimes I think if I don't remember somebody's name soon I think I'm gonna go nuts, naked-ass nuts, just running down the fucking street, screaming, 'Medic, medic,' and nobody's going to hear me—is that what you're talking about now?"

She pulled him closer and nuzzled in closer. "I don't think of it that way, no. I don't holler for a medic. I holler for Ma. Do you know I go to her grave every day?"

"Every day? Jeez, I knew you went a lot. But you go every day, really?"

"Every day until yesterday. I told her I had to stop comin' for a while, it was gettin' too hard. I told her I had to get a job or I was gonna go crazy in the house. Like all the old ladies who used to go crazy in the house after their husbands died and their kids moved. And I told her that my husband was still alive and she would be glad to know that, but . . . and this is a really big but . . . but he was workin' like a goddamn rookie cop and he was gone more than ever and I was talkin' to myself and I was boring myself to tears 'cause I didn't have anything to say that was worth hearin'. So I'm not gonna go back for a while, I mean, except to take petunias there . . . she loves petunias. . . ."

"Hey, you want a job, you wanna find out what it's like out there in America, huh? You wanna leave all this luxury, go 'head," Balzic said, hoping that she was hearing it as the sardonic joke he intended it to be.

"God, Mar, you're such a silver-tongued bastard. Your head's cement, but your tongue's pure silver."

"I was hopin' you'd say that," he said, hoping further that she really meant it.

71

"The trouble is, I'm absolutely unqualified to do anything. When people ask me whether I'm familiar with WordPerfect, I, oh god, the first time somebody asked me that, I said, 'Huh? Word what?' This lady told me it was a computer program and all I could say was, 'Lady, not only don't I know anything about computers, I never even took typing in high school. I never had a job. I got married. I know how to keep house, what is this WordPerfect stuff,' oh god, I was practically hysterical when I came out of there."

Balzic looked down at her and squirmed around so that he was facing her. "You been goin' on interviews and stuff? Huh?"

" 'You been goin' on interviews and stuff?' " she mimicked him. "No not 'interviews and stuff.' I've been to the community college three times. I went last week, they had this seminar, or whatever, it was for 'women who were trying to get back into the workplace' or some bullshit like that. I told them, look, I'm not 'trying to get back in,' I was never in there in the first place, you know? And fortunately, or unfortunately, however you wanna look at it, it turns out I wasn't the only one. Half the women there, god, they were just like me, we were pathetic, what a bunch. I mean really, Mar. I felt so sorry for this one woman. Her husband died, she was like sixty-something, she didn't have a clue, he never told her anything, she didn't know where the checkbook was, didn't know how to write a check, people callin' her up, really harassing her about these bills, and she didn't know where the checkbook was or where he kept the bills or anything. Lived here for sixty some years, Mar, and she was like, well, this really funny lady, she said, 'It's okay, honey, it's just you're from Zorgon, the planet of the lost women, and you got shipped here by mistake,' and everybody just broke up, even this woman, but then she started to cry, oh, it was just shitty, I felt so bad for her. I mean I felt bad for her, but at least I know how to pay the bills, I know how to write the checks,

72

god, I may not know how to make the money but I do know
how to spend it."

"And a damn fine job you do of that," he said, poking her
playfully in the ribs. "So you really been goin' on interviews
and stuff, huh?"

"Oh come on, I've been to the community college three
times I said, that's not interviews. I mean, holy hell, all I'm
finding out is about the only thing I'm qualified to do is baby-
sit."

"Aw come on."

"No, I'm serious, Mar. That's about all I can really think
about tryin' to do, really. There's nothing—I mean, what the
hell kind of job am I supposed to look for? I mean, it's either
baby-sitting or workin' in a stop'n'rob."

"Well that's out, period."

"Yeah, so, what's left—I mean if you can't type, what's left?
W-O-P, that's what's left. Now there's a whole new meaning
for WOP, it doesn't mean some dag' 'without papers.' Now
it means 'watching other people.' You either watch other
people's kids or you watch other people's parents—"

"Aw come on—"

"You keep sayin' that, Mar, but it's true. Half the women
in this class, that's what they do. And there was this one
woman, the one who told this other lady she was from Zorgon? She's really funny, she is. She messes up words so bad
and she doesn't know it, like she says 'sangwich' instead of
sandwich and 'afaghan' instead of afghan. But she was talking about how these were supposed to be her 'golden years,'
when she was supposed to be taking it easy, she had everybody cracking up, really, but this poor woman is watching
kids sometimes seven days a week, most of the time twelve
hours a day. The only meal she doesn't make for them is
breakfast, she bathes them, takes them everywhere she goes
'cause her husband got hurt at work, fell off a ladder and
landed on his head or something, I'm not sure how he got

hurt, but he can't drive, so she has to take them with her everyplace she goes. You know how hard it is to load kids into cars and take them shopping? And she's sixty. That stuff's real hard on the back when you're twenty. I mean she was laughing and she's really funny, but she said she didn't have any choice—she didn't know how to type—"

"Why's everybody so convinced you gotta know how to type?"

"Mario, it's computers. If you want to do something besides work in a stop'n'rob, if you go into anybody's office, that's all you see is computers and if you don't know how to type, I mean, what are you going to say when they say do you know WordPerfect or Lotus or Apple something or DOS. This woman said, 'What the hell is this DOS?' all she hears is DOS this, DOS that. And somebody said it may as well be Italian if you don't know it. And this woman says, 'Well, hell, I know Italian, why don't they make computers out of Italian?' "

Balzic was looking at her intently, not even smiling.

"I guess you had to be there," Ruth said.

"You mean, uh, you've been out there three times now talkin' to people and that's it? Huh? That's what you learned about what you could do—watch other people?"

"Well to tell you the truth, it was sort of good just to be in this place with all these women who were pretty much in the same boat. Well . . . that's not true at all. I mean I wasn't in the same boat. I don't have to W-O-P sixty, seventy hours a week. What's happened, Mar? I mean, there's something I don't get. I know everybody has to work for a living, but god when you talk to these counselors and these people who run these seminars, they tell you about all the people, especially the women, the old women, who are really scrapin' and scufflin' just to hold it together—"

"It ain't just old women, dearie. The guy I took up the hospital, he told me straight out, he's a, how'd he put it? He's a 'fugitive from capitalism.' Hasn't worked since Volkswagen shut down. Twenty-six weeks of unemployment, then I guess he got another extension on that, and now his wife's on food stamps and, uh, he's gettin' hassled by the state to take minimum-wage jobs, and then he's gonna have to get out of his house in order for his wife to collect welfare. On top of that, he can't sell his house, and if his wife signs up for welfare the state's gonna put a lien on it, so he says he works strictly for cash. 'Cash, barter, and poach,' I think he said.

"But believe me he's not the only one. Wildlife officers I talk to tell me deer poachin' is the worst it's been in their memory. One guy told me he could be bustin' guys every day if he had the time and wanted to do the paperwork. Says all he has to do is drive his Jeep out into the woods at night and just sit there with the windows down. He says within a half-hour, no more, he'll hear the guns goin' off. Hell, he says it's so bad in Fayette County, the wildlife guys down there call the people the Fayette Cong, says you can't get a conviction for huntin' out of season to save your buns. Says you cannot convict anybody 'cause when you show up at the prelim hearing, there's ten guys waitin' to give alibi testimony. And if it's just one wildlife officer bustin' one poacher, the magistrate's gonna go with the alibi witnesses every time—'cause he lives there and sooner or later he has to run for retention."

"Well god, Mar, how'd it get like this? It's like the Depression all over again."

"You askin' me? I'm the guy who can't figure out how to not be ridin' around like a rookie, remember? I can't find enough bodies to keep one black-and-white on the streets some times, remember? I drive around town, I swear all I see is old people and kids. It's like there's a whole generation disappeared in there somewhere, I don't know what happened to 'em. All I know is they're not workin' around here, that's for sure. Look at that blue jay, god, isn't it pretty?"

"Do you know that's one of the few birds where the male and the female are both the same color, identical?"

"Yeah? You think you're so smart, so are starlings and grackles and pigeons. All I know about blue jays is, long as the mills were workin' around here I never saw one. D'you ever remember seein' one? When d'you see the first one, you remember?"

Ruth shrugged. "About ten years ago. I never saw one before then."

"Neither did I. So there ya are. Either you have the mills workin', spittin' smoke and god knows what all else into everybody's lungs, or else you have blue jays."

"It ought to be a better choice than that."

Balzic snorted. "You would think so, wouldn't you. Noisy bastards, ain't they? You'd think bein' that good-lookin' would be enough for 'em, but nooooo, not them. They gotta be big mouths on top of it."

"That reminds me," Ruth said, "we're almost out of bird-seed."

"I thought you weren't feedin' 'em in the summer, thought we agreed about that."

"Yes, that's right, we did agree, but if you don't put something out there for the squirrels, they eat your house, remember? Look at the screen. I just put this screen on the end of May, look at it already. Two holes started."

"Well, see, there's a job you could get. Screen replacement. Get you some cards printed up, trade in the car on a van, buy you a couple rolls of screen, get you a baseball hat with, lemme see, Ruthie The Replacer on it. T-shirt too. And there you go, whole new career."

"Oh great. Ruthie The Replacer. Right. You hungry?"

"Not really. Too hot. That there, what you're makin' right there looks good to me."

"Okay, get some silverware and clear off the table. We have to talk."

"I thought that's what—whatta you mean we have to talk? What the hell were we just doin'?"

"Oh, Mario, really, we were—the talk hasn't even started. That was just the warm-up, that's all. I have to learn all over how to talk to you. But so you do too, buster. I'm not the only one has to learn how to talk to my spouse, uh, my partner."

Balzic rolled his eyes and shrugged and sighed and opened the drawer where the silverware was. He collected the silver, stopped at the phone stand to get some placemats out of the bottom drawer, then went into the living room to the round oak table Ruth had put together from a kit she'd bought in a hardware store. They'd been using it for a dining table for the past year or so. Balzic said it reminded him of one of the tables at Muscotti's; Ruth said it reminded her of a table at an outdoor café, but bigger, so they both liked it.

Balzic put the placemats down and laid the silver out and started to pick up the paper when Ruth called from the kitchen, "Did you really read it, Mar?"

He tossed the paper onto the couch and sighed. "Yeah, I really read it. I told ya I did."

"Well what did you think?"

"I don't know, maybe if you could type I wouldn't have such a hard time understandin'. . . ." It was not coming out funny as he thought it would; it was coming out smart-assy, and he was already wincing.

She came around the corner from the kitchen carrying the salads and her lips were pinched tight. "That is not the way to keep this goin', partner."

"I'm sorry, okay, really, that sounded funny in my head, but as soon as it came out, I knew it was all wrong, I'm sorry."

"Okay fine," she said, sitting down. She folded her hands and looked to Balzic as though she was getting ready to say a prayer, which was not something either of them did as a general rule, so it surprised him.

"Uh, excuse me, but, uh, what're you gettin' ready to do, huh?"

77

"Listen, partner, and you shall hear."

"Oh-oh."

"Ummmm," Ruth began, clearing her throat, "we who are about to dissolve this marriage—"

"We who are about to do what?!"

"—just listen, just listen. Um, we who are about to dissolve this marriage in search of a better, more mutually satisfying relationship which I want to call a partnership, um, we who are about to do that, we salute you, whoever you are, man, woman, or committee."

Balzic's mouth fell open and he hunched forward.

"If you don't close your mouth, Mar, you're gonna start to drool."

When Balzic regained his composure, such as it was, he said, "Hey, in all those sixteen pages you wrote it didn't say anything about dissolvin' any marriage!"

"Not in so many words, no, it didn't. I didn't. But, I mean, if you're going to start a new relationship, then the old one's got to go, that's all there is to it. Can't make an omelet without breakin' the eggs."

"Yeah well go where? You talkin' lawyers here, huh? Jesus Christ, Ruth, are you talkin' lawyers here, you talkin' courthouse here or what? What the hell's goin' on? I mean, Jeeeeee-sus."

"Well see this is one of the things I no longer want to have go on, and I wrote that—that I made as clear as I could make it. I wrote, as clear as I know how, that I don't want you raising your voice to me anymore—"

"Raisin' my voice! You're talkin' dissolvin' the goddamn marriage and you're worryin' about me raisin' my voice!"

"Mario, Mario, raising your voice is one of the reasons the marriage is already dissolved."

"Already . . . huh? Whatta you mean already dis—what the hell you talkin' about?"

"Lower your voice about eight notes, one whole octave,

remember octave? Hmmm? First you lower your notes, then you lower your volume, then maybe we can find out what I'm talking about."

Balzic put his knife and fork down and his hands dropped into his lap and his shoulders sagged.

"Look at you, Mar, honest to god it's comic sometimes—now don't get mad—I'm not laughin' at you, okay? But in order for you to lower your voice and lower your volume, you have to lower your whole body, honest, it's funny. . . ."

"I guess you have to be there. Over there. Where you're sittin'. 'Cause the last thing it is where I'm sittin' is funny."

Ruth put her hands in her lap and waited. "I mean it, Mar. I don't want to be talked to like that anymore." She was smiling, but her eyes were glinting hard.

He tried to straighten up, to pull his dignity up by pulling his shoulders up while swallowing several times as though swallowing could bring his voice down. He didn't know what he was doing, or what he was supposed to do. He heard himself taking long, noisy breaths.

"Uh, do I, uh, is this, uh, do I raise my voice, uh, do I talk loud a lot?"

"Yes. Yes, you do. You have always talked loud a lot. But you don't talk. You shout. When somebody or something pisses you off, you shout. I don't know what you do out there," she said, nodding in the general direction of the front door, "but in here, when something gets you, you get loud."

"When 'something gets' me? You're not talkin' now about when I get mad at you—"

"Well. Now *there's* a start. I mean admitting that you do get mad at me—occasionally. That is something—do you know that is something you have never admitted in all the years we've been married—that you get mad at me?" She was still smiling, but the glinty eyes were softening.

"Well I wanna know, I mean, is it, uh, is it when something out there pisses me off, you mean I come in here and get

79

loud about it, or do you mean when sometimes, uh, when sometimes, like every once in a while—"

"Oh for crissake, Mario, you can say you get mad at me. You won't die. I won't die. I won't go away if you say you get mad at me."

Balzic peered at her, his eyes squinting, his mind wandering in spite of himself to when he was eighteen somewhere out on the Pacific Ocean, only god and the navigator knew where, they used to say, and god wasn't talking and the navigator wasn't allowed. Who was that *they* who used to say that, Balzic pondered, and then he came back to Ruth.

"That's it, isn't it?" Ruth said. "You think if you get mad at me, if you allow yourself to admit that you get mad at me, I'll go away, huh? That's what you think, don't you?"

He put his elbows on the table and folded his hands and rested his chin on them. He sighed. "I could say something real smart-assy now about how that sounds like real good psychology, like it ought to be right, and now that you told me, everything should just be fine, like on TV. We have a little talk, lasts for a half-hour, we get everything worked out before the last commercial, then we all go out for dinner or something."

"Oh, Mario, that would sound real smart-assy. Really, it would, and I hope you don't. Don't say it like you mean it, please. Please don't believe it."

"Well, see, that's what I think I was tryin' to say, that it does sound like good psychology, but if I just say that, I mean, if you just say that and all I do is, uh, lemme think, if all I do is just hear the words, then, really, that's all there'll be to it. I mean, I was glazin' over there, I know I was, and I was back on that ship goin' over, and I was tryin' to think how I was then and all I can remember is how sick I was, god, I was so sick, I mean everybody was sick, you can't imagine what that ship stunk like, it was god-awful, really, and I kept thinking, Jesus, how're we supposed to fight anybody, I mean guys were so sick they couldn't stand up, for a couple days I thought I was gonna die, I thought my stomach was gonna come up through my mouth and there we were gettin' ready to go fight, hell, we didn't know where we were supposed to fight until a couple days before we got there, not that it would've made any difference to anybody, not to me, that's for sure. I'd never heard of Iwo Jima. Hell I was lucky if I could've found Japan on a map then. What am I ramblin' on like this for, you know?"

"I think it's 'cause you're trying to remember what you were thinking and feeling, about the guys you were with maybe, before it started. I think you were thinking whether you were, uh, maybe you were trying to remember if you were mad at them before it started. What do you think?"

Balzic put his hands on the table and looked at the salad. He picked up the bowl and moved it aside. "All of a sudden I'm not very hungry. Thinkin' about that ship got me queasy as hell."

Ruth started to say something, sitting for a long moment with her mouth poised to talk, but then she closed her mouth and cleared her throat.

"Yeah, I know I know," he said, "it's not just the ship or thinkin' about the ship, it's all this. Christ, Ruth, you're scarin' the hell out of me with this stuff, I mean, holy shit, dissolvin' the marriage? I don't know how to deal with this. I mean, if talkin' loud really bothers you, I mean I'll have to learn a whole new thing here, I'll have to really watch myself, and I don't know if I can. I mean, Christ, here is where I blow it off, you know?"

She nodded many times. "Yes yes, exactly. That's exactly it. I want you to stop blowin' it off at me, you know?"

Balzic jumped up and almost knocked his chair over backward. "Well shit! I mean who'm I supposed to blow it off to then?"

"Mario, this is exactly what I'm talking about," she said as calmly as she could, though her voice was quavering ever so slightly. "Please sit down. Please?"

Balzic paced around the room, two circuits around the chairs, in front of the couch, to the kitchen door, words roaring up to his tongue in great clumps of air, and then stumbling back into his mind because he knew he couldn't say them. He was sputtering and he heard himself sputtering and he thought that it would really be good if he could laugh, well maybe not laugh out loud at himself, but maybe if he could show Ruth that he saw himself as a sputtering, blustering fool just by bringing up a small chuckle or two, maybe he could make some sense here, but he couldn't. He was—and this took a great stretch of his courage to admit even to himself—he was more afraid of looking foolish in front of her than of anything else.

When he sat down again, he was not quite scowling but very sober, somber, because he was trying to look angry, he knew it, because he had trained himself to look angry to scare street punks, and here he was doing it in his own living room to his own wife and he couldn't stop, but because he was caught in his own grim joke about it, he couldn't manage his best scary look and he certainly couldn't manage a smile, so he thought the only face left was a fool's face and the best way around that was to try to look sober and somber. Which probably meant he must have been looking really foolish now. Maybe she was right, maybe he only knew two emotions—fear and fury.

Ruth cleared her throat again and reached over and touched his forearm. "Mar, we don't have any choice. If we're going to stay together, we have to learn how to talk to each other—and you have to believe me when I tell you that I'm not just pickin' on you here. It's as much my fault as it is yours—"

"I'm not just two emotions, am I? I mean, I'm a little more

complicated than that, no? Huh?" As soon as the words were out, he thought he sounded like a child. It made him cringe.

"What do you mean—sure you are, hell yes you are, but lots of times you get confused about how you handle stuff out there and how you're supposed—no, not how *you're supposed* to do it in here, no, that's not what I mean. I mean how I would *like* you to handle things in here, that's all I'm talkin' about, Mar, honest to god I am, really."

He didn't know what to say.

"Mar, remember how you used to practice mugging in the mirror, remember that? Remember how you used to practice looking really crazy tough, hard, so you'd know what kind of face to make?"

"I didn't know you knew I did that."

"Oh god, Mar, do you think I would have told you then that I saw you? It was like, uh, oh god what's the word, it's right on the tip of my—Peeping Tom! I, uh, one day, you left the bathroom door open a crack and I saw you in there, you were shaving, uh, and you were makin' these terrible faces, oh you looked really, uh, scary, honest to god, I said, *Who is this man, what is he doing*? I wouldn't have figured it out except I ran into, oh, what's-her-name, she's dead now, so's her husband, but he used to be a sergeant when you were a patrolman, never mind who they are, but for some reason I got up the nerve to ask her about it, and she got the biggest boot out of it, she said, 'Yeah, they all do it, they're all a bunch of hams.'"

"Well I don't know if all cops do it, but I know I did it, because I wanted to know everything I could know that would keep me from gettin' into a physical thing with somebody, that doesn't make me any ham, goddamn actor or somethin'."

"Well that's just what she said, I didn't say that, you don't have to defend yourself."

"I didn't say you did, but I just want you to know why I

83

did it, that's all. Knowin' what kind of face to make is just as important as knowin' what kind of questions to ask. It can save you a lot of grief, believe me. Knowin' how to look mad when you're not, like when you're just disgusted with anybody who could do somethin' so stupid, that takes some practice, you know?"

Ruth was nodding her head repeatedly. "I understand," she said. "And what I'm tryin' to tell you right now—and I don't know why I never thought of this before—what I think it would be really good if you could do around me is, I don't see why you can't practice in front of a mirror, just like the old days, only this time maybe you could practice looking patient and understanding, how about that? Instead of practicing how to scare people, how 'bout practicing looking interested and concerned and patient and understanding, and and and, most of all, practice lookin' real calm, how about that, huh?"

Balzic put his face in his hands and shook it. "God this is bizarre," he muttered into his palms.

"It's not bizarre, Mario, it isn't. You have to practice things. Everybody expects everybody to know how to do things, everything, but you don't know how to do something until somebody shows you. And then you have to practice. I mean you don't expect people, guys, just 'cause they think they're tough, you don't expect them to know how to be a cop, know the law, know first aid, know, uh, how to shoot, everything you have to know, I mean, you have training. You train them yourself, or you send them to the state police to get training and you're always trainin' them—"

"Used to always train 'em, past tense, babycakes, not anymore. Don't have the people, don't have the money—"

"But you would if you could is what I'm saying. And you wouldn't think your whole department was goin' to hell just because you found out you had one guy in it who didn't know how to do something, would you?"

He shook his head thoughtfully.

"Well, then, uh, just look at it like it's a training class, that's all, like you had the money and you heard about this guy who was an expert in some other department and you hired him to come in to tell you about something you need to know, like he was an expert in if, uh, somebody was holdin' their kid hostage and their wife was screamin' she was goin' in the house to get him or something. I mean, you wouldn't have any problem doing that, would you?"

"No. Not if he really knew what he was talkin' about and knew how to talk, no. And if I had the money, no," he said, shrugging. " 'Course not."

"Well, Mar, all I'm asking you to do is go back in front of the mirror in the bathroom, you know, when you're shaving, and practice looking like I'm a really nice wonderful person that you want to become, uh, partners with. And you know that lookin' angry and talkin' loud really upsets me and you don't want to upset me and so you have to practice. I mean, think of it like it's a first-aid class. 'Cause that's what it is, Mar, really. We need to both practice. Honest."

"Yeah?" He knew that he was looking suspicious and it wasn't because that was a face he'd ever had to practice. His mother used to say he was born suspicious. "And while I'm practicin' this first aid, uh, just what're you gonna be practicin'?"

She slumped, took a deep breath, then pulled her shoulders up and let the breath out, tucking her diaphragm in. "I'm going to practice how to be a person—all on my own. A person who's a partner with a man. A man who used to be my husband. A person who doesn't go running off to the cemetery complaining to a dead person, a person I loved more than I loved my own mother, but I can't go off complaining to her about what I don't know anymore and expecting her to tell me how to see things and what to do. My god, Mar, I'm fifty-four years old and I couldn't take care of

85

myself if I had to. If something happened to you, I mean, god, Mar, what would I do?" Her eyes were brimming with tears and her chin was quivering.

He slid down to his knees and scooched over to her side and wrapped his arms around her and she started to cry hard. "God, I miss her so much," she said.

"I know, I know, I know," he said, but it was just words, that's all it was because he knew he didn't know. It was just another of those times when saying that he knew something when he didn't was just a different way of making soft, appealing grunts, another of those times when he felt about as smart as animals that dragged their knuckles on the ground when they walked.

He held her like that for a long while, almost a minute, then he had to get up because his knees hurt and then his hips hurt and then his back. He sighed and sat back down again and rubbed his knees and watched her wipe her eyes and blow her nose.

She looked at him and laughed and said, "God, ain't we a pair."

"Yeah? Well are we? Or aren't we?"

"I don't know, Mar, you tell me."

"Ruth," he said several times, stopping each time to shake his head and start over. "The older I get the less brains I think I have—"

"There's nothing wrong with your brains—"

"Nah, no, lemme finish. I mean, I been havin' a hellofa time with some things now, god, for years. I mean . . . I mean I really got rattled when I first started hearin' the rumors about Kennedy messin' with the mob guys from Chicago. I mean, everybody around here, all the Catholics, they were so happy about that, when Kennedy got elected, Jesus, Ma was nuts about Kennedy. But I said to myself then—to nobody else, believe me, I didn't tell anybody about what I was thinkin', nobody. But I had real bad feelin's about that when

I first started hearin' things, real bad. I mean, I understand you got to make accommodations with people, 'cause Americans, you know, they're the most goddamn self-righteous people—well, I shouldn't say that because I've never been anyplace else except the war, but people here, man, they love to have it both ways. They love to tell other people what they think ain't good for 'em or what they ain't supposed to want. They wanna make laws for how everybody else is supposed to behave, but, man-oh-man, they sure don't want those laws to apply to them.

"And I don't have to tell you what kind of deal I've had here with Muscotti, I mean, he does his thing and I do my thing, and sometimes it might look to other people like those two things are real blurry. And sometimes they are. I know that better'n anybody. But, godalmighty, Ruth, I never went to him and asked him to hit somebody for me. I never did that. I told him plenty of times to get some people to wise up, get smart, stop makin' fools out of people, but on my mother's grave, Ruth, I never asked him to do something for me because I couldn't do it myself the way it was supposed to be done. When I heard about Kennedy and those Chicago guys, I said, Hey, this is over the line, this is way over the line. And I sure as hell didn't know half the facts—I didn't know 'em then and I still don't know most of 'em now, but one thing I do know is that's when I first started askin' myself whose side I was on. And the more that's come out in the news, like about that maniac Hoover and how he ran the FBI and how Kennedy was buggin' the guys who ran the steel companies and how the newspaper that was all hot to get Nixon for the Watergate thing, how the guy that ran that paper knew all about Kennedy buggin' the steel guys and never said a word, I mean, hell, Ruth, I've been havin' day-mares about some of this stuff. It just goes on and on and the older I get the more I keep askin' myself what the hell am I doin' it for? Like now, I mean, Christ, I know you think

I'm nuts for ridin' around in a black-and-white, but you know what? It came to me the other day, hit me between the eyes like a brick."

"Do I know what about what, I'm not following you," Ruth said.

"I know I'm goin' in circles, but I'm gettin' to it. The other day I was ridin' through the Flats and this juicer's staggerin' around in the middle of the street, wavin' his arms, bitchin' at the world, you know, and I pulled over and got out and came up behind him and he swung around and saw me and just froze. And he looked at me and said, you know, just slobberin' and spittin' all over the place, he said. 'Well if it ain't old Balzic. Look at you. You know what, Balzic? You been a cop as long as I been drinkin', but I'll bet I know why I keep drinkin' better than you know why you're still a cop.'

"So I was tryin' to get him in the backseat and tellin' him not to throw up in my car, blah blah, and he looks at me, this guy who's drunk out of his skull, stinkin', clothes are filthy, and he says, 'Every day I get up, I suck on this bottle, it's my tit. But every day you get up and suck on that badge. And you don't even know it's a tit.' And then he passed out."

"Well, jeez, Mar, I wouldn't—no, I'm not going to say what I think. What did you think—what do you think?"

"I think I do what I do because I don't know what else to do. And I don't think there's anything that shakes me up more than that. I mean, you're talkin' about us startin' something new here, you've been thinkin' about what we are and what we've been doin', and so you sit down and write, man, sixteen pages about what you think we've been doin' and what you don't want to do anymore and what you do want to do, but I look around inside my brain and some drunk hits me between the eyes and tells me I'm as addicted to this goddamn badge as he is to his bottles and I think he's right. And what's worse, I've been thinkin' for years that I didn't know whose side I was on or whose side I was supposed to

88

be on—or if there were even sides for crissake. And now, now, man-oh-man, I don't know. I just don't know sometimes. I just don't know what the hell I'm doin' and I think it's just gonna get more confusing as it goes. Like I cannot think of us not bein' together, but I don't know, I mean right now, I don't know if I ever knew how we really were around here. And I don't know if I have the kind of brainpower it's gonna take to be what you want me to be. Like, I don't know if I can practice this kind of first aid you're talkin' about. I just don't know. All I know is I'm real scared, Ruthie. Honest to god I am."

"Me too, Mar. Me too." She stood up and came beside him and leaned down and put her arms around his shoulders and kissed his hair. "Me too."

*   *   *

July had been hotter than any other July on record in Rocksburg. And August was hotter than July. The Municipal Water Authority had requested that a voluntary curtailment be imposed on all its customers because the Conemaugh Reservoir was at its lowest level since 1942, when the dam that created the reservoir had been built. The curtailment meant, among other things, that people were not to wash their cars or water their lawns or gardens and that drinking water was to be provided in restaurants only upon request. People were asked to not flush their toilets as often and to not let their faucets run when they were shaving, or brushing their teeth, or doing the dishes, and to take shorter showers and to bathe all their small children in the same tub if at all possible.

Hardware stores couldn't keep fans in stock, department and discount stores couldn't keep air conditioners in stock, and County Emergency Management was appealing to people to look out for their elderly neighbors and to letter carriers to nose around if mailboxes were starting to fill up. The

89

Rocksburg Gazette was interviewing "health care professionals" about the warning signs of heat stroke, and the "health care professionals" were advising people to drink plenty of water and to soak in cool tubs if they didn't have fans or air-conditioning.

Balzic was grousing to himself about the advice from the "health care professionals"—didn't anybody call them doctors and nurses anymore?—as he was driving across the Rocksburg line into Kennedy Township. Goddamn pill-rollers are telling people to soak in cool tubs and the goddamn water authority is trying to get the county commissioners to make excessive water use a third-class misdemeanor.

There seemed to Balzic to be a kind of communicable disease going around, a kind of flu that started out with just the sniffles and the headaches and muscle pains, but the longer it lasted the more it turned into its main symptom, which was a rising intolerance for things other people did, and the only medicine the infected people could take was to persuade some equally infected lawmaker to turn their intolerance into an indictable offense. The trouble with this disease, as far as Balzic could see, was that once the sniffles and aches and pains went away, it was left to the cops to figure out how they were supposed to arrest the violators and left to the courts to figure out how to prosecute them.

It was fine to make a speech about how excessive water use was wrong and a crime and punishable by a fine, et cetera, et cetera, but who was going to read the meters? Who was going to make the arrests? And which level of the courts was going to hear the cases? It sounded to Balzic a whole lot like the baloney about the DUI laws: everybody was for getting drunk drivers off the roads in the same way everybody was for not abusing children. But when it got down to actually putting drunk drivers in jail, jail space disappeared the first weekend after the state DUI law was passed. If the state pols were serious about putting every drunk driver in jail who was busted, they'd have to pick out two or three of the largest counties in the state and lay double strands of concertina wire around them to make a concentration camp. The actual result of the DUI law was that almost no first offender was going to jail. In practice, at least in Conemaugh County, a third offense might get you forty-eight hours—if there was room.

So it wasn't just the heat that was making Balzic surly as he pulled into the driveway at 108 Avon Drive, Stratford Acres.

Stratford Acres was a housing development that had sprung up about 1986 or '87 when the officers of Rocksburg Savings and Loan had decided that the real-estate-development boom erupting across the country was passing them by, so instead of just lending money for home mortgages—which they knew something about—they set up their own development company—which they didn't know anything about. So they hired people who claimed to know about housing development: housing development consultants. And these consultants then hired architects, who drew the plans and hired the contractors, who rented the bulldozers and highlifts and trucks and hired the subcontractors, who hired the men to operate them. In what seemed no time at all, all the trees had been eliminated and so had most of the humps and gullies on 110 acres just off Route 66 north out of Rocksburg. The roads and underground utility lines went in, the lots were marked off, and dozens of two-story boxes, half brick, half aluminum siding with attached two-car garages, started to stick up out of the brown, devegetated dirt. There were six different floor plans, but no matter how they were laid out, they each had three bedrooms, two baths, eat-in kitchen, living room, dining room, laundry and mud room, and heat-pump whole-house heating and air-conditioning. One model floor plan could be told from another by the colors of the aluminum siding, summer-sky blue, or cornsilk yellow, or vanilla white; or by their shingles, forest green, or russet brown, or sparkly charcoal. The starting price was $79,500, with 10 percent down, plus points, thirty-year mortgages at only 10.25 percent, twenty years slightly higher.

The finishing price was seven indictments, one plea bargain, five convictions, three prison terms, one probation, one death by cardiac arrest at the arraignment, and a sign in the window of the main office of Rocksburg Savings and Loan that it was now the property of the Resolution Trust Corporation of the U.S. Government. The sign in the window did not say so, but the U.S. Government had purchased the RS&L at the remarkably low, low price to U.S. taxpayers of only $17 million.

Of the 220 houses in the original proposal submitted to the Kennedy Township Planning Commission by the Rocksburg-Stratford Development Co. Inc., the wholly owned subsidiary of RS&L, 66 had actually been built, and 17 had actually been bought. The four roads that had actually been paved were named Shakespeare, William, Avon, and Bard. Enough suits and countersuits had been filed in the prothonotary's office to keep lawyers and bureaucrats busy until probably the next millennium, if they didn't milk it too hard. Balzic had learned all of this from Panagios Valcanas, who had finished his lesson by saying, "My friend, don't look so glum. When life gives people lemons, somebody's got to make lemonade. And nobody knows that recipe better than lawyers."

Balzic pulled off Avon Drive in front of 108, got out of his cruiser, and started walking up the steps to the front door of a model with vanilla siding and sparkly charcoal shingles. The more he looked around, the more he thought he was wasting his time. A lawn was in, and while it was as brown as the dirt under it, given the weather, somebody had made an effort at least. A red maple tree in the middle of the front yard, wilted though it was, still had support ropes holding it upright, and there were lots of juniper bushes around the

92

foundation. Somebody had been trying to keep the front yard from turning into a desert, but good landscaping didn't have anything to do with abusing kids, or anything else.

Nothing had anything to do with anything else. After sixty-four years on the planet, Balzic thought that of all the dumb ideas he'd ever heard, the dumbest was that just because somebody was good at doing one thing, that meant they were good at doing some other thing, or just because somebody wanted to do something good or bad, they would naturally want to do something else better or worse. It was avalanche thinking and all you could do was try not to get buried by it. Avalanche thinkers believed that once a kid smoked a marijuana cigarette, he would naturally progress through all the illegal drugs until he was dead in a dingy room with a needle in his vein with the syringe lined with the residue of every form of cocaine, every form of opium, and every designer drug any renegade chemist had ever dreamed up. A subscriber to *Playboy* would naturally progress through every form of pornography until he was dead in a dingy room, exhausted from sex with women, men, boys, girls, and domestic animals, all of which had been tied and beaten into submission and were now carrying the AIDS virus, which every reader of T&A magazines got from the ink.

Balzic used to be surprised whenever he encountered ava-lanche thinking, but he was hearing it more and more, not only from people he used to dismiss as fanatics but from newspapers and television shows. He couldn't get through a food market checkout line without having to pass racks filled with four or five tabloid papers carrying the most outlandish headlines imaginable. He and Ruth read those headlines to each other for laughs, and sometimes he'd even buy one of those papers to pass around at the station because it said things like, "Wife Loves Sex With Torsoless Husband," or "Woman Loses 140 Pounds On Diet She Got On UFO." His personal favorite was the one that went: "Mental supermen lock in ESP duel—then . . . FAMED PSYCHIC'S HEAD EX-PLODES. Secret mind warfare experiment ended in tragedy, say detectives."

More and more he was encountering people who didn't laugh when they read those papers. And the religious channels on TV were filled with warnings about the devils and demons that were possessing everybody except them, which would have been okay except that more and more thugs were coming into court claiming that one or another devil made them do it. If it wasn't demon drugs that made them do it, it was ol' demon rum, or their demon mothers or demon fathers or demon girlfriends or demon wives or demon ex-wives or demon foster fathers or the neighbor's demon dogs.

Balzic was beginning to think that this wonderful Judeo-Christian tradition politicians liked to say the country ought to get back to was nothing but a system for evading responsibility. If somebody did right, it was because he'd been born again and had seen the light; if he did wrong, it was those dirty demons who made him stick white powder up his nose and pick up his girlfriend's little boy by the legs and slam his head against a wall. No matter what the law said about mitigating or extenuating circumstances, more and more indicted people were coming into court claiming somebody else or something else made them do it, and more and more lawyers were arguing that it was so.

Then again, he grumbled to himself, it's probably always been that way. Just seems like it's getting worse.

He had to stop and think for a moment why he was there. That had been happening more and more lately, too. He'd find himself getting ready to knock on a door or dial a phone and he'd have to think once again to recall why. Just now he remembered the girl with the child who had said her boyfriend was going to hurt this guy, this Farley Gruenwald, because he was abusing the boyfriend's kids. Mostly what Balzic remembered was that he was bored with riding around

94

in the black-and-white, which he'd been doing primarily to show people in Rocksburg they still had a police department. Then, too, he'd gotten a dance-around from the Children's Bureau, and he wanted to find out about that, which all combined to make him surly, but mostly he was just bored and hot.

Before Balzic rang the bell or knocked, the door was pulled open the width of a man's face. Balzic felt stupefied from the heat. "Uh, I know this is gonna sound dumb, but did I knock or ring the bell?"

"Naw. I just saw you pull in and walk up here and I come to see what's up. So?"

"Good, I'm not losin' my mind," Balzic said. "You Farley Gruenwald?"

"Yeah. So?"

Balzic got out his ID case and held it up. Gruenwald stuck his head forward and squinted. "Chief of police of Rocksburg? This ain't Rocksburg, this is the township, whatta you want?"

"Just wanna talk to you for a little bit. Got information that somebody was real upset with you."

Gruenwald pulled the door all the way open and leaned forward with one hand on the knob and the other on the jamb. He was wearing cutoff jeans, no socks or shoes, and a faded black T-shirt with a Harley-Davidson motorcycle logo on it. He had about two days' growth of graying beard.

"Oh wait, was that somebody a little scrawny chick with a kid, a little kid, maybe three, four maybe?"

"As a matter of fact, yeah."

Gruenwald hung his head and shook it from side to side. "See, everything you do comes back on you, I swear to god it does." He picked his head up and squinted again at Balzic. "Come on in, all my AC is blowin' out the door here."

Balzic walked in ahead of him and waited. The house looked pretty much like it had been furnished from Sears or

Penney's, nothing expensive but the stuffed furniture still had that new smell to it. More to the point as far as Balzic was concerned was there was no evidence that any children lived there. He didn't see one toy, one ball, not a foot mark on the couch or chairs in the living room, not a high chair in the dining room. The wall-to-wall rugs in the living room and dining room were beige and went up the stairs to the second floor and there was not a spill spot on any of it. Gruenwald led him out to the kitchen, where ledgers and checkbooks and stacks of bills and receipts were arranged in orderly piles on the formica-covered table. There was no high chair there either, no baby bottles near the sink.

"I'm really, really glad you come out here," Gruenwald said, motioning for Balzic to have a seat at the table. "Want some coffee?"

Balzic shook his head no. He didn't want anything to interfere with the comfort of the air-conditioning.

Gruenwald topped off a cup on the table with a coffee maker suspended under a cabinet near the sink. "My rig's in the shop, tore up the front end, some damn water line broke and I drove through this puddle, you know, just not thinkin', not payin' attention, and drove it in up to the goddamn axle, man, what a mess, losin' jobs, pissin' people off, losin' money, god am I losin' money. Anyway, this chick, I shoulda never done it, never done it before, I guaran-fuckin'-tee you I ain't never gonna do it again, but there she was, standin' along the goddamn road, it was hotter'n hell, and, uh, she had this kid with her, and I asked her like a goddamn fool if she wanted a ride. I don't even take my wife in my rig, not when I'm haulin', I mean she's been in it, but not when I'm haulin' 'cause I don't want nobody or nothin' distractin' me, you know? I don't know what in the fuck I was thinkin' about, I musta been feelin' sorry for the kid or some goddamn thing, I don't know."

"You picked her up?"

"Yeah I picked her up—no, it wasn't no goddamn pickup, it wasn't like that, I mean I wasn't tryin' to get laid. I don't fuck nobody but my wife, and I sure as hell don't fuck nobody in my truck. It ain't like I'm a goddamn saint or anything, but I had a buddy get the AIDS from some whore in a truck stop in Jersey, I told him a dozen times if I told him once, you don't know who them whores been fuckin', you don't know where them needles been they been stickin' in 'em. Think he'd listen? Huh? Fuck no. Man, I wanna tell you, the last couple weeks of his life he was beggin' me to shoot him. Called me some terrible names when I told him I couldn't do that. Maybe I should have, and the more I think about it the more I think I should have, but I just couldn't. So if you think I picked that chick up to ball her, that's not it, man. I wouldn't do that to me, never mind my old lady. It ain't about me bein' saintly, man, or about marriage vows or anything like that. It's about them diseases out there, man, they're scary as hell."

"So you picked her up 'cause it was hot and you felt sorry for the kid, is that it?"

"Yeah, man, swear to god. But we weren't a half-hour down the road, man, I knew that chick was runnin' on moon time. Man, talkin' to her was like talkin' to a guy I knew once, sombitch used to toke up a joint, put his headphones on, and turn the volume up to fuckin' number nine, man. About two LPs later, he'd take them earphones off, man, he was liable to say any-fuckin'-thing, you know? Well that was her, man. All I could think of was, you asshole, you had to go and paint your name all over this truck. Got it on both doors, my phone number, my address, and I gotta feel sorry for this headcase 'cause it's hot. Honest to god, man, she's been hasslin' me ever since. Called my wife here one day and told her I was the father of that child for crissake! So I been all over hell and half the courthouse, man, tryin' to get somebody to pay attention to me. I been to Family Court, I been to the DA's office, they sent

97

me to the state police, the fuckin' state police sent me to a magistrate, and they all look at me like I'm fulla shit, like, right, you balled this chick and now your wife knows and and and you're tryin' to make out like it's some *Fatal Attraction* shit, you know that movie? You ever see that movie, huh?"

"No, but I've heard about it."

"Yeah? Well honest to god, man, I did this little girl a favor, I took her to Uniontown, she said she wanted to go see her old man there or somethin', I don't know what, but by the time we got there I was just hopin' she'd shut up, man. So I dropped her off in the middle of fuckin' Uniontown, and a week later, seven goddamn days, she starts callin' here, man, drivin' my old lady nuts. And I'm on the road, I'm gone three, four days at a time, man, sometimes five, I try never to be gone longer than five in a row, but sometimes you can't help it, you know?"

"She called your wife and said you were the father? Of her kid?"

"Yeah, man, swear to god! I mean any-fuckin'-time anybody wants me to take a blood test to prove that's bullshit, here's my arm," he said, holding his right arm straight out. "Pick a vein. Just get me inside a courtroom where somebody'll listen! You know? I mean, you're the police, man, you tell me what I'm supposed to do, I'll listen, just say it."

"You don't have any kids?"

"Me? You mean me and my old lady?"

"Yes."

"Man, my old lady had to have a complete hysterectomy when she was sixteen years old, which was two years before I ever met her. If she's got any kids, man, she's got 'em hid someplace. What? Is that what that chick said?"

"Something like that. You married her boyfriend's first wife and took his kids and now you were abusin' them and he was gettin' ready to put a job on you."

Gruenwald laughed and shook his head. "Oh, man. I

mean, oh man oh fuckin' man, I ain't got any kids, man. Me and the old lady been talkin' 'bout adoptin' some, but that's out 'cause I used to be a hell-raiser, you know? I used to run with the biker-boys, man, you know, I thought when I grew up I wanted to be a Pagan. Damn near made it too. Almost, yessirree." Gruenwald shook his head ruefully. "So I married her old man's first wife, is that the story now? Wait'll my old lady hears that one, man, no shit. You know what a complete hysterectomy is, man? Huh? All the pipes are gone, you know? I mean we joke about that. She says all her friends get PMS for free, she has to buy hers at the drugstore."

Balzic didn't get it.

"Hey, that's a joke, man. You know? If you're a woman, you know, if you got all your plumbin', you get your PMS for free, get it? But my old lady has to go to the drugstore to buy her hormones. She got a prescription . . . I guess your mind's on somethin' else. Anyway, the only way we could have a kid is if her sister had my sperm injected into her and she carried it for us, you know? Oh man, what'm I gonna do about this chick? Come on, man, you got to help me out here. What do I do?"

"Uh, before I get into that, where's your wife now?"

"My old lady? Workin'. Oh, you wanna double-check me out, huh? Fine, go right ahead, man. She works up at the Giant Eagle, the one below the Rocksburg Mall. Five days a week she's workin' one of the registers, man. Just ask for Tracey Jane Gruenwald. Maybe she'll tell you where she got the kids hid, she sure ain't told me, 'course I only been married to her fourteen years so I don't know every-fuckin'thing about her."

"Uh, you got a rapsheet?"

Gruenwald shook his head. "Only juvey shit, man. What you see now is an independent trucker. President and chief executive officer of Farley Gruenwald Trucker Inc., man. I'm legal. I got a lawyer, I got a certified public accountant,

99

I don't break the weight rules, I don't cheat on my taxes. Only rule I break is that stupid-ass fifty-five-miles-an-hour speed limit, which'll put you in bankruptcy court if you're a trucker, man."

"You said you, uh, wanted to be a Pagan when you grew up?"

Gruenwald nodded his head many times, "Yessir, I did, I surely did. Thought they was just the nuts, man. And the berries. Thought that was the way it was done, man, you know? Get the wind in your face and tell the world to go fuck itself. Man, I loved to party and those guys knew how to party, man. Drink beer until you thought you were gonna pass out, then pop some crank, drink some more beer, pop some more crank."

"Yeah, sounds great," Balzic said, smiling crookedly.

"Hey, man, for a long time they was only family I had. I just didn't understand some shit, that's all. When I understood it, I knew they was lots more fucked up than my own family, which until then I thought was the most fucked-up family in the history of the world."

Balzic canted his head and peered at him. "So what happened?"

Gruenwald's knee started to bounce. "So, uh, you tryin' to jerk me around or what?"

"No I'm not," Balzic said. "I'm serious. What happened? How come you, uh, how come you—"

"How come I split?"

"Yeah."

"You shittin' me, you really wanna know?" His eyes were nearly squinted shut and his knee was bouncing hard.

"I'm not shittin' you, I really want to know."

Gruenwald scratched his scalp and thought for a long moment. "You want—lemme get this straight, you wanna know how come I split from the Pagans, do I got you right?"

"Yeah I told ya, I'm not jaggin' you off here. You said they were the only family you had for a while, and then you just walked away from it. I mean, how'd you do that? What made you do it?"

"What? You gettin' ready to quit, or what? Huh? Retire, is that it?"

Balzic hesitated, then found himself nodding. Is that what I'm thinking about? And now I'm asking for advice from a guy who split from the Pagans? Well, why not. Biker gangs are organized like anything else. Got their leaders, their grunts, their rules, their business. Just because you don't like their rules or their business is no reason not to want to know how one guy decided to walk away. Balzic was still nodding and then he heard himself say it out. "Yeah, yeah. That's what I'm thinkin' about."

Gruenwald's knee stopped bouncing, his eyes lost their squint, and he settled back in his chair. "Well," he said, poking his tongue against his cheek and running it around his lower lip to the other cheek. "Ain't this the damnedest conversation I ever had."

"I've been in stranger ones," Balzic said. "So let's get on with it. How'd you do it?"

"I'll just bet you have been in some strange ones." Gruenwald thought for another long moment. "Okay. Okay, you wanna know, I'll tell ya. They dealt crank, mostly. That and PCP. But mostly crank. And mostly to truckers. I was never in on it, I never even got to the point where I saw it go from their hand into somebody else's. I wasn't *in* in, you know? I was just a pup, hangin' around to get patted on the head, you know, get my belly rubbed, but I knew what they was doin', 'cause every time they scored, they partied, and I was right there, partyin' down with 'em. Man, I was lovin' it, every-fuckin'spoonful, man, just eatin' it up. This was long before they started dealin' coke, man. Or if they was, they never talked about it around me, you know what I'm sayin'?"

Balzic nodded.

101

"So anyway, so I'm doin' some heavy crank myself, you know? I mean, beer and crank and cheeseburgers, them was the three food groups, man. And I started, you know, I started havin' these nightmares, man, 'cause I didn't know what else to call 'em. I didn't know what heavy crank does to ya. I didn't even know what the word *hallucination* was, you know? I'd never heard it. But your sleep gets so fucked up, you don't know sometimes how long you been awake or what. So we used to joke about it, like if you're awake, prove it, you know? Like if you ain't dead, prove it. You know? I mean, I hear people worryin' about dyin' all the time, man, you know, all them fuckin' holy rollers on TV, man, that's all they're talkin' about, like what's gonna happen after you die, you goin' to heaven if you're good or you goin' to hell if you ain't, you know, and I just laugh, 'cause I think about all us dumb fuckers, asshole bikers skied out of our fuckin' skulls on beer and crank and arguin' about whether we was alive or dead and how could we prove either one. And it turned out the only thing we could do was prove we was awake enough to do wheelies, you know, with our lights out in the middle of some fuckin' campground somewhere at four o'clock in the mornin'. And then when you'd come back, these assholes'd be lookin' at you and sayin', 'Okay, okay, so what's 'at prove, you alive or you dead? You in biker heaven or you in biker hell and how the fuck would you know, you're so fucked up you don't know your own fuckin' name.' I mean, it was crazier'n hell and I know it, and I knew it then. But the thing I learned was, nobody knows whether they're alive or dead, man, I mean if the only thing you can do is a wheelie in the middle of the night with your light off, man, I mean, what the fuck does that prove?"

"And that's why you wanted to get out?"

"No no no, that was only the start of it. I mean that was just bullshit, you know? After I split, when I was tryin' to get straight, I went back to the community college to get my

GED, you know? High school diploma? I don't even know what GED stands for anymore—"

"General Equivalency Diploma."

"Huh? Oh, yeah, right. But anyway I went back and was takin' a course to study for it and one night after the class, you know, I went into this bar and there was a couple of the professors hangin' out, you know, and drinkin' beer, and goddamn if they weren't arguin' about the same bullshit, how could they prove they was alive, you know? Just like a coupla asshole bikers, only they was usin' real big words, you know, and just goin' back and forth, this guy said this and that guy said that and somebody else said this and on and on. And I just looked at 'em and thought to myself, These fuckin' guys with all their education and all their diplomas, they don't know any more about whether they're alive or dead than a bunch of asshole bikers."

"So that's what made you want to get out? I don't understand," Balzic said, getting impatient.

"No, man, that was after I already made up my mind to get straight. Long time after. Nah, no, what made me get out was one night we was on a run somewhere, I don't know where we been or where we was goin', but we come up on this rig, man, goin' onto the turnpike in Irwin, you know? Off Route 30 there, and so, we're just like the fuckin' tourists, you know, we gotta pull over and go gawkin' at this poor fuck." Gruenwald paused and swallowed several times. "Still gets to me. Still chokes me up, you know?"

"What?"

"Oh man, this sombitch is twisted up in his rig, man, and he's just skied, he's flyin' on crank, you could see his eyes from twenty yards away, no shit. He was pinned in there and they was waitin' on that tool, you know, that Jaws of Life, to pry him outta there, and man, he was just screamin', just fuckin' screamin' and it was all about how he only had a couple more hours and he'd be home, just a couple more

103

hours, that's all and he'd see his kids. And I recognized him. I mean, as fucked up and all covered with blood as he was, I saw he was a guy was a regular customer, you know? I mean he was gettin' his crank from us—not from me, 'cause I wasn't dealin', but I remember seein' him at the truck stops, you know, where we went, and he was always doin' business, you know? And I turned around to this guy who was like my daddy—well I was hopin' he was like gonna be my daddy, you know—and I said, 'Hey, that's a guy buys from us,' or somethin', I don't remember exactly what I said to him, but I remember what he said to me, man, I'll never forget it. He said, 'The rules of the road, sonny boy, is if you can't keep it on the road you ain't fit to rule. And that mothertrucker ain't goin' be in nobody's road no more.' And I thought, Shit, you know, the dude was just tryin' to get by, you know, just tryin' to do his thing, and all the crank he bought, he sure made it right for us to do our thing, so that was a pretty shitty way to talk about him like that. I mean that's what I thought, I didn't say nothin' that's for sure, but I remember thinkin' it."

"And you just quit? Just walked away, never looked back?"

Gruenwald shook his head no. "Oh I had troubles for a long while. I had troubles with my head, troubles with them, but everybody just said the same thing when I wanted to talk about it, you know, it was shit or get off the pot, smoke or get off the pot, smoke it or give it up, drink it or pass the jug, you know, a hundred different ways of sayin' it, but it all come down to the same thing—do or die, and if you died, then so long, motherfucker. And every time I'd see in the paper about some trucker goin' over, you know, I'd be wonderin' was it some guy buyin' from people I knew so I could party? And every time I wound up thinkin' about that poor sucker on Route 30, it started to eat me up, man, that was all there was to it. Somebody said to me once, I forget who it was said it, but whoever it was said the Pagans had about as much conscience as worm snot, and for a long time I didn't have any more than most of them did. And I didn't even know it was conscience. All I know was, I'd get to feelin' bad every time I read about a truck goin' splat somewhere. And little by little I just stopped runnin' with 'em." Gruenwald shrugged. "I was never a member, you know, I never went through the shit, whatever it is, so they never come after me. I see 'em, lots of 'em, they're still sellin' their shit, you know, the ones ain't in jail. They pretty much let me alone, they know I ain't buyin'. I run on caffeine and nicotine, man, and if that don't make it, I pull over and go to sleep. That rig's more'n half mine, and I ain't about to fuck it up 'cause I'm crank-blind, you know, drivin' seventy miles an hour with your eyes wide open and you ain't seein' a thing, man."

Gruenwald stopped talking. He got up and refilled his coffee and sat down again. "You lookin' kinda spacy, chief, you okay?"

"Huh? Oh yeah, sure. Just thinkin', that's all." He stood up and started walking toward the front door. "Your wife's name is Tracey Jane? Right?"

"You got it. Giant Eagle, at the mall."

Balzic nodded and continued walking. Gruenwald stopped him at the front door. "Hey, uh, ain't you gonna give me some advice about what I'm supposed to do, huh?"

"Who's your magistrate? Your district justice?"

"Uh, some woman in the mall, downstairs, I forget her name."

"Yeah, Paulich. Rena. You go see her, tell her I sent you, tell her you want a peace bond, tell her you want three of 'em, one for you and your truck, one for you and your wife here, one for your wife at her job. Tell her to write it up so this woman's not allowed within a hundred feet of you or your wife no matter where you are. She'll send copies to the state police, and that's it. This woman comes near you, just call the state cops and they'll come bust her. They have to. Once that bond's on record in their barracks, they got no

105

choice, they gotta do it. The first time they do it, she's gonna lose her kid, and I think that'll be the end of it. I think she likes that kid, enough anyway that she won't risk losin' it. On the other hand, she may be so far gone that she oughta lose the kid, I don't know. Anyway, thanks for talkin' to me. I appreciate your cooperation. Hope you get your rig back on the road soon."

"Hey, man, thanks, really. I appreciate that. Damn, peace bond, awright. Oh, and thanks for not askin' me to wear a wire."

Balzic was halfway down the walk to his black-and-white. "For not doin' what?"

"For not wearin' a wire, you know, state cops really leaned on me to wear a wire against the Pagans. You know, in the truck stops and that."

Balzic snorted and shook his head and laughed. "Take it easy, I'll see ya around maybe. Have any trouble with the magistrate, give me a call."

Balzic got in the black-and-white, turned the engine on, then the AC, and got back out for a couple of minutes to wait for the AC to kick in. Wear a wire? Is that what he said? To get evidence on druggies? He laughed to himself. If I had a wire, I wouldn't know what to do with it. If I had a wire I don't have anybody who knows what to do with it. I'm lucky we got people to show up when there's an accident with injuries. No injuries? If traffic keeps moving, we tell them to call their insurance agents, maybe they can get a claims adjuster there inside of an hour. Only time we show up is if traffic's got to be rerouted or if people are bleeding bad. Wear a wire, Christ. That's almost as funny as listening to some politician talking about the war on drugs. Might as well be listening to McGruff, the cartoon dog on TV, talking about taking a bite out of crime.

Balzic drove to the Rocksburg Mall and found Tracey Jane Gruenwald in the Giant Eagle. He talked her supervisor into

106

letting her take a break and she confirmed everything her husband had said, which Balzic knew she would. Maybe people could hide children if they knew a cop was coming, but there was no way they could rid a house of every sign that children lived there without a long warning time, and the Gruenwalds' house didn't have a spill spot on the carpets. Anyway, Balzic had to pick up a few things, some generic rolled oats and some buttermilk, and talking to Gruenwald's wife was just a way to let Gruenwald know that Balzic followed up. It was Balzic's kind of public relations, and it had become so much of a habit that he did it without thinking.

*   *   *

Balzic didn't remember where he was when he heard that President Bush was ordering troops into the Middle East because of Iraq's invasion of Kuwait. He hadn't really paid much attention to it. It was just something he'd heard on the news or more likely somebody else had heard it and told him, Ruth probably, he wasn't sure. But when he walked into Muscotti's, it was the main topic of conversation, and Vinnie was one unhappy bartender.

"It's about fuckin' time," Vinnie snapped at Balzic. "Jesus Christ I called you guys a half a fuckin' hour ago."

"Take it easy, take it easy," Balzic said. "There ain't no guys, you know, it's just me and a dispatcher, I can't be every place. So what's the problem?"

"Him!" Vinnie snapped, jabbing his thumb over his shoulder toward the other end of the bar. "He's the fuckin' problem, the Mad Russian—"

"Yeah fuck you too with that Mad Russian stuff, that's all I been hearin' my whole life, the Russians this, the Russians that, the e-vil a-the-is-tic com-mie bas-tard Russians." Myushkin was at the end of the bar swaying his head in time with each syllable and bonking his knuckles on the bar in the same rhythm, grinning goofily.

"He's been in here makin' speeches since I opened up this morning. You gotta get him outta here, I ain't gonna listen to his bullshit all day—"

"You wouldn't know bullshit from cowshit, mine or anybody else's, you wouldn't know chickenshit from ratshit. You know why? 'Cause you never looked at any of 'em, it's all just shit to you. You're like all the other goddamn sheep in this fuck-ing so-called mo-dern in-dus-tri-a-lized rep-re-sen-ta-tive de-fuck-ing-moc-ra-cy."

Vinnie splayed his hands. "You hear that? Huh? Since nine o'clock I been listenin' to that. Chased everybody outta here. All my best customers come in, take one listen to him, boom, they're gone, the fuckin' jagoff. You gotta get him outta here I'm tellin ya."

"Slow down, slow down," Balzic said, as much to himself as to Vinnie. He forced himself to walk slowly down the bar and took a seat on a stool one away from Myushkin. "So, uh, what's the problem?"

"The problem," Vinnie said, hustling down the bar, "is he's givin' out the same old shit. He's the same old goddamn Mad Russian—"

"Same old Russian?" Myushkin howled. He gawked at Balzic. "What's he talkin' about, same old Mad Russian, huh? He got eyes but he don't see. Look at me. I'm new! I'm improved! I'm lemon scented, for crissake! My wife says she don't know whether to make love to me or spray me around the house, for crissake! She don't know whether to make love to me or bottle me and sell me, for crissake!"

Vinnie threw up his hands and bowed slightly toward Balzic as though to say, see? You want explanations? From me?

"Gimme a glass of water, will ya?" Balzic said, sighing.

"I'll give ya a bottle of wine you get him outta here."

"Just the water, huh? Okay?"

"You got it, water, comin' right up," Vinnie said, whirling around for a glass and whirling back to fill it and slide it in

108

front of Balzic. Balzic picked it up, took off his glasses, and held the glass to his forehead for a moment.

"So, uh, what's the problem—"

"Hey!" Vinnie snapped. "What the fuck you askin' him for? I'm the one with the problem. He's the fuckin' problem—"

"Vinnie, yo, Vinnie," Balzic said, trying to interrupt Vinnie's tirade. "Do me a favor and go watch traffic, go on, go up the other end of the bar, okay?"

"—what the fuck's with you, Mario? Huh? I'm the one called you, I'm the one with the problem, what the fuck you care what his problem is—"

"Vinnie . . . Vinnie . . . Vinnie, go to the other end of the bar and let me handle this, huh? You called me, right? So let me do my job."

Vinnie blew out a derisive sigh, let his hands fall to his thighs, and turned and stomped away, muttering and cursing.

Balzic turned back to Myushkin. "So?"

"We back to me now, huh? My turn?"

Balzic nodded. "Yeah, so what're ya, bustin' Vinnie's balls or what?"

"Of course I'm bustin' his balls. What else do you do with Vinnie? Talk to him? You mean like have a conversation? About what?"

"Okay, so talk to me. And try not to say it too loud, okay?"

"Okay, so quietly, I'll tell you. My kid's in the airborne. He's on his way over to the Gulf, you know, if not today, then tomorrow, next week, whenever. And my wife thinks I'm a baby killer or something."

"So, uh, what? D'you make him join up or somethin'?"

"Of course. Hell yes. I mean, he did it, it was his decision, but I sure as hell laid some influence on him. Jesus, he gets out of college, he's layin' around the house, he's turnin' his stomach into a beer keg, you know, he's doin' nothin' but growin' a beer gut, so I took him aside and I explained the

109

facts of life to him. I told him, hey, the army was good enough for James Jones, it was good enough for me, it's good enough for you."

"James Jones?"

"James Jones, yeah. You never heard of James Jones?"

"I know lots of Joneses. In my line of work, after Smith, Jones is the name I hear the most."

"No, man, no. James Jones is the guy who wrote *From Here to Eternity*, you know? Among other things. You never read that book? Huh? Robert E. Lee Prewitt, Milt Warden, Karen Holmes, Fatso Judson, Maggio, Jack Malloy?"

Balzic shrugged. "What is it, fiction?"

"Yeah, of course it's fiction. It's damn near the only way left to tell the truth in America."

Balzic shrugged again. "I don't read much fiction. Not anymore."

"You didn't see the movie either? Huh? Montgomery Clift, Burt Lancaster, Deborah Kerr, Ernest Borgnine, Frank Sinatra—Jack Malloy wasn't in the movie, they didn't know what to do with him. But you didn't see that?"

"Yeah, maybe, I think. Long time ago. So, uh, what—you joined the army 'cause you read a book? You make your kid join the army for the same book?"

"No, nah, it wasn't like that. For poor people, the army's a fact of economic life, that's what you learn from James Jones. When I got outta high school, I mean it was the mines or nothin' for me, and I was goddamned if I was gonna spend my life gettin' black lung. I had to go in a mine one time, some goofy teacher thought it would be a good idea, you know, since most of the kids' relatives worked in the mine, she thought it would be great if we all went to see what it was like, you know? I mean, that's all we been hearing all our lives, what it's like in the goddamn mines, from our fathers, from our uncles, our cousins, this teacher thinks she's gonna show us somethin', right?"

110

"Maybe she was tryin' to learn something herself."

"Hey, very good, that's very good. Really, not too many people would've had that perspective. I like that."

Balzic dismissed the compliment with a wave. "Yeah, so, uh, back to your wife and your kid. What's goin' on?"

"What's goin' on is my wife is nuts with me because White House Boy Georgie gotta get his oil fix, you know? He's been runnin' this campaign to find a new Willie Horton, you know? So he looked around and he found one, you know, this short, ugly guy with a black moustache, and he's been runnin' around shoutin', you know, 'Hey, everybody, look, it's Adolph Hitler.' Remember? The guy who was the boss of the bad guys in *Raiders of the Lost Ark*?"

"Wait a minute wait a minute," Balzic said holding up both hands. "You're talkin' about the president? Bush? And Willie Horton—"

"Yeah yeah, exactly."

"—and Adolph Hitler and the *Raiders of the Lost Ark*? I thought that was a movie." Balzic began to wonder if maybe Vinnie wasn't right about this guy. "How'd you get from the president to a movie?"

Myushkin looked truly surprised. "How? The same way Rocketcock Ronnie got from *Star Wars* to space-based missiles, you kiddin' me? Ronnie boy saw Stevie Spielberg do it with special effects, you know, him and George Lucas, so Ronnie figured, hey, if they can do it in Hollywood, it oughta be a pop cinch for the Generals, you know, General Dynamic, General Motors, General Electric."

Balzic felt his mouth dropping open. "Uh, maybe you oughta go home for a little while."

"Hey, look, Balzic, you gotta keep up, you know? You gotta understand how myths get made in America, I'm just givin' you a real short course here. I don't have the time, you don't have the time for me to go into all the details, but believe me, what you're watchin', what this whole country's been watchin'

111

for the last eight, ten years is one of the greatest con jobs in the history of the world. And these guys don't care who they use—the Russians, you know, the Evil Empire, which was Reagan's favorite Hitler, or that welfare queen with the nine kids by nine different fathers, you know, showin' up in a white Caddie convertible to sign up for her checks and food stamps. Then Boy Georgie needs a job and abracadabra, Willie Horton becomes an overnight success, you know, one minute he's just a thug, and the next, you know how the poem goes, don't you? 'In America, America, you can be a star, with the right PR, with the right PR, in America, America.' "

Balzic held the cool glass up to his forehead again. "I must've missed that poem too. So, uh, listen, how much you had to drink today?"

Myushkin screwed up his face and pointed at the cup and saucer in front of him. "This is coffee, you kiddin'? I haven't had anything to drink. You mean alcohol?"

"You mean you just get naturally wound up like this, huh?"

"I'm not wound up, man, what're you sayin'—I'm nutso or something—'cause Vinnie doesn't understand what I'm talkin' about? You gotta be kiddin'. Vinnie's a fuckin' bartender, man. A thief. He robs his customers, he steals from his boss. That's his entire world. It's like he got an ant's eye view of the universe, man, don't you understand? If I told Vinnie there were such things as mites and some of them lived out their entire life cycle in his eyelashes, Vinnie would need a strait jacket, you know? I'm not puttin' Vinnie down, understand, Vinnie's Vinnie. But that's all he is. I mean, if Vinnie can't steal it or eat it or drink it or fuck it, it has no meaning for him, understand? So when I come in here and put two things together that Vinnie thinks should not go together, hey, Vinnie immediately thinks one of two things: either I'm drunk or I'm flipped out. Now you wanna take me and Vinnie down the station and analyze our breath, go right ahead. What you will find is that Vinnie's had a lot more to drink than I have. You wanna take me up to the mental health clinic, go right ahead. But I'm not a danger to me or anybody else, so they're not gonna keep me, and I know you know that as well as I do, so what's the gig here?"

"Well the gig I guess is you lower your voice and quit scarin' the other customers."

"Yeah, well that ain't gonna be as easy as it sounds."

"Why not?"

" 'Cause I'm really worried about my kid. I mean, Jesus Christ, I did put him there. And my wife's . . ." Myushkin's shoulders sagged. "My wife's really pissed at me. I mean, she's been pissed at me for a long time about a lotta things, but this, man, this is the capper here. I mean there was a time when, when she looked at me all she saw was the glitters, man. Gold and silver and spangles and baubles. I was birthdays and New Year's Eves and . . . shit. Now. Man. Now, all she sees when she looks at me is brown and yellow. I ain't what I do anymore. All I am is what comes out the ends. All I am is the work you gotta do when the party's over, when everybody goes home." Myushkin hung his head.

"Sounds to me like you got a real bad case of the pities. I think maybe the best place for them is someplace else."

"You think this is self-pity, man? Is that what you think?"

" 'At's what it sounds like to me."

Myushkin ground his molars and squinted. "Yeah, right, probably from your point of view that's what it would sound like. I mean, what the fuck're you, right? The voice of authority. You're the guy who carries the gun that all power comes out of the barrel of, right? I mean, you're the guy who delivers the warrants, right? And if the people don't wanna pay attention to the courts, if they wanna mock the warrants, you're the guy who shows 'em how wrong they can be, right?"

"I don't carry a gun," Balzic said dryly.

"You personally may not carry a gun," Myushkin said.

113

"That ain't the point. The point is, you know who does carry the guns, and if some citizen gives you static, you call the guys who do carry the guns. So what you want is peace and harmony and positive goody goodness and everybody smilin' and happy and dancin' politely in the dance halls, and none of this rock'n'roll either. When a guy like me comes along and tells you the fuckin' president, the bossman himself is nothin' but a goddamn oil junkie, as hooked on oil as any nigger hooked on crack in the ghetto, that's an idea you can't conceive of, because your whole life is devoted to upholdin' the flag, the Constitution, the Pennsylvania Consolidated Statutes, the city ordinances, the bench warrants. You don't question the fuckin' law, you enforce it. That's your job. But see, I'm a writer. That ain't my job.

"The government don't pay me, not a fuckin' dime, not a penny. They don't pay me to apologize for their laws or to explain their laws or to rationalize their laws or to justify 'em. I ain't on their goddamn payroll . . . and you are. I don't apply for their fuckin' grants. I ain't one of them pansy artistes who goes grubbin' to Uncle Sugar, man, sayin' 'Oh me oh my, I just have to have my money pie,' and then when Uncle Sugar gives it to 'em, they throw a bitchy, hissy fit when Senator Claghorn says, 'Hey, y'all cain't be showin' them pitchurs of guys french kissin', not with tax money, y'all cain't,' and them artistes have a conniption fit, you know, 'Censorship, cen-sor-ship! The censorship sky is falling!' It takes a lotta balls to panhandle money from Uncle Sugar and then complain when Uncle gets pissed 'cause you show him up, you know, make an ass out of him. I mean, bureaucrats get pissed when you tell 'em they're bureaucrats. I mean, bureaucrats are the people who think bureaucrats are the people who work across the hall."

"You do tend to ramble, don't you?"

"Ramble?" Myushkin's eyebrows shot up. "Man, Robert Frost said thinkin' was just putting one thing beside another

114

and lookin' at 'em. What you call ramblin' is what I call thinkin'. But that takes me right back to my original point—"

"Which was?"

"Which was, when I say something that goes against your grain, the first thing you think about is how much have I had to drink, you think I'm drunk, and then the second thing is you think I'm nuts. In that respect you ain't no different from Vinnie there. But I ain't neither. I just ain't buyin' the party line here, that's all."

"You bought it enough to join the army."

"Very good, Balzic. Very good. Most people don't have that much of an attention span. You got potential."

"I also got other things to do," Balzic said, "and whether I agree with the party line or not, whether I carry a gun or not, I think I can make a pretty safe prediction. If you don't get outta here, I'm gonna have to come back, and if I have to do that it'll be because several people are pissed off, so how about if you find some other place to make your speeches today, okay?"

"Aw, man, you don't understand. I really like it in here. I really do. Lots of my friends' ghosts are in here. It's not just a saloon for me, you know? It's a repository for some good souls. Some of the best drinkin' buddies I ever had in this life, I met right in here. Sometimes I need to talk to 'em. Vinnie thinks I'm talkin' to myself down here. Hey, I'm talkin' to Pete and Lenny and Billy and Jaybird and Jimbo and the Snake. I miss those fuckers, I really do. And I know they're in here. It doesn't bother me to talk to ghosts, you know? Some people gotta go to cemeteries to do it, but I just come in here. So naturally Vinnie thinks I'm talkin' to myself so I must be nuts or somethin'. But it's hard to find guys to talk to, man. It really is."

"Well, uh, maybe they hung out in other places, whatta ya say? Any chance of that?"

"Okay okay, you made your point." Myushkin stood up and sauntered down the bar toward the front door. "See, Vinnie? See, I'm goin', ya happy now? Huh?"

"Get the fuck outta here, don't come back till some fuckin' head doctor drills a hole in your head, lets some of that pus outta there."

Myushkin stopped at the door and put both his hands on his chest. "Vinnie, you hurt me when you talk like that, you know? My delicate little heart can't stand it when you evil-mouth me like that." He got this goofy lopsided grin on his face, bowed deeply from the waist, and came up with his eyes crossed and his tongue stuck out the right corner of his mouth. Then he opened the door and was gone.

Balzic sipped the water and in between sips held the glass against his temples and forehead. When the glass was empty, he put it down and headed for the front door.

Vinnie, who had been attracted to something out on the street, suddenly remembered about Balzic and turned around and said, "Hey, whatta you gonna have, huh? Lemme buy you somethin' here."

"Some other time," Balzic said.

"Come on come on. I owe ya one for gettin' him outta here. He woulda been in here all day, the fuckin' jagoff."

Balzic stopped at the door. He looked at Vinnie and was going to say that what he always liked about Vinnie was that to him life was always simple, but he knew he couldn't keep the sarcasm out of his tone or off his face, so he just gave a little wave and went out to his cruiser.

He spent the next hour in the Flats on Washington Street trying to placate Mrs. Bohince that her neighbors were not out to personally antagonize her by stealing her newspaper every day and by not cleaning up their dog's droppings off the sidewalk in front of her rowhouse. Balzic knew it was going to be a lot more difficult than he first thought when he learned after two phone calls, one to the *Pittsburgh Post-*

Gazette and the other to the *Rocksburg Gazette*, that Mrs. Bohince did not subscribe to either paper. Nobody was home on either side of Mrs. Bohince's house, so Balzic couldn't be sure whether they had a dog. He was reasonably sure that he heard no dogs barking in either house when he knocked on the doors and rang the bells. Maybe the dogs were deaf.

"Look, uh, Mrs. Bohince, how long the newspapers been missin' now, can you tell me that?"

"For years, for years," she said hotly. She was a round woman, short, but round in almost every way. Her face, her arms, her fingers, all had a puffy roundness to them, everything except her hair, which was so sparse her scalp was plainly visible. She had dyed her hair black and it was grotesquely stark against the grayish flesh of her scalp.

"You never called about it before, is that it?"

"Sure sure I did. I called plenty of times, but younz never come. Never."

"Uh-ha. Yeah. Well, see, I been lookin' around here on the sidewalk for any, you know, evidence that the dogs do their business here and, uh, I don't see it."

"Well sure sure. That's 'cause I clean it up. Whatta you think?"

"Uh-ha. So what do you do with it?"

"Huh? What do I do with it?"

"Yeah," Balzic said, shrugging. "I mean, whatta you do with it? Where do you put it after you clean it up?"

"I put it down the sewer, whatta you think? You think I keep it in the house or somethin', jeez-oh-man. I might not be too smart, but I ain't crazy."

Balzic scratched his chin for a long moment. "Well, see, Mrs. Bohince, I got a problem here. I mean, you say you were gettin' a morning paper and I called both the morning papers that deliver around here and neither one of them ever heard of you. I mean, I don't know what to do with that information, you know? I mean, how do you explain that?"

117

"Well sure sure that's what they say, but I oughta know whether I get a paper or not, right? Huh? Doncha think?"

Balzic had to agree that she ought to know. "But see, then there's the other thing about the dogs here. I mean, there's no evidence, I mean, I been lookin' around on the sidewalk here and I don't see anything—"

"But I just got done tellin' ya I clean it up all the time."

"—yeah, yeah, you did, but you say you put it down the storm sewer, so, see, what you got to understand is I have to deal with evidence. You know? I mean, there's gotta be somethin' I can see, you know? That somebody actually did some of the things you say they did—"

"Sure sure, I know that. But I'm givin' you the evidence. Right now. I'm tellin' ya what the evidence is. That's what I'm tellin' ya. I mean, I'm the evidence. I'm right here. Look at me, you keep lookin' away from me, down at your feet."

"I'm lookin' at the sidewalk, ma'am, for evidence that the dogs are leavin' some stains or something, you know?"

"Well they don't leave no stains 'cause I bring a bucket out here with Mister Clean and I scrub it off. That's hows come there ain't no stains."

Balzic folded his arms and chewed his lower lip and rocked on his heels. "Look, missus, I'm sure the people here, the neighbors, I'm sure they're givin' you a bad time about something, but I don't know what. What I'm also sure about is if you used to get a paper every morning, you're not gettin' one anymore—"

"That ain't true, that's a story somebody's makin' up about me—"

"—maybe it is, maybe it is. But, see, I'm a policeman, ma'am, and when I gotta deal with the lawyers and the judges, see, they don't let me come in and just start accusin' people, I mean, you can understand that, can't you? Huh?"

"Well huh yourself. How 'bout the people accuse me? How 'bout them?"

"People accuse you, ma'am? What do they accuse you of?"

"Huh? Oh. I'll tell you what. People always accuse me of hollerin' at 'em, turn their radios down. This little girl over here," she nearly knocked herself off balance by nodding twice toward the rowhouse over her left shoulder, "this little girl over here, she says I'm knockin' on the walls all the time, and I don't do that. I would never do that. But she says I do. Is that accusin' me or what? Huh?"

Balzic scratched his neck and his chin and sighed. "Look, missus, I gotta go check some things out, okay? I gotta check out the evidence here, understand? So here's my card." He fished a business card out of his ID case and handed it to her.

She nodded and pursed her lips and canted her head and murmured "Oh" many times. She was clearly impressed.

"And see? Right there at the bottom is my personal office number. You call that number and if I'm in my office at that time, I will answer the phone, I guarantee it, and you can talk to me about what's goin' on here, you know? Whatta you think?"

"Well. Well. See, that makes me, I mean, well. I feel a whole lot different about this. I mean, man-oh-man, you damn tootin'. Now we're gettin' somewhere." She was smiling so large her cheeks were getting pink from being squeezed.

"I have to go now, missus. I gotta check some things out, okay? We all set here now, hmmm?"

"Oh you betcha. Damn tootin'." She read the card again. She was still reading it when Balzic crawled back into the blessed air-conditioning of his cruiser and drove slowly out of the Flats, pondering what his wife would have to say about that performance. Then he found himself defending himself. No papers, no subscriptions, no dogs barking, no dog crap, what was I supposed to say? An hour ago, a grown man admits he talks out loud to people when what he's really doing is talking to some goddamn ghosts of people who used to hang out in Muscotti's, and now here I am, defending me

119

to Ruth, who's doing god knows what, but whatever it is, it sure doesn't have a damn thing to do with what I'm doing here, trying to handle this daffy lady. Hell, she ain't any daffier than any of the rest of us, she's just lonely as hell, that's all. Hell, I didn't *handle* anybody. I finessed her, that's all. Put a little grease under my feet and slid right out of there, what the hell's wrong with that? Jesus Christ, I ain't Jesus Christ. What the fuck am I supposed to do about these people? Give her my card and show her my number and hope to hell she never calls me, 'cause I'll be bored stiff in twenty seconds, no matter how much I tell myself it could just as easily be me. 'Cause that's what I'm scared of. 'Cause if I quit this, how the hell do I know I won't be callin' the station myself and makin' up some cockamamie story about the neighbor's dogs. Christ. Just to get a little conversation. . . . The president's an oil junkie? . . .

*　　*　　*

Balzic trudged up the steps to his house. There was no question he was getting older—who wasn't?—but this heat was starting to slow him down, starting to make him feel his age. Here it was the last week of August, with no sign of a break in the heat, and he was wondering if maybe he wouldn't feel as tired if he didn't spend most of his time thinking about cold water and air-conditioning. For almost a month now he'd been talking to everybody he knew, trying to figure out what his payments would be, whether it would be worth it, and so on, if he hired somebody to install whole-house air-conditioning. So far all he'd come up with was his own indecision.

When he got inside, he found Ruth steaming angry, going from kitchen to living room and back in a stomp with the dishes and flatwear and the supper.

"What's the matter with you?" Balzic said. "You look mad enough to chew nails."

"Oh god, I just saw the most disgusting thing I think I've ever seen in my life."

Balzic was stripping off his coat, tie, and shirt, and draping them over the newel post to the upstairs, and watching her.

"So? What was that? Around here? Somethin' happen?"

"No no. Not here. On TV. That goddamn Saddam Hussein. He had all these people. Hostages. And he was patting this one little boy on the head, my god, the kid was scared to death. Just petrified. That slimy bastard. He was acting like he was their uncle, telling them they weren't hostages, they were guests. Guests! Can you imagine the gall of that sonofabitch. It was disgusting, honest to god. Using little kids like that."

Balzic sat down at the round table, the one Ruth had built from a kit. "Hey, cakes, politicians kiss babies, you know? That's what they do."

"Kiss babies! Mario! This wasn't some guy runnin' for office, kissin' babies. My god! How can you say that?"

"Hey hey hey, take it easy, okay? Number one, I didn't see it. I'm just goin' on what you said you saw. And, I mean, I can see you're really pissed about this, you know, but, even without seein' it, I mean, this Hussein guy's no different from any other politician—"

"Mario, wait just a minute here. I mean, using children who are clearly hostages, using them to make yourself look like Santa Claus almost—"

"Ruthie, I know this guy turns your stomach, but believe me, he's in the stomach-turnin' business. That's what politics is, you know? You don't want kings anymore, then you gotta put up with guys who wanna be kings but who try to let on like they don't. So this guy's over there pissed off about how the Kuwaitis are screwin' around with the price of oil, and, uh, he's claimin' Kuwait was always a part of Iraq anyway, and our guy in the White House, he's takin' everything real personal. You know, everything he says, it's about how pissed

121

off *he* is. *He's* really startin' to lose *his* temper or *his* patience and *he's* gettin' real ticked off or whatever, and the whole goddamn thing's about oil, only our guy's talkin' about how this Arab's the new Hitler, you know? I mean, I hate to hear myself say it almost, but, jeez, Hitler was Hitler. Nearly fifty years after Hitler's dead, I mean, every time somebody needs a new bogeyman, why's he always have to be a Hitler?"

"So what are you saying? I'm not listening to how dumb my own leader is?"

"No no no, that's not what I'm sayin' at all. I'm just sayin', you know, don't be so quick to get pissed because this guy's usin' kids, that's all. I mean, I don't have any crystal ball, but, knowin' what I know about the world, our guy's gonna be usin' kids real soon, believe it. I mean he'll be usin' kids to kill kids, that's what they all do. I mean, I was just a goddamn kid when I got used. You know? Iwo Jima? Remember? I look at eighteen-year-old kids now, I think, Jesus Christ, they're babies. But that's how old I was when I was over there. What the hell did I know about what was goin' on? Huh? You think I understood any more about what was goin' on then than those kids you're talkin' about today? The ones you saw on TV?"

"Oh, Mario, my god, these were children! Five, six years old. There's a big big difference between five and eighteen. A huge difference."

"Sure, when you're five you're allowed to show how scared you are. When you're eighteen, you say you're scared and you ain't gonna do what they want you to do, they put you in jail. You damn right there's a difference."

She leaned forward and canted her head at him. "Did I miss something? What happened today? Why don't you understand this? Why don't you understand how mad I am?"

Balzic shrugged. "Nothing happened. I understand how mad you are. I just get real discouraged when, you know, the whole world starts crankin' up their propaganda ma-

122

chines, and all of a sudden, everything's either you're with us or you're against us, like the last thing you're allowed to be is somebody who says, "Hey, piss on the both of you, you're both a coupla scumbags."

"Are you saying I'm not smart enough to understand when I'm bein' lied to? When politicians are givin' me a snow job? My god, Mario, I'm married to the chief of police. I had to learn something about politics whether I wanted to or not."

"Oh, so we're still married?"

"Huh? Oh, well, no, I mean, officially of course. That's not going to change. But unofficially? See? That's when I quit going with the party line, with the husband and the wife business. The wife part's the part I don't like. That part about being twisted, turned, wrapped up like being hidden, that's what the dictionary says. You know. Out of sight? Out of mind?"

"What're you gettin' all defensive about, huh? I didn't twist you up or turn you around or wrap you up. I didn't make up the words, you know? Or where they came from."

"Well the meaning's here whether you made them up or no matter who made them up," Ruth said. "I hope you're not gettin' sick of cold suppers. God, I can't bring myself to turn the stove on in this heat."

Balzic couldn't help laughing out loud. He had to cover his mouth to keep from expelling food. "Spoken like a true nonwife."

"God what a conversation this is," Ruth said. "We start out talkin' about Saddam Hussein and look at you now. You look like one of the Three Stooges. Almost spit your food out laughin' at me."

"I'm not laughin' at you," he said, covering his mouth with his hand, as though that would make a difference. He was weaving and rocking with laughter.

"Some two-bit Hitler is using kids to show what a sweet guy he is, and my householder is practically spittin' his food out laughin' at me. Good god," Ruth said, shaking her head. "No, not *my* householder. The householder I live with."

"Well I'm certainly glad you made that little distinction. I mean, by god, if you're not gonna wear a veil around here and walk two steps behind me, then by god I ain't gonna be *your* householder."

"Very funny," Ruth said. "Very funny. Keep this up and I'm gonna have to be retrained to learn how to turn the stove on again."

"There's no law says food gotta be hot when you eat it. Ice cream'll make your blood just as lumpy as melted butter. And I know where the fridge is."

"You saying you don't need me even for a cook now?"

"All I'm sayin', my darlin', is, you know, what I heard Marie tellin' Emily once, they didn't know I was listenin'—"

"Eavesdroppin'—"

"Bein' a good father, right, that's what I said. And Marie was tellin' Emily that love is not based on need. It is based on want. Love based on need, she said—I think she was about seventeen—love based on need was 'sooooo juvenile.' I almost got a hernia tryin' to get away before I laughed."

"Well seventeen's about right for that. God I thought I didn't need you. I thought I wanted you, shows you how smart I was. But if you listened to all these people on Phil and Oprah, everybody who needs anybody is an addict. Co-dependents. Dependin' on somebody is a disease worse than cancer."

"Is it dependin' on somebody or is it *sayin'* you depend on somebody that's worse? Comin' out in public and admittin' you depend on somebody. Honest to god, all these people think they don't need anybody else, think they can get along by themselves, they crack me up."

"No, really, Mar, it's like the worst thing you can be now, the worst thing you can say about yourself is you're addicted to this person, you can't live without this person."

"Well that all started with the guys who said alcoholism was a disease. See? It's got so I can't even say it without usin' their words for it. Alcoholism, crap. Gettin' drunk every day. Stayin' drunk. But what I mean is, these guys who run these detox clinics, the only way they could get rich was first they had to con the insurance companies into payin' for what they do, and they couldn't do that until they turned drinkin' into a disease. Once they pulled that one off, hell, cakes, it was only a slip-slide and a jump away from everything you can't handle is a disease. There are billboards all over town, all they say is, 'Disease is an addiction, addiction is a disease.' How long's it gonna take before somebody says, 'Love is only love if you can walk away from it'? Huh? That's what Marie was tryin' to tell Emily, right?"

"And does that mean, my precious householder, that you are unable to walk away from me?"

Balzic thrust out his chest and threw his head back. "I can walk away from you anytime I want. I don't need you. What do I look like, some kinda goddamn addict? Love junkie? Huh? Need a fix of you every day? Huh? Crap. Double crap. I can take you or leave you, woman. Twisted up, wrapped up, turned inside out or upside down."

Ruth threw out her own chest. "That goes double for me, buster. You can start washin' your own clothes anytime you want, ironin' 'em too. And you can start with makin' your own breakfast tomorrow morning. I don't need to boil water for your instant coffee to demonstrate how much self-esteem I got. I ain't no love junkie either."

They giggled at each other.

"These people get paid for goin' on these talk shows, huh? Whatta you think? I think if they get paid, we maybe got a whole new career ahead of us, you know? We could go on all of 'em, tell the whole country how much we don't need each other."

"If you want to go on talk shows, big boy, if you want to

125

find out whether they pay those people, you're gonna have to make the calls yourself. I don't need to make calls for you."

"Yeah, yeah, okay. The calls I can make myself, but, uh, about this washin' clothes and ironin', that was just a joke too, right?"

Ruth clapped her hands over her cheeks and made a tiny pursed circle with her mouth. "Is my little householder not sure when his ex-wife is making a joke, hmmm?"

"C'mon, Ruth. Get serious for a minute here. Washin' clothes and ironin', you're just kiddin', right? 'Cause I don't know how to run the washer, you know I don't."

"Awwwwwwwwwwwwwww, poor baby."

"C'mon, Ruth, don't be screwin' around with me now. I'm serious. Washer's got more dials and do-hickeys on it than an airplane."

"Awwwwwwwwwwwwww."

*   *   *

Labor Day came and went. And the next day, as they had done for as long as anybody could remember, the schools in Rocksburg opened. And working the corners on the north side of Third Street Elementary School was Councilman Egidio Figulli's daughter, Philomena Marie Figulli, or as she was known, Jockey—not to her face of course. The nickname rose out of what was a more or less normal evolution of nicknames: Philomena, Phil, Philly, filly as in female horse, and Jockey, as in skinny and ugly with a long face and an eager willingness to ride on her father's political back. She would have helped herself more, it was said around the station, if she had been less eager to remind everyone whose back she was riding on and which direction she was riding.

She told Patrolman Larry Fischetti and Patrolman Harry Lynch on her first day on the job, a week before the start of school, that she was going to be chief in ten years, maybe sooner, it all depended on how the rate of attrition went. Her

126

actual words to Lynch were, "It all depends who gets attritted out." The reason Balzic knew about it was that Lynch had never heard the word *attritted* before and went and asked Fischetti who'd never heard it either and came and asked Balzic about it.

"It means who retires, who croaks, who flunks his physical and can't get insurance so he has to go on disability, like that."

Fischetti looked glum. After a long moment, he said, "You think she can really make it? In ten years? No shit?"

Balzic shrugged. "What do I know, huh? What're you askin' me this for? Don't you have someplace you're supposed to be, huh? Like in a black-and-white?"

"Hey, Mario, this is serious, this, uh, this, uh . . ."

"Go drive around, pretend you're protectin' the people, you know? Maybe you'll think of what you wanna say."

Fischetti walked out of the station and got into his black-and-white, shaking his head in what appeared to be deep dejection.

Balzic decided the best thing he could do was observe School Crossing Guard Figulli in action, so he left the station on foot, walked across in back of city hall past the animal shelter and across Fourth Street and down Pennsylvania Avenue until he came to the intersection of Third and Pennsylvania, where he hoped to take a position on the front porch of the library, behind the tree growing in the front corner of the lot. He would have done this too, except that Councilman Figulli had had the same idea and was already there, peering through the branches and leaves at his daughter, who was stopping and starting traffic and leading small groups of children safely across Third Street to their first day of school. Councilman Figulli was barely able to contain his pride. He was fidgeting as much as ever, but he was also grinning and shaking his head from side to side, as though to say, There, see? That's how a crossing guard works. See? That's my

127

daughter. She has a degree in criminal justice. She's going to be chief someday. But first I want her to start at the bottom, learn the ropes, work her way up. She'll be the youngest chief in the history of Rocksburg.

Balzic was going to turn and slip-slide out of there when Figulli happened to spot him. Figulli then began to wave and bob and weave around, a whole series of hypercontortions in an effort to summon Balzic to his side while not calling attention to himself, or at least giving the appearance of trying not to call attention to himself. Considering his usual tendencies to advertise himself at every opportunity, this current reluctance to be noticed struck Balzic as hilarious.

"Now what's this goofy sonofabitch gonna tell me," Balzic muttered to himself as he headed toward the library and to where Figulli was dancing around behind the tree. Figulli kept waving his arm for Balzic to come on, all the while mouthing giant whispers, "Hurry up, come on! Hurry up!"

When Balzic finally arrived at Figulli's side, Figulli motioned for him to lean down so he could talk into Balzic's ear.

"This is the proudest day of my life, Balzic," Figulli said. "My little girl's wanted to be a cop as long as I can remember. Honest to god, I'm so proud I could bust a gut. Look at her down there. Go on, look! Ain't she a sight?"

Balzic peered through the branches of the tree and down into the next block where School Crossing Guard Figulli was working traffic.

"Lookin' good," he said. "Yessir. She's lookin' good."

"Damn right she's lookin' good, Balzic," Figulli said. "That girl's gonna be chief someday. Mark my words. She's got a degree in criminal justice from Indiana University of Pennsylvania. One of the finest criminal justice programs in the state. She could've taken a position with some very large city police departments, Balzic. I said to her, 'Little girl,' I said, 'if you want my advice, you'll stay right here in Rocksburg. Start at the bottom. Work your way up. Learn the ropes. So when you get to be chief, you'll know. You won't just know out of books. You'll know from out of books *and* from your experience workin' your way up.' That's what my advice to her was, yessir. And thank god, I raised a child who respected my advice. Yessir."

Balzic suddenly needed a very large glass of wine. "Uh, Councilman, I'd like to stay and observe your daughter, I mean, Crossing Guard Figulli, but I have some business I have to attend to, so if you don't mind, I'll be on my way."

"Certainly, certainly, don't let me hold you up. I just saw you comin' up the street there and I knew you wouldn't want to miss the opportunity to see the start of a wonderful career. I knew you'd be as proud of her as I am. And you know, there's too much negativity in the world today, Balzic. Really, too many people have all these bad things to say about our young people, but really, they need to see some fine young people at work, don't you think?"

"Oh absolutely. Couldn't agree more."

"I think, you know, I don't wanna rush things, but I think, maybe, you know, after a little time passes, she gets to know her way around, I think I'm gonna go down the *Rocksburg Gazette* and talk to some reporters I know down there and say, Look, did ya ever think, you know, about doin' a picture story of somebody's career, you know, like from start to finish, you know, like every coupla years, you do a story, sorta follow up on how this person's doin', you know, progressin' right along there. Every coupla years, you put a complete picture story in the paper there, two three pages, you know? See how that person has been progressin' right along, huh, whatta ya think, Balzic? Think I oughta go down there and tell them, huh? You know, half them goddamn reporters, they don't know a good story when they see one. Whatta ya think?"

"Oh I think it'd be a great idea, yeah. Absolutely. Sure. You know, from crossin' guard to chief, right. What a record that would be. Absolutely, right in the paper there. Every

129

couple of years." Balzic patted Figulli on the shoulder and said, "Look, I really hate to go, I'd like to stay and discuss this with you, but you know how it is, huh?"

"Oh absolutely. Go on, get outta here. Get to work. I know how busy you are," Figulli said. "I'm just gonna stick around for a while. Ouu, look, there he is!"

"Huh? Who? There who is?"

"Up on the roof of the post office. See him? I hired a guy from Jimmy D'Alfonso's shop to get some pictures of her on her first day. Christ, this is great. I was thinkin' he wasn't gonna show up, I was gonna have to go down there and chew Jimmy a new ass, but, hey, he's as good as his word."

"I gotta go, Councilman," Balzic said, hustling away.

"Sure sure," Figulli said, waving Balzic away, even more deeply absorbed by the scene playing out before him, down Third Street and on the roof of the post office.

Balzic hurried toward Muscotti's. He hadn't walked this fast since the end of April, so fast he'd walked himself into a shirt-sticking sweat in less than half a block. Photographers on the roof, picture stories every couple of years, chief in ten years, hell, why stop there? Why not go for the White House? President Figulli. Hell yes, why not? Couldn't be any worse than what we got now, Balzic grumbled to himself.

*　　*　　*

Balzic woke up the morning of January 17th to the sound of the television in the living room. It was much louder than he thought it ought to be. In this moment of his first wakefulness, his face creased and puffy from sleep, his lips stuck together at the corners, his teeth gummy, his throat and sinuses dry from the forced-air heat, he thought immediately that something was wrong or else Ruth wouldn't have the sound up that high. He swung his feet off the side of the bed and stumbled around the bed and down the hall into the living room. He was scratching the sides of his belly and trying to remember where he'd left his glasses when he made it into the living room and saw Ruth standing, her hands wrapped around a mug of coffee, her shoulders hunched, her face pinched into a scowl, glaring at the TV set.

"They finally did it," she said. "The sons of bitches finally did it."

"Huh? Did what?"

"Started bombing. The planes. They started last night after we went to bed, must've been right after we went to bed, or maybe I'm mixed up about what time they're sayin' it started."

Before Balzic could reply, the phone rang. He padded over to it and picked it up.

"Mario? That you?"

"Yeah. Royer?"

"Yeah. Hate to do this to you, Mario, but we got shots fired."

"Huh? Shots? Who the hell's shootin' this time of day? What the hell time is it?"

"Some asshole is settin' bottles up on his back fence or in his backyard and shootin' 'em, the woman was a little nuts, you know, so I'm not real sure what's goin' on. The address is either one-zero-one or one-one-one on Braddock Street down in the Flats, that's the one about two over from the football field—"

"I know where it is," Balzic said. "So anybody down? Just shots or what? And what time is it?"

"Far as I can tell, just shots. Nine-one-one called first and then I had two other calls and the board's still lit up, so lemme talk to somebody else and I'll get back to you."

"Oh hell, don't bother. I'm on my way. Call the state cops, you know, just wake 'em up case I need anybody. I'll let you know as soon as I know."

He hung up and said to Ruth, "Gotta go. Somebody's shootin' down in the Flats. What time is it?"

131

"Well why not," she said sourly. "Isn't that what everybody does? When they don't get what they want? Start shooting? Just look at the damn TV. God, look at it, Mario. Just look."

Balzic sighed. "Don't have time, cakes. Gotta go." He wobbled off to the bedroom and put his clothes on and was starting for the front door when Ruth held out a vacuum bottle. He took it from her, kissed her on the cheek and squeezed her arm and hustled out to the cruiser in the garage.

In ten minutes he was parking in front of 108 Braddock Street in the Flats, so called because it was a low area on the south shore of the Conemaugh River. He got out and listened for about thirty seconds or so but didn't hear anything. He went to the door at 108 and knocked. An elderly woman with no teeth, pulling the collar of a frayed and fading flannel robe tight around her neck came to the door.

"You call the police, ma'am?"

She shook her head no and quickly pushed the door shut.

He went to the next front door, 106, in the row and knocked and rang the bell. Nobody came.

He trotted across the street. The moment his foot hit the other sidewalk he heard the shot and the explosion of broken glass. Good God, he thought, some asshole really was shooting bottles in his backyard.

He didn't have to knock at 107. A woman, fiftyish, also in a robe she was pulling tight across her neck, was waiting for him.

"You call the police, ma'am?"

"You damn right I did. That crazy man is shooting." She was pointing to her left. "He's in the end house, one-oh-one, and you're gonna have to call an ambulance for Mrs. Ogorodny. I saw her go down, Jesus god almighty, you know how many times I been tryin' to call younz guys? Everybody asleep up there? Goddamn line's busy every time. Whatta they, take it off the hook and go to sleep?"

132

"You're not the only one callin', ma'am. Call 911, and ask for an ambulance, would you please do that? Huh, okay?"

"That's who I'm callin'! Nine-one-one!"

"Well call 'em again, ma'am, please?"

Balzic tiptoed down the sidewalk to 101 and sneaked a look inside the diamond-shaped window in the front door. There were no curtains in that window and there was a light coming from somewhere in the back, but he couldn't see beyond the newel post and banister to the upstairs, so he crept over to the two windows to the left of the door. He could see the light was coming from the back room of the house, probably the kitchen, so he had no trouble seeing inside, but he couldn't see any movement. There did not appear to be a whole lot of furniture in the room he was looking into. The only two pieces of furniture that he could see were lawn furniture, aluminum with plastic webbing, a folding chair and a chaise lounge.

He tiptoed to the end of the building, got down on his hands and knees, and peeked around the corner. Scraggly brush and weeds blocked his view. He eased up slowly to try to see over them. Just as he did, there was another shot and another explosion of breaking glass, but this time he saw the glass exploding and flying to the ground. Well, he thought, whoever it is, at least he's shooting in the direction of the Indian Mound.

The Indian Mound was a centuries-old burial ground a couple of hundred yards long, fifty yards wide, and thirty or so yards high at its highest point. It was between the Flats and the Conemaugh River, and its base started about twenty-some feet from the ends of the half-dozen streets of row-houses like Braddock Street. An unpaved alley ran between the streets and the Mound. Balzic himself couldn't have picked a safer stop for the bullets than the Mound, so the shooter wasn't a total crazy.

Looking at the Mound, watching the newspapers and

candy wrappers and grocery bags blowing up and around and down it, Balzic couldn't help but think of the three days in the early seventies he'd spent trying to deal with two members of the American Indian Movement who'd come to the Mound to reclaim it from the whites who had been desecrating it for centuries, "ever since the first one came with his measuring tools"—that was how they described the surveyor George Washington. Then, just when Balzic thought he'd reached some kind of understanding with them, not the least by giving them some kolbassi sandwiches and by arranging a meeting with officials from the Carnegie Museum in Pittsburgh, where many of the skeletons and artifacts from the mound had eventually wound up, somebody in the U.S. Justice Department decided it was nothing less than an "occupation by a radical group" and ordered in the FBI. The FBI, about two dozen more than seemed necessary to Balzic at the time, and most carrying automatic weapons, "surrounded the occupying group of radicals," arrested them, and took them away in every kind of restraint known to law enforcement at the time, all the while patronizing Balzic and the rest of his department as well as every other Rocksburg official for "their lack of sophistication in understanding the problem radicals presented" and in their "lack of resolve" in dealing with the "clear and present danger the radicals presented." Balzic had no trouble remembering the words because they were in the report the Justice Department sent to Rocksburg City Council and which was read into the minutes of a council meeting over his protest. The whole incident made him almost as disgusted as the miners' strike at Edna No. 3.

He shook himself out of that memory and hurried back to 107 and pounded on the door. Just as it opened he heard another shot and another explosion of breaking glass.

The woman had a phone to her ear and thrust it into Balzic's face. "Listen to this. Nothin' but busy signals."

Balzic shrugged. "Uh, ma'am, anything you can tell me

about who that is in one-oh-one, anything at all? Name, age, anything."

"He's a guy, that's all I know. Moved in about three months ago. Maybe four, I don't know, maybe five months. He's a guy, that's all I know. He comes, he goes, he don't say nothin' to me, I don't say nothin' to him. All I know is he talks to himself a lot. He don't got a job, I know that. 'Course around here he fits right in."

"Anybody else in there with him?"

"No. At least I never seen anybody. But I never been in there, I don't know."

"No woman, no kids?"

"I just told ya, I never seen anybody."

"What's out back, ma'am?"

"What's where out back?"

"In the back, you know, on the other side of your back door? Is it another row of buildings, some garages, a wall, what?"

"Oh. There's a, it's my little backyard, you know, and then there's the alley, and then there's a, the houses over on Washington Street. The backs of 'em."

"I have to come through your house, ma'am, see what I can see? Hope that's okay with you."

"I don't know," she said, her hand over her mouth. "I don't know. What if he sees you and starts shootin' up this way? Jesus god almighty."

"C'mon, ma'am, I need to get inside to get a look at him. Besides, it's cold as hell out here, I'm freezin'. Was it supposed to get this cold, huh? D'you hear a weather report say it was gonna get this cold?"

"It's January," she said. "You surprised it's cold?"

"C'mon, ma'am, I gotta get inside, please?"

"Jesus god almighty, all right, c'mon, c'mon, all my heat's goin' right out the door, hurry up."

"All these places laid out pretty much the same way?" Balzic

135

said, coming in and starting toward the back of the house, cupping his hands and blowing on them.

"How should I know? I only been in this one and the one next door, Mrs. Ogorodny's."

"Well is her place pretty much like yours?"

"Yeah. Sorta. I never paid any attention. Every time I'm over there it's 'cause she called me 'cause she was gonna pass out."

Balzic stopped and turned around and said, "She calls you when she's gonna pass out? You call an ambulance every time she does?"

"No. Why would I do that?"

"Then why you wanna call for one now? You think she's been shot or what?"

"No no, I didn't say she was shot. I think she probably had one of her spells. The guy he makes her real nervous, he's talkin' to all these people over there and nobody else ever comes out. That's what she says anyway. I just figure he's talkin' to himself. What else could it be, I mean if you don't see nobody?"

Balzic mulled that one over, took another deep breath, and turned and went to the back room of the house, the kitchen. There was a door to the left and a window to the right, over the sink. He went to the sink and pulled the curtains back, being careful to not knock over a row of tiny glass and ceramic animals, dogs and seals and cats and elephants, atop the frame of the bottom window.

"Hey watch my animals!" the woman shrieked.

"I'm watchin' I'm watchin', Jesus, lady, don't scream like that anymore, okay?"

Another shot, another explosion of glass.

Balzic couldn't see anything from the window. He eased the curtain back down, being careful not to touch the ceramic animals, and went to the door. He pulled back the inner door, which was wooden and had a window in the top half, and he leaned as close to the glass in the aluminum storm door as he could get, but he still couldn't see anything. He fiddled with the handle of the storm door until he found the latch that worked the lock, opened it, and then pushed the storm door open a crack, then wider until he spotted the man two yards over. He was bent over. All Balzic could see was the man's rump and legs and the rounded hump of his back. The man took some moments to straighten up and he had his left hand on his back as he did. When he was erect, he walked slowly and stiffly to the wooden fence at the end of his yard and set a beer bottle atop the fence. When he turned around, Balzic's mouth dropped and he shoved open the door and went barging out into the backyard. Two chain-link fences separated Balzic from the man, who spotted Balzic as soon as he went charging into the yard. The man began to grin sheepishly and scratch his head with the barrel of the revolver he had in his right hand.

"Myushkin, what the hell're you doin'? Jesus Christ, you got people scared outta their minds, what the hell are you doin'?" Balzic was up against the chain-link fence separating this backyard from Mrs. Ogorodny's. He looked all around the fence for a gate and finally found it straight back from the door he'd come out of and went to the gate and through it and down the alley toward Myushkin, who was still standing in his backyard with his left hand holding his right wrist atop his head, still grinning sheepishly and slumping from foot to foot.

The fence around Myushkin's yard was wooden and rotting. The gate into his backyard was hanging by one hinge and when Balzic pushed through it, it came off in his hands. He looked at it for a second and then looked at Myushkin, who said, "Just like everything else around here, comin' apart and goin' to hell fast as it can."

Balzic dropped the gate and wiped his hands to get the rotted wood and old paint off them. "What the hell're you doin', man, Jesus Christ, you've got people scared outta their minds, what the hell're you doin'? What's your problem today?"

"Oh, Balzic, what is my problem, lemme think, what is special today, hmmm. Is it cause I'm broke? Hmmm? No. I was broke yesterday. Is it cause I'm hungry, hmmm? No. I was hungry yesterday. Is it cause I'm cold? No. I was cold yesterday, gas company turned my gas off end of December. Is it cause my back hurts and I can barely stand up, hmmm? No. My back's been killin' me for damn near two months now. Hmmm. I'll tell ya, Balzic, I don't know what it can be— oh wait, wait. I remember now. It's cause we're in a goddamn war, that's what it is. How could I forget about that little detail? Went to bed last night, we were at peace with the world, woke up this mornin', turned my radio on, and White House Boy Georgie got himself another war. The one in Panama didn't satisfy him, nossir, he had to get him a Hitler, man. I mean, if ol' Frankie Roosevelt could bag him a Hitler, why, goddamn, no reason why White House Boy Georgie couldn't bag himself a Hitler too, even if it was a little ol' stinkin' Arab kinda Hitler—"

"You drunk?"

"There you go again, Balzic, thinkin' the only two possible states of consciousness I could be in is in-toxication or insanity. Hell no I ain't drunk. I'm just out here testin' my marksmanship skills. I could be called up at any time to defend my president's right to fish outta his high-speed, gas-guzzlin' motorboat. I mean when my president wants to— how'd he say it? Oh yeah, when he wants to 'pru-dent-ly recreate,' by god, I gotta turn into Johnny-get-my-gun, gotta run, gotta run. Hell, Balzic, you can't be drunk when you get your gun, gotta run, gotta run."

Oh Christ, Balzic thought, why me. "Oh, Christ," he grumbled, and went over to Myushkin's side and said, "Come on, Christ almighty, let's go inside, it's freezin' out here."

138

"Well it ain't gonna be much warmer in there, I can tell you that right now," Myushkin said, allowing himself to be led into his rowhouse.

When they got into the kitchen, Balzic could see by his breath that Myushkin had not been exaggerating. It wasn't much warmer. "They turned the gas off on ya? In December?"

"Yep-pie," Myushkin said, going over to a wobbly wooden chair at the equally decrepit table and easing himself stiffly down onto the chair. In the middle of the table was a thousand-round box of .22-caliber long rifle cartridges. There was nothing else: no cups, plates, pots, nothing to show that this table was used for food. Except for a cast-iron frying pan and a small aluminum pot coated with Teflon on top of the apartment-size electric stove, there wasn't another cooking implement in sight. The same could be said of the rest of the kitchen. Either Myushkin was very tidy, or he ate someplace else.

"You still got electricity?"

"Yeah, they haven't turned that off yet. Fact, I got a letter a couple days ago askin' me to come in and talk about some easy payment plan. So, I got electricity and water, just no gas, no heat. 'Course, none of it's gonna make any difference 'cause I'm about to get evicted anyway."

"Little behind in the rent too?"

"I ain't behind. I promised to wash the walls and paint 'em, you know, patch 'em up, in exchange for a couple months' rent, but my back's been so screwed up I can't get on a ladder. I mean I can get on one, but I can't reach up with one hand for more than a couple seconds at a time, so, you know, the guy's been real nice about it, but, hell, everybody's got a limit. Ain't that the message from Iraq today, huh? Everybody runs out of patience sooner or later? I mean, White House Boy Georgie, hell, he's been tellin' us for how long now he's ticked off, he's gettin' real mad, he's runnin' outta patience with this Saddam Hitler, and, hell, now I guess we gotta believe him, right?"

Balzic took his hands out of pockets long enough to blow on them and rub them together, and then thrust them back into his raincoat. "Listen, give me your word, okay? No more shootin' till I get back, okay?"

"Where you goin'?"

"Next door, see about the old lady."

"What, she conk out again? Hell she'll be okay. She's got high blood pressure and she thinks once she takes all the pills in one bottle she doesn't have to take any more. Then she tries to stand up fast and she gets dizzy and over she goes. She'll be all right. She just needs to start payin' attention to her doctor, that's all."

"You, uh, you don't think anything you do in here has anything to do with it?"

"Anything I do in here? Like what?"

"Well like shootin' bottles for one—"

"This is the first time I ever did that—"

"Oh. So that would mean she wouldn't have any history of passin' out when you were shootin' bottles then, right?"

Myushkin hung his head and grinned sheepishly up at Balzic.

"And talkin' to yourself in here, apparently that wouldn't have anything to do with it either, right?"

"Hey, Balzic, I write stories, man. That's what I do. And I talk to myself while I'm doin' it. I mean, how the hell else do I know the dialogue's gonna sound right if I don't say it out loud first. Then I read it out loud after I got it down. I mean, I can't help it the walls are about an inch thick here. Hell, I hear her talkin' to herself too, you know? Writers and lonely people, they talk to themselves, man. Most people play the TV or the radio, you know? Why the hell you think there's all these goddamn talk shows and call-in shows, huh? 'Cause there's all these lonely people in this goddamn country, don't

140

know how to talk to each other. That's why we have the pros, man. Pro talkers do it for us. That's why there's Phil Donahoe and Phil Musick and Myron Cope and Sally Jessy What's-her-face. This old lady next door don't have a TV or a radio. She's over there talkin' to Jesus. I offered to give her my radio, but she said she didn't want nothin' to do with it. She didn't give me a reason. I told her, you know, if you don't start listenin' to these people, they're gonna lose their jobs and they're gonna wind up livin' next door to you just like me, but she didn't get it. Or if she got it she didn't laugh. Maybe I didn't tell it right."

"God, you are a rambler," Balzic said, shaking his head, and heading out the back door, stopping at the door to admonish Myushkin one more time about not shooting until he got back. "I got to check this old lady, not that I doubt you, you know. . . ."

Myushkin grinned lopsidedly. "Right. Why would anybody doubt me?"

Balzic was back in less than a minute. He came in, blowing on his hands, and said, "Turns out you were right, she's okay, or she is for now anyway."

"Told ya."

"So before I arrest you," Balzic said, "what the hell's this about?"

"Woooeee," Myushkin said. "You mean you ain't gonna arrest me till I tell you? Look out Sche-her-a-zade!"

"Yeah. More or less," Balzic said, not sure who Scheherazade was but squinting and scowling because he remembered how this man liked to ramble.

"Well I'll be delighted to put the light on it for you."

"Cold as it is in here, you better do more than put light on it. You better generate some heat too. A lotta heat."

"Hey, generate heat. That's pretty good, Balzic. Pretty good. Stories will now be weighed by their caloric content. Damn, you could have a whole new school of criticism named

141

after you, man. The Balzic school of literary criticism, fiction damn near good enough to eat. Hey, then for the gourmands, there would be the high-cholesterol school, you know, and for the Puritans, the low-cholesterol school—"

"Okay okay okay, skip the bullshit and get to it."

"Well sir, it's like this—oh, before I start, I got a couple pairs of gloves if you wanna put some on."

"Cut it out, Myushkin, goddamnit. Get to it."

"Okay, okay. It's like this. I'm sittin' here in my condo by the Conemaugh, see, tryin' to figure out how come I'm not doin' as well as, say, oh, William Buckley, you know? I mean, he's up there in New York City, and he does what I do, you know, puts words on paper, and every time he thinks about takin' a couple months off, you, he goes and rents a schooner or something and sails it across the Atlantic—or the Pacific. Me, I can't even get a rowboat out on the Conemaugh, you know, captain of my fate I am not."

"Yeah, right. So you're not a captain. So go 'head."

"So, I was just thinkin', you know, I worked for Volkswagen for ten years, you know, best job I ever had, most money, worked for 'em as long as all their tax exonerations lasted, all their exemptions from real estate and school taxes, after the state of Pennsylvania built 'em a four-lane highway complete with a goddamn cloverleaf, built 'em a rail spur, you know, and the goddamn month their tax exemptions and exonerations run out, that's the month they suddenly can't sell any more Rabbits, man, boom, shut it down, man. Almost to the day, you know?"

"No I didn't know that."

"Well they did, man, you can check me out on this. Go look it up. Go talk to the tax collectors in the school district and in the township there, man, you'll find out."

"This is why you're shootin' bottles? Huh?"

"It's part of it, yeah. It ain't all of it, but it's part of it. I mean, the state, the county, the township, the school district,

142

hell I don't know who all was involved in bringin' VW over here to make cars—probably the same bunch that's involved in gettin' Sony into the same goddamn plant—and I don't think anybody knows how many millions and millions of dollars, hundreds of millions, man, when you add up the costs of the road and the rail spur and all the taxes they didn't have to pay? You kiddin'? I mean, there was government handouts flyin' around, the pols couldn't hand it out fast enough, but I never heard ol' William Buckley piss and moan about those handouts, did you? I mean, the only kind of pissin' and moanin' you hear ol' Billy Boy doin' is when it comes to welfare and unemployment for the grunts. I mean, look at me, man. Look around."

"I am lookin' at you, Myushkin. I'm right in front of you. But I ain't gettin' any warmer, so you better start tellin' me somethin' good."

"Hey, Balzic, I got nine books in the Library of Congress. Nine! I got those books in eight languages around the world. I mean, my stuff's been sold in England, man, Scotland, Wales, Ireland, Canada, New Zealand, Australia. My stuff's been translated into German, Dutch, Swedish, French, Spanish, Italian, and Japanese for crissake. And here I sit. I'm fifty-five years old for crissake. I can't live in my own house 'cause the welfare guys won't give my wife any money if I'm there. I ran outta unemployment so long ago I can't remember, beginning of '90 I think. I got no heat, I'm broke, my back's killin' me, and I'm about to get evicted. You wanna tell me why it is guys like Buckley think guys like me are bums? How do you suppose he got to the place where he can't see that the handouts those fuckers who run VW took from the state ain't any different from the handouts he thinks guys like me took for a while—a damn short while, too, pardner. Damn short.

"Meanwhile the bastards that run Volkswagen are back in Germany, you know, skiing in the Alps and shootin' crap in

Monaco. Here I am, I don't even have the price of a Lotto ticket, man, can't even get in the door to play Bingo at the goddamn Loyal Order of the Moose."

"God, Myushkin, you really are feelin' sorry for yourself—"

"Sorry! Sorry? Sorry my ass! I'm gonna tell you some things, Balzic, things you never thought about in a hundred years, man about this mighty fine country of ours, and how the fuckin' taxes work."

"Uh, before you tell me about how the taxes work, maybe I should tell you about how the law works."

"Aw come on man. What're you gonna tell me? Huh? About *Title 18 Crimes and Offenses, Pennsylvania Consolidated Statutes*? Come on, man."

"Okay," Balzic said. "So you know everything. But if you do, you're not puttin' what you know with what you're doin'. 'Cause you come in front of the wrong judge, and he wants to play hard-ass, that gun you're holdin' is a guaranteed five years, and nobody's been able to beat that one."

"Hey, so maybe it'll be a little warmer in jail than it is here, whatta ya think?"

"I'm serious, Myushkin. That pistol's no joke. I mean, the very least you did is you violated a city ordinance. Dischargin' a firearm inside the city is thirty days, a thousand-dollar fine, or both."

"In my case I guess it's gonna have to be the thirty days—if you guys got room in the jail. I guess I don't have to tell you, but, you know, the jails are so crowded, man, even the *Rocksburg Gazette* is disturbed about that. They're writin' editorials about how we're all gonna get stuck with another big bond issue for a new jail, you know?"

Balzic folded his arms and rocked on his heels and toes and looked down at the floor. There wasn't much linoleum left. "Will you get to it?"

"I'm to it right now, man. You think I'm talkin' in circles,

144

but I ain't. All this stuff, everything I'm gonna tell you is part of it, honest to god it is."

"Well speed it up, I'm cold. And you're sittin' there holdin' a piece and I'm not real thrilled about that."

"And well you shouldn't be thrilled, Balzic. The gun in America *is* America. We are what Mao Tse-Tung said: 'All power comes out of the barrel of a gun.' 'Course we never say that because he was a commie pinko bastard and we ain't allowed to repeat commie pinko bastard truth even if we live it every day of our lives. Hell, man, even as I sit here and you stand there, our president, White House Boy Georgie Himself, is sendin' hundreds of thousands of gun barrels to free Kuwait from our monster of the moment, ain't he? And who was it who said, 'Before we kill our enemy, we must first make him a monster?'—who said that? Nietzsche? I can't remember now, but it sounds like somethin' he would've said. Anyway, it's the thought that counts, not who says it.

"Well, Balzic, what you're gonna find out from me is I'm no different from anybody else. I'm exactly like everybody else in America. You wanna ride the bus in America, you gotta have the ticket. And the ticket costs money. You want your garbage collected, you gots to pay. You can't get it done by writin' the garbage collectors a great review. You can't get 'em to collect it by sayin' you never saw anybody empty cans the way they do, such style, such power, such grace. And they don't bang the cans! The most important new voice in garbage collection in years! The most sensitive garbage collector in America! The *New York Times* says nobody collects garbage like ABC Sanitation!

"Balzic, you want your garbage collected, you gotta pay 'em, or they leave it on the curb. No amount of emotional currency is gonna make 'em pick it up. They want cash. Well goddamnit so do I. People been tryin' to pay me emotional coin for twenty-five years. I got great reviews up to my ankles, man. Guess what? I can't take 'em to the market. I can't take

145

'em to the gas station. I can't take 'em to the state store. If I take the whole goddamn pile to the state store I can't buy one bottle of Vino Duva."

"Uh, excuse my ignorance," Balzic said, "but you lost me back there a ways. You got 'great reviews' up to your ankles?"

"I was speakin' metaphorically, man. I don't really have 'em to my ankles. It was a figure of speech—"

"No, uh, I mean 'great reviews', uh, I don't even know how to ask the question—"

"Reviews is what gets in the papers and magazines, you know. After you write the damn book, if you're lucky it gets read by people who work at newspapers and magazines and they tell their readers what it's about and whether it's any good, like that."

"And you got 'em up to your ankles?"

"Yeah, metaphorically speaking, yeah."

"And they're all great?"

"Well not 'great' great. I mean, what the hell, I gotta exaggerate a little bit, you know."

"Well don't exaggerate. Tell me straight. You got 'em or not?"

Myushkin nodded several times. "Not all of 'em, of course. But most of them are. Lots of 'em, man, I honestly could not have written them better myself, man, more complimentary, I'm not jokin'. And see, that's what really bugs me. I mean, I get these reviews that say my stuff's worth readin' and damn near the only people who buy it are libraries, man."

"Well what's wrong with that? Somebody's buyin' 'em."

"No, naw, you don't get it. This is what I want to explain to you, man. This is what I wanna tell you about taxes and America, man, and writin' and war, Jesus—"

"Hey wait a goddamn second here," Balzic said. "I said I wasn't gonna arrest ya till you told me, but you said yourself everybody got limits, remember? And my old joints ain't gettin' any warmer, so hurry the hell up. Just leave out all the stuff about the war—"

"Hey, man, my joints ain't a whole lot younger'n yours. Why you think my back's killin' me, huh? I don't even have money to join the Boys Club. If I had the dues, man, I could go down there and get a hot shower every day. Christ, I can't believe it. I was born down here in the Flats, man. That was the way my whole damn family used to get cleaned up—well not my mother. My old man, my brothers and me, during the Depression we all used to go to the Boys Club, get a hot shower every day. Imagine this shit, man, forty, fifty years later, books in nine languages and I haven't had a hot shower or bath since the end of December, and this is what, the seventeenth? Seventeen goddamn days. It's no wonder my back's in knots for crissake."

"You're ram-bling, Mis-ter My-ush-kin. Get to the god-damn point."

"Hey! That *was* one of the points goddamnit! After all the work I've done in my life, hey, and not just writin' books either, goddamnit! I did a four-year enlistment in the United States Army. Honorably discharged, man. I have never once cheated or lied on my income tax, man. I been payin' Uncle Mother-Fucker Sam taxes since I was fifteen, I never missed a year, man. I don't belong to any church, man, and I don't write down on my tax forms that I give any money to any goddamn church either. I don't use any charity dodges to beat my tax rap, like the whole fuckin' ruling class does in this country. And you may not think any of this is part of the problem with me today, but everygoddamnthing I just said is part of the problem."

"Well it may be," Balzic said, "but you better start puttin' it together so I can understand it. I mean, if you're such a hotshot writer, you better start grabbin' my attention, don't ya think?"

147

Myushkin licked his lips and shook his head from side to side and squirmed on the chair and then started rapping his fingertips on his thighs. "I can explain it, man. I can. But you got to be just a little bit patient, you know? I mean you can't say everything you know in one sentence or one paragraph. I mean, there've been times when I set out to say somethin' and three hundred pages later I found out I said somethin' else, man, it wasn't anything like I started out to say, you follow' me here?"

"Well I sure hope to hell that's not what's gonna happen now," Balzic said sourly. "And, uh, for starters, how 'bout if you hand over the gun, whatta ya say?"

Myushkin shook his head. "Hey, man, don't game me that way, huh? I give you the gun, you're gonna walk right out that door. I mean, I know how to tell a story, man, but I also know there are some people, piles and piles of 'em in America, who don't wanna hear good fiction, man. And I remember a conversation we had in Muscotti's not too long ago, you told me straight out, you said, 'I don't read much fiction.' That's what you said and I figure what you really meant was, you don't read fiction period. So I give you the gun, far as I'm concerned, I lost about ninety-nine percent of my attraction here. I mean, let's be honest, Balzic. Without the gun, you wouldn't be here, am I right or not?"

Balzic ran his tongue around the inside of his lower lip. "So get on with it. Oh, one thing first. If you got all these, uh, these great reviews, how come I never heard of you? I mean, why hasn't there ever been anything in the papers about you? I never read anything about you in the *Rocksburg Gazette* or the Pittsburgh papers. I may not read fiction, but I would've remembered something like that, you know, hometown boy makes good."

"First place," Myushkin said, blowing on his own hands, "my hands are turnin' to ice cubes. There's a couple pairs of gloves on the chair in the front room, man, you wanna go get me a pair, please, okay?"

Balzic went into the front room and saw that he'd been right about the furniture: there were only two pieces, lawn furniture, a chair and a chaise lounge. The gloves were on the bottom of the lounge. He put one pair on and took the other pair back into the kitchen and handed them to Myushkin.

"Thanks, man," Myushkin said, putting the gloves on after he'd motioned for Balzic to back up to the other side of the room.

"Lemme see, how come you never heard of me? Hmmm. Well, see, Balzic, it's like this. I had to choose. Did I want to write, or did I want to be a star? The first is a verb, *to write*, the infinitive, man. It's action, it's doin', it's lookin', it's seein', it's observin', it's rememberin', then it's writin' it down as close to the bone as you can get it. Most people think of writin', they don't see it as action, man, as labor, but it is. It's physical labor and don't let anybody tell you it ain't. It's as hard as humpin' hod, man, hard as mixin' cement and carryin' bricks. The second one, bein' a star, that ain't a verb, man, that's a malignancy. That's bein' the object of veneration. That's bein' worshipped, man. That's wakin' up everygoddamnmornin' and knowin' that there are people by the bunch out there just waitin' to take your picture and get your name on paper and touch you and get a button that fell off your coat or if one doesn't fall off, man, they reach out there and rip it off. And all because they think you're special and the only way they're gonna be special is by gettin' close to you, man. That's a sickness, man, a disease. And in America it's a goddamn epidemic."

Balzic was smiling in spite of himself. Looking around this kitchen, looking at this man, listening to his words, Balzic could not make his face not smile.

Myushkin smiled back. "You think I'm fulla shit, don't ya? Huh? You think I'm sittin' here in the middle of this dump in the middle of the goddamn Flats, busted out, no heat, no food, about to get evicted, and you think I'm trippin' out, huh? Flyin' on delusions of my own grandeur, ain't that right, Balzic?"

Balzic looked at his shoes and tried to make his face sober and stern and professional. "Well you have to admit, given, uh, where we are, I mean, the thought that you're an object of veneration, well . . ."

"I didn't say I was, Balzic. I said I had to choose whether I wanted to write, whether I wanted to do somethin', be a verb, a livin', breathin', movin' animal—or be a star. A fixed thing, up there, not in my mind, but in the minds of the people who come out at night to look up to try to find me. Didn't you ever contemplate why people in churches and mosques spend so much time on their knees and lookin' down and then lookin' up? What's 'at mean to you, bein' on your knees and lookin' down? Or lookin' up and askin' for somethin' from somebody you can't see? You ever wonder why all those chickees used to scream when Frankie Sinatra sang? Or when Elvis shook his ass? Or when the Beatles got off the plane? Or when Michael Jackson waves his sparkle glove around? Or when Madonna points her tits at somebody and grabs her crotch?"

"Well I don't know why all of 'em scream," Balzic said, "but I imagine a few of 'em are gettin' paid to scream. The rest of 'em I guess just do what comes naturally."

"That may be one reason, I don't doubt that, but what I'm talkin' about, man, is there's this huge need in people to believe there's somebody more important, more special, more gifted, more beautiful, more powerful than they are. It's somethin' that's been in people as long as there have been people, man, I mean it just didn't start here, you know, last week. It's been around as long as there's been writing and

150

painting and sculpting. But it's somethin', it's, uh, it just makes me cringe, man. It just makes me go queasy inside to think there are all these people who think so little of themselves, man, that they spend their whole lives lookin' for somebody's feet to kiss. And I didn't want to be part of that, man. And I know, I mean, I can see you lookin' around here and tryin' hard not to laugh in my face, but you got to believe me, man, I could've been part of that. I could've been one of the somebodys whose feet they were lookin' for, man. And I said nothin' doin', I ain't playin' the star game, not in this life I ain't."

"So that's why I never read about you in the *Rocksburg Gazette*, is that what you're tellin' me?"

Myushkin nodded his head several times. "That's half of it, yeah. The other half is they wouldn't pay me."

Balzic burst out laughing, he couldn't help himself.

"Yeah yeah, I know, I know," Myushkin said. "You think, yeah, that's it. *That's it!* That's the real reason. But I'm tellin' ya, man, that's the other half of what I'm talkin' about."

Balzic had to get a hanky out to wipe his eyes and nose. He tried to make it look like it was because of the cold, but it was because of his laughter and there was nothing he could do to hide that.

"See, Balzic, come on, man, settle down here and pay attention. I'm tryin' to tell you somethin' now. Keep your mind open. 'Cause the one thing feeds into the other. I'm serious, man. Listen to me."

"All right, all right, I'm listenin'. But I'm tellin' you, Myushkin, I'm not gettin' any warmer."

"Okay, okay. Stick with me here. See, once you refuse to play the celebrity game, once you say you're not goin' to be part of that, you have to deal with all the people who're in the game only they think they're not. And that's all the reporters who got all this space to fill every day, every week, every month. See, the papers, the magazines, they got this

151

advertising gig goin', and they gotta have somethin' to put in the spaces between the ads. I mean the ads is how they make their money—or how they hope they make their money, but when they sell the ads, man, they have to have something to put in the rest of the space, get it?"

"I think I understand that," Balzic said.

"Yeah, you think you do, but you don't understand the part I'm gonna tell you now. 'Cause, see, when the reporter from the *Rocksburg Gazette* or any other newspaper, when he's sittin' around pickin' his nose, and his boss tells him get off his ass and do somethin', see, he gets this bright idea to come talk to me and here's the way the conversation goes, man. He asks me if I wanna sit still for an interview. I tell him no. He says why not. I say how much. He says how much what? I say how much you gonna pay me? He says I'm kiddin', right? I say no, I ain't kiddin', how much. He looks at me kinda stupefied. I say to him, you gettin' paid by your paper? He says of course. I say, is your paper gonna charge money to the people who want to read the paper that day? He says of course. I say, is your paper gonna charge money to the people who bought ads in the paper that day? He says of course. Then I say, so if your paper's gonna be sold for money to the people who wanna read it, and if your paper's gonna charge money for the people who wanna advertise in it, and if you're gonna get paid for askin' me questions, then what's so hard to understand about payin' me for answerin' those questions? And he goes, Huhhhhhh? Then he says, all bug-eyed and grinnin', hey, think of all the free ad-ver-tis-ing you're gonna get. And I say, no, *you* think of all the free advertisin'. What I'm gonna think about is I'm in the same business you and your bosses are in—the word business. And if you and your bosses are gonna make money askin' me questions, then I'm gonna make money sellin' my answers, or I'm not gonna say a word, understand? And of course he doesn't, because every reporter is convinced, deep down in his guts, that the only reason he hasn't written a best-seller yet is 'cause he hasn't had time, 'cause he thinks that if he had the time, he could knock one out in, oh, you know, two or three weeks, bing-bang-pow, and he would lovvvvve to get out there, be in that position where people were wakin' up every day with the first thought in their minds was to try their damnedest to find where he was so they could get first shot at tryin' to kiss his feet. And when a guy like me comes along and says, uh-uh, I ain't ridin' that bus, that bus they want with everything that's in them to be on, man, they get real pissed off at me. And that's the third reason I don't play that game, man. You get it, man? I don't wanna be adored 'cause I ain't adorable, I don't care what moves people to adoration. I wanna get paid for my words 'cause words are my trade and that means not only when I'm writin' 'em but also when I'm talkin' 'em. And I'm tired of explainin' this to reporters who get pissed off at me for not bein' what they think they'd be if they were me. So that's why you don't read about me in the *Rocksburg Gazette*, man, or in any other newspaper. I mean, I gave interviews, man. Three of 'em. I wouldn't have learned what I know if I hadn't. But after the third one, I said that's it, no more of this freebie bullshit. You want my words, you gotta pay me."

"Except for now."

"Huh?"

"You wanna get paid when other people wanna ask you questions, but when you wanna talk, you, uh, how do I say this? You either talk to your ghost buddies in Muscotti's and drive Vinnie crazy for free, or else you, uh, give a whachma-callit, a command performance. Only in reverse. For me. Right?"

Myushkin hung his head again and shook it slowly, peering up under his brows at Balzic.

"Okay," Myushkin said. "So it's a little extreme, shootin' bottles. So I'm havin' a little problem with my readership—

153

god I hate that fuckin' word. Readership. It's like worship, you know? Worshippers? Readershippers? Do I hate it? Really? Or am I just bullshittin' myself, you know, 'cause I got so damn few of 'em I can't keep the weather off my ass?

"I keep tellin' myself, we gotta make time for the stories, man, 'cause we gotta understand the difference between fiction and faction, between the lies from which we learn truth and the lies from which the truth is kept from us. This is what I been tellin' myself for the last thirty years, man. I tell everybody, I say, see, what I do is make fiction. What those bastards, those white-bread bastards who run the country, what they do is make faction. You know when you read my fiction that it's a lie. But those scum in Washington, when they give us faction? When they stand there and tell us the truth, the whole truth, and nothing but the truth—when they do that, man, it's run for cover. 'Cause when they're givin' us their truth, only their real good buddies know who's gonna get screwed that day."

Myushkin's eyes turned to slits and his face darkened. "Fiction is a lie, man. But down there in the middle of it, right at its center, if it's good fiction it's a lie to help us get at what's goin' on. You don't know how many people I talk to, man, it's pitiful, they don't have a clue what fiction is, what it's for. Most people I talk to about this, they think if a writer calls it fiction, he can just make up any goddamn thing he wants. Whatever he writes doesn't have to conform to the laws of physics, or the laws of ballistics, or the laws of the federal government. You ask the first hundred persons you find to explain how a tax-exempt foundation works and you won't find ten who even heard the phrase and nine of them won't be able to tell you how it works.

"You ask the same hundred persons how this savings and loan mess got out of control, you won't find five who have a clue. But you ask them to tell you what fiction is and they'll tell you, damn near all of 'em, sure, they know what it is. It's whenever a writer makes stuff up, pulls it out of the air, it can be about anything, the more farfetched the better. Put it in another time, another place, a hundred years ago. Put it in Tombstone, Arizona, make up some bullcrap about gunslingers, make it about Billy the Kid, or Wyatt Earp or the Lone Ranger or Tonto or John Wayne, it's all mixed up in people's heads here.

"The most pathetic thing I ever saw on the news was a coupla actresses cryin' in front of Congress—this was years ago—sayin' how John Wayne ought to get some medal before he dies because he was such a great American, such a great defender of the American way. And Congress gave him the goddamn medal! As an actor, man, he had three faces and one walk, that was his whole schtick. But to the people who can't wait to get down on their knees every morning to worship somebody, he was the Green Beret, the Texas Ranger, the All-American, the marine who gets shot in the back by the Japs on Iwo Jima all rolled into one—"

"Okay, that's enough, you can stop right there."

"Huh? What?"

"You heard me. I said stop right there. I don't wanna hear anything about Iwo Jima."

"I wasn't talkin' about Iwo Jima, Balzic. I was talkin' about John Wayne playin' a marine who gets shot in the back by the Japs in the movie *Sands of Iwo Jima*—"

"I know exactly what you were talkin' about. What I'm tellin' you is knock it off. I don't wanna hear any more about it."

"Touch a nerve, huh? John Wayne one of your personal faves?"

"Aw man John Wayne's dead, okay? I'm not talkin' about John Wayne. I'm talkin' about you. I don't wanna hear anything you have to say about Iwo Jima, understand?"

"Not even if what I have to say is the truth?"

"What truth?"

"That John Wayne was never in the service, that truth. That he never fired a gun during World War Two or Korea or Vietnam, that the only guns he ever fired was on a movie set, that truth."

"Who cares?" Balzic said. "Lots of guys who were in World War Two never fired a gun, guys who were carryin' the guns, guys who were supposed to be firin' 'em didn't fire them, so I'm supposed to be impressed because some actor was in war movies but he was never in a war? Who cares?"

"I'm tryin' to make a point about fiction and faction, man. I'm tryin' to tell you how screwed up people are in this country because they don't understand fiction. When people start confusin' the actor for the roles he plays, the country's in big trouble. Christ, that's how we got Reagan."

"I've heard this all before, you know?" Balzic said. "I've been listenin' to Mo Valcanas bitch about this for, God it seems like forever. It's nothin' new."

"'Course it's not new. I'm not makin' any claim for originality here. Never had an original thought in my life. Not one. Everything I ever thought, somebody else thought it first. You write fiction, you don't get points for the originality of your ideas, man. You get points for creatin' characters. Those characters can have the dumbest ideas in the world, that ain't the point. It's whether a writer can make you believe a character could think all those dumb ideas and still make you keep turnin' the pages to find out where those dumb ideas are gonna take the character, that's what makes a fiction writer, not how he'd do in a debate with Socrates."

Balzic ran his tongue around his molars on the left side and wondered how long he was going to have to listen to Myushkin. It was Balzic's experience that people who spent too much time alone tended not to know when to shut up once they'd found somebody who would stop and listen, and it was more than obvious that Myushkin hadn't found anybody willing to listen to him for a long while now, which

156

meant that Myushkin had built up a headful of notions as well as a gutful of determination to get them out. The only real problem from Balzic's point of view was the gun, which he recognized as an Ivor Johnson, a nine-shot revolver. Balzic had no idea how many live rounds were still in it; he couldn't see the open end of the cylinder from where he was standing because Myushkin would either point it toward the backyard or toward the front room. He'd never once pointed it at Balzic, not so far.

"Well okay, look. I won't talk about Iwo Jima, honest. I'll just try to make my point. We've been lied to for so long, lies look like truth. John Wayne looks like a hero, Ronnie Reagan looks like a president, and all they were was actors. You know how many times the actor who played Perry Mason on TV talked to groups of lawyers? You ask those lawyers what that was about, they'll give you this crap about, 'Oh, it's just a lark, that's all it is. It's a joke, what'samatter, you lost your sense of humor?' That's what they'll try to tell you. But they're lyin'. 'Cause it's not a lark, it's not a joke. Everything's startin' to blur in this country. You know why that's a problem, man?"

"I'm not gettin' any warmer, Myushkin. This stuff may be what's eatin' at you, but it ain't makin' me any warmer, you know?"

"I know, Balzic, I know, but just listen. For a long time, the brain-strainers, the guys who tell us who's nuts and who's not? They been tellin' us the problem with the criminals and the addicts is they don't know where they leave off and where everybody else begins, you know? It's like every baby goes through this period when he thinks he and his mother are one and the same. And if he develops normally, he starts to find out he and she are different persons about the same time he learns to say no. That's when he starts makin' his own personality, character. He starts to figure out that he has fingers and she has fingers and they don't pick up the same thing at the same time just because he thinks about reachin' for it, whatever it is."

Balzic cleared his throat and said, "I'm gettin' colder, man, I'm sure as hell not gettin' any warmer."

"Yeah, well, I'm tryin' to make my points, but they can't all be done in one breath. My point is, no matter when babies do it, eventually they do do it, if they're gonna develop into anything even remotely approaching their own person, they do go through that stage when they discover that they end when their fingers stop and the rest of the world begins. But the criminals, man, and I'm surprised you don't know this—"

"I didn't say I didn't know it. I'm just patiently freezin' to hear you make your point, that's all."

"—okay, fine. I'll make it then. With criminals and addicts, that's one of the problems they have with life. They can't distinguish between where they stop and where other people begin—that's what the brain-strainers been tellin' us. But see, look at the president right now, man. He can't believe America stops where Kuwait starts, see? 'Cause to him and all his cronies in the oil biz, Kuwait may as well be around the corner from the White House. It's at the end of his arm, man. The end of their arms, the end of their fingers. America is wherever the oil comes from, man. And no two-bit Hilter's gonna screw around with America's fix, with Bush's oil."

"From what I've been readin' in the papers, we don't get oil from Kuwait," Balzic said. "The Japs do, not us."

Myushkin blew out a blubbering, blustering sound of derision. "Technicalities, man. Details of geography. Who the hell do you think created Japan? Us. The U.S. of A. Since 1945, man, you know this as well as I do, don't tell me you don't: Japan is what we made it. It was just one junkie turnin' on another one to pay for his habit, man. The fact that oil from Kuwait happens to go to Japan instead of us is a matter of contracts. It's like the Red Sox playin' the Yankees during

158

the regular season instead of the Dodgers. It's all baseball. Which does not subtract from my point, which is that America does not know where it stops and where other countries begin. And the guys who run it, oh, man, they make all these speeches and write all these books about America this, America that, in the modern world there are no borders, this is the global village, man, they drag Marshall McLuhan into it, anything, man, they'll make up any lie and call it faction, man. They're exactly like junkies. You ever talk to a junkie about his habit, man? A drunk? You listen to all the lies they tell themselves about why they're hooked? They got a million reasons, man, and I know you've heard 'em all. But down there at the bottom, when they're stealing from their own families to get money to get their fix, man? You know who they are, huh? They're blurrin' the line, man, between where they leave off and where other people begin. You know what I'm sayin' here, Balzic, don't tell me you don't 'cause I know you do. Say somethin'."

"Whatta you want me to say? That I agree with you?"

"Hey, don't agree just to be sociable. You agree or not? You tell me. How can people steal from their own mothers and fathers, brothers and sisters, wives and children, if they aren't able to con themselves that they aren't really stealin'? You tell me."

"You want me to say that addicts steal from their own families because they're sayin' what's mom's is theirs, right? Because they never got past the stage in their development where they had to find out that there was a point where they ended and the rest of the world started, is that what you want me to say?"

"I don't want you to say anything you don't want to say, man. I'm not lookin' for affirmation here. I'm just tryin' to tie my opinions to your experience, that's all. So does it or doesn't it?"

"Look, I'm a cop, I'm not a drug counselor. I have a phone

book. When I have to deal with somebody who maybe might benefit from talkin' to somebody instead of goin' through the courts, I call a pro. But other than that I stay out of it. I can talk theory as well as anybody on the next bar stool, but I'm not gonna go messin' around in somebody's head."

"So pretend we're down at Muscotti's. C'mon, I wanna hear what you know. Jesus, man, you've been chief as long as I can remember. How long you been a cop?"

"Too long."

"C'mon c'mon, how long? Exactly?"

Balzic heaved a sigh, his shoulders rising and falling deeply. He could feel the tension radiating outward from his neck to his shoulders. It wasn't the same as he'd felt in the middle of his Iwo Fever, but it was too similar to quibble about. And thinking about how long he'd been a cop and what he'd do when he wasn't anymore was not something he wanted to discuss here and now.

"Look," Balzic said, "I know you want to pursue this, whatever this is here, but I got a problem. Problems. And you're only one of the problems. So get on with it. I'm bein' patient as hell here. Stop jerkin' me around."

"Okay okay okay, I'll get to the point. The point is, man, it's how we define property in this country. It's how we say who owns what and who has to defend it. I mean, you get guys like Buckley, they get the fancy diplomas, man, then they get the government jobs, then they learn all these five-syllable words so they can snow the shit outta people, and then when guys like Bush need to kill somebody 'cause they're fuckin' with his connection, guys like Buckley root around in their closet, you know, where they keep all their justifiers, and they find the right Roman or the right Jew in the great Judeo-Christian pantheon of justifiers, man, and they say, Ho, hey, I got it! Saint Such and Such said it's peach-y fuck-ing keen if you wanna blow these Arabs away 'cause they're fuckin' with your oil—ta da!—'cause they're baby killers! Yeah, absolutely! They kill babies, right there in the incubators, they kill 'em—"

Balzic shook his head and sighed. "Good god, Myushkin, are you ever gonna come to the point?"

"I am, I am! This is ALL the point. Man, during World War Two I must've seen thirty movies where Japs or Nazis were bayonetin' defenseless people, mommies with little kids, pregnant mommies, beheadin' prisoners and shit, machine-gunnin' guys in parachutes. It's the bullshit, man. It's the hype. It's how rulers get the ruled to do their killin' for 'em. Peaceful people just don't go off killin' strangers, man, not without a reason. That's where guys like Buckley come in, you know? Some other word hustlers make the monster, and guys like Buckley, they do the research, come up with the pretty words from out of the right book by the right saint, you know, and ta-da! The monster's ready for killin'. Once you got the monster built, hell, even the dullest dimwit knows it's his duty to help kill it."

Balzic rocked back on his heels and toes and then rose up and down on his toes and swung his arms from front to back and did it all again, everything to keep moving, generate some heat. "What, you wrote a letter to this Buckley guy once and he didn't write you back, is that it?"

Myushkin nearly snarled; he did everything with his face except make the noise. "You asked me why I'm doin' what I'm doin', man. You asked me why I was out in my backyard blowin' bottles up with this .22 pistol. I'm tryin' to explain it to you. Why you gotta make jokes?"

Balzic did his own snarl. "I'm makin' jokes because you said you were gonna throw some light on this, remember? And I said I hoped you were gonna throw some heat on it too, remember? But so far, Myushkin, all I been hearin' is a ton of ramblin', you're goin' here, there, everygoddamn-where, and I'm still right here freezin' my ass off!"

"Exactly my point, Balzic. 'Cause that's what I'm doin'—

161

freezin' my ass off too, you know? I mean, you can leave anytime you want, get in your city-bought car and turn the heater on. I can't! I'm stuck! I'm stuck here in the goddamn Flats, where I started. And I'm tryin' to figure it out, man, that's what I'm tryin' to do. How'd I get in this fix, you know? I mean how'd I wake up this mornin' and discover that the only thing I could do that made any sense at all was get a .22 pistol and shoot bottles. I mean if that isn't the goddamn bottom of frustration I don't know what is. If that isn't use-lessness carried to its absurd conclusion I don't know what is. It may be the dumbest goddamn thing I have ever done in my life."

"Well you get no argument there."

"Well la-de-fuck-ing-da, we have reached an agreement, an understanding. A small one, yessirree, but it's a start." Myushkin jerked his left hand up and pointed with his thumb over his shoulder toward the corner of the kitchen. "See those boxes Balzic? Huh? See 'em?"

Balzic nodded. "Yeah. So?"

"They're filled with letters, Balzic. My epistolary legacy. My ten years of futility with representative democracy. Letters to my congresspersons, you know? Corrupt bastards of every gender, though they happen to all be male. Ten years of writin' to those bastards to make them reexamine certain parts of the United States Constitution and certain other parts of the Infernal Revenue Code. You know why? So I wouldn't wind up in the position I'm in right here, right now. This is what's called irony, man, you know? I'm sittin' here, freezin' my ass off, tryin' to explain in—how much time you gonna give me, Balzic, huh? Another fifteen minutes?"

"Why don't you just get on with it? Who knows? If you tell it right, and you get my interest, maybe I'll give you sixteen minutes. I'm flexible." Balzic took the gloves off, blew on his hands and rubbed them together hard to get some friction heat, then put the gloves back on and put his hands deep into his pockets.

"Okay okay, hold on to your hat, here goes. I don't know why I'm doin' this, I really don't, nobody else's paid any attention to me—"

"Get on with it for crissake!"

"Right. Here we go. United States Constitution, Article One, Section Eight, Powers of Congress, Paragraph Eight, 'Congress shall have the power to promote the progress of science and useful arts, by securing for limited times to authors and inventors the exclusive right to their writings and discoveries.' With me so far?"

"So far."

"Right. Good. Stay with me now. Same document. Fifth Amendment, last part. 'No person shall . . . be deprived of life, liberty, or property, without due process of law, nor shall private property be taken for public use without just compensation.' Still with me, huh?"

"Still here," Balzic sang.

"Lemme flesh these out for you, man, as they apply to me. Oh oh oh, I almost forgot about the first power of Congress, very important, don't wanna forget that one. The power 'to lay and collect taxes, duties, imposts and excises, to pay the debts and provide for the common defense and general welfare of the United States'—it goes on but that's the important part far as the fuckin' Infernal Revenue Service and the moth-er-fuck-ing House Ways and Means Committee is concerned."

"So?"

"It all ties together, man, just bear with me. Ever go to the library, man? Huh? Ever get a book out of the library?"

"Certainly I been to the library. Most of the books I read, I either get from the public library or from the law library. So what?"

"So whatta you think it means when it says in the Constitution that Congress has the power to give to writers the exclusive right to their writings, huh, what's that mean?"

"Uh, don't know, never thought about it."

"Yeah, right, neither did most of the people in this fuckin' country, includin' guys like Buckley who're all the time defendin' the goddamn Founding Fathers and what they meant when they said such and such in the constitution."

"So what's it mean—and forget about this Buckley. Stick with you and stick to the point, I'm tellin' ya, I'm runnin' outta patience here."

"It means, and this can't be explained all in one breath, Balzic, so let me say it all, all right?"

"Get on with it!"

"First you gotta understand that even though books have been around for a long time in this world, the first time, the very first time, writers ever got a proprietary interest in what they wrote, man, the very first time, was in England in 1710 in what was called the Statute of Anne. Up until that time, Balzic, you got to understand this, this is very important, man—"

"I'm listening, I'm listening!"

"Okay. Until that time, man, writers, all they had was a common-law interest in their writings. It was the publishers, man, whoever had the right given by the king to publish, it was the guys who owned the printing presses, in other words, who had the proprietary thing goin' for them, see. But now! Now, when the Statute of Anne is passed, for the first time it's a goddamn law that writers—WRITERS, man—the people who put the words together, not the people who *print* the words, but the people who actually put them together, man, the government finally recognized that the writers had a right to their own work, their own words, and that right didn't mean shit, didn't mean a thing, if the writer didn't have the right to *sell it*, man, get it? I mean, puttin' the words

164

together and *ownin'* the words, for the first time, man, so the writer could make a profit, that never happened until 1710."

"And you're shootin' bottles to celebrate, is that it? 'Cause you can't afford fireworks?"

Myushkin's shoulders sagged and his hands fell into his lap. "C'mon, man, this is serious."

"Are you gonna go from 1710 to now? How often you gonna stop? I mean, if you're gonna explain somethin' from each century, that's one thing, but if you're gonna stop, like, say, every ten years, uh-uh, game's over. I ain't ridin'—"

"No no no, just a couple more dates, honest. In 1734, ol' Benji Franklin, the granddaddy of good ol' American prudent business his own self, he opens the Library Company of Philadelphia. This is the same guy who is also the founder of the first abolitionist society in America—"

"You gonna give a lecture about slavery too, huh?"

"You goddamn right I am! Slavery's exactly what I'm talkin' about, but you gotta pay attention. Listen. In 1833, the first tax-supported public lending library opens in Petersborough, New Hampshire. One year later, 1834, one hundred years after Benji Franklin starts up his library hustle, the British Empire outlaws slavery. The U.S. doesn't get around to outlawin' slavery for another thirty years. Thirteenth and Fourteenth Amendments, man, outlaw slavery except as a form of punishment and say the states—remember they already said it about themselves in the Fifth Amendment—now they're sayin' the states can't deny anybody life, liberty, or property without due process, that's what the Fourteenth Amendment does, man. Confirms the Fifth for the states.

"Yet here we is, one decade away from the second millennium, man, and public lendin' libraries, tax-supported by taxes directly and by tax-dodgers indirectly, they deprive me of my property six days a week, every goddamn week of the year, and that's how's come I'm in the fix I'm in—"

165

"Whoa whoa, wait a goddamn second, hold it," Balzic said. "How the hell'd we get from Benny Franklin, in, uh, seventeen-somethin' to you bein' in the fix you're in, you gotta run this one by me a little bit slower here—"

"Well there's a switch. Couple minutes ago I couldn't go fast enough, now I'm goin' too fast. Wonderful."

"Well back up and slow down. You lost me between Franklin and this library in New Hampshire and the Fourteenth Amendment."

"Okay, okay. The Fifth Amendment, remember? It ends with the phrase that the federal government can't take anybody's life, liberty, or property without due process and it says, 'nor shall private property be taken for public use without just compensation.' That's the important part, man. The federal government says itself that it ain't allowed to take property without payin' for it."

"Right right, eminent domain. I understand that," Balzic said, nodding his head. "If the state wants to put a road through your backyard, they gotta pay you for it. What the fuck's this have to do with libraries?"

"Hey man! Books are my backyard! The books I write, that's my backyard. The libraries, that's the state, from Washington, D.C., man, the Library of Congress right down here to the Rocksburg Public Library, man, that's the roads that are runnin' through my backyard."

"Wait a minute wait a minute," Balzic said, holding up his hands and shaking his head. "You gotta explain better'n this, I don't know what the hell you're talkin' about."

"Okay, lemme go back," Myushkin rubbed his face and mouth with his left hand. He licked his lips and sniffed. "Listen, I told you about the Statute of Anne, see, the whole point of that was publishers were gettin' ripped off, by pirates, you know, knock-off artists, copiers, you know, people makin' copies without payin' the publishers, and the publishers got pissed, man, that this was happenin', but so did the

166

writers, they said to the publishers, you know, if you guys are gettin' screwed, ripped off, we're gettin' screwed worse. So what the Statute of Anne said was, yeah, right, writers didn't just have a creative interest in what they produced, they also had a proprietary interest in it. And what that means, Balzic, is, hell, man, this goes right to the heart of everything this country stands for, man. Property! Ownin' property doesn't mean a thing if it doesn't mean you have a right to sell it. You know? Sell it? At a price you can get? I mean what good does it do to own property, man, if you can't sell it! What the hell's the point?"

"Oh hell, Myushkin, lots of people own things they have no intention of sellin'," Balzic said.

"Whether they intend to sell it or not, that's not the point. The point is, if they wanna sell it, it's their right because it's theirs. If they wanna just sit around and look at it, whatever it is, that's their right too. But if they wanna sell it for a profit or a loss, according to the Constitution, that's their exclusive right. That goes to the heart of all the laws about theft, which is something you oughta be very familiar with, am I right or not? I mean, when X takes Y's property without his consent and sells it, what're we talkin' about here, huh?"

"Theft."

"Yeah, well you know as well as I do there's all kindsa theft. Theft of property, theft of services. But I want you to open your mind a little about books and libraries, man. They steal from me every day. Every goddamn day, libraries rip me off in direct violation of the Fifth, Thirteenth, and Fourteenth Amendments, me and every other writer in America. 'Nor shall pri-vate pro-per-ty be tak-en for pub-lic use with-out just com-pen-sa-tion,' man. When I get a copyright on my words—you know what a copyright covers, man? Huh? You ever think about this?"

Balzic shook his head. "It's not somethin' that ever came up before."

167

"Well listen to this, man. A copyright is the legal thing, the legal instrument that is the basis for me to make a licensing agreement. Whenever I sign a contract with a publisher, all I'm doin' is givin' him a license to reprint my work and to sell the reprints. The work, man, that's mine, that's what's protected by copyright. And the work is not the letters of the alphabet, it's not the individual words, it's not the ideas, it's not the title, it's not the paper or the ink or the covers or the glue or the binding, it's not the book. It's the arrangement of the words, man, it's the way writers put the words together, that's what's their property, guaranteed by law, statute, and case law all over the goddamn world, man, I mean except for the thieves and pirates. Very important, man, for you to understand that distinction between the way the words are arranged and what they're printed on. 'Cause I didn't relinquish—I didn't give up ownership of the way I arranged the words just 'cause somebody sold you a copy of the way I arranged those words—"

"Huh? Hold it. Say that again."

"Okay okay. Here, lemme say it this way. Say you buy one of my books, man, right? Okay? That's yours. When you go in a bookstore and put down your money, the clerk takes your money and gives you a copy of my book and a receipt. That receipt is proof, along with your possession of the book itself, that that copy is yours, get it?"

"Yeah, yeah, I get it."

"But the fact that you bought a copy legally, and the fact that the publisher, the retail bookseller, and me, the fact that all of us made a profit from that sale—if we're lucky—that still doesn't mean that I gave up the right of ownership in the way I arranged the words that are in the copy you bought, you get it?"

"No."

"Oh man you have to get it! Jesus Christ, if you don't understand this part, nothin' else is gonna make any sense—"

"Well explain it better! You're the goddamn word-man here, not me."

"What I'm sayin' is, just because you bought a copy of my words, just because you can carry it around, you know, it's a physical thing, it has weight, it takes up space, it has dimension, you know, that's yours. You bought it, you paid for it, and everybody who had a hand in sellin' it to you, we're all supposed to make money from it, that's the American way, right?"

"That part I understand," Balzic said. "it's the part about you still keepin' ownership, whatever, that's the part I don't understand. If I bought it how come it's still yours?"

"The copy you bought ain't mine! That's the distinction you gotta make here—"

"Well *you* make it, goddamnit! I mean for a guy who claims it's your trade, you're doin' a pretty shitty job of it if you ask me, wanderin' all over the place, Benjamin Franklin, Christ, I mean, the libraries buy your books, don't they? You're not tryin' to tell me the libraries steal 'em—"

"No no no, they buy 'em, hell yeah they buy 'em. That's not what I'm sayin' at all—"

"Well then what the hell are you sayin', 'cause, believe me, I mean, I don't see what's the big deal. Christ, if I buy your book, when I'm done readin' it, you tellin' me I can't give it to my wife? Huh? 'Cause to me that's what it sounds like you're sayin'."

"No no no that's not what I'm sayin' at all! You have—you buy the book, you have every right to give it to whoever you want. That's part of the right of property—"

"Then what's your bitch with the libraries, I mean if they buy your books, what're you bitchin' about? Sounds to me like they do the same thing I do, which you just said is okay with you. I buy the book, I read it, I give it to my wife, she reads it, she gives it to our daughters, so what do the libraries do that's so different?"

169

"Hey, Balzic, next time you're down the post office, you know? Turn around and look up at the words on the top of the library. It's says 'Rocksburg Public Library.' 'Public,' that's the word. Man, that's what changed everything. EVE-RY-THING! That place is supported by taxes! Taxes, get it?"

"So am I! So what? I've been supported by taxes all my life, since I got outta high school. I been a marine and I been a cop. Governments have been payin' my way since I was eighteen. So what?"

"It ain't just the fact that taxes pay for the libraries, man. It's the way the taxes are collected, who pays 'em and who doesn't. It's the fact that a place, a public place—remember the Fifth Amendment? 'Nor shall private property be taken for PUBLIC use,' remember that? When you finish readin' the book, man, and you give it to your wife, and she gives it to your kids, the one thing that ain't, the one thing that is not, is a public transaction supported by tax dollars—and I don't care who pays you personally, so forget about where your salary comes from. But when it happens in a public library, man, that's public use of private property without just compensation, think about it, really, man."

"I am thinkin' about it, what the hell do you think I'm doin' here? I'm tryin' to understand it, you know? And I don't mind tellin' you, if don't understand it, you're in a lotta trouble."

"Oh shit, Balzic, how much more trouble could I be in? My kid's halfway around the world in a war that started last night and I'm the one who talked him into it, and my wife's so pissed off at me about that she don't even wanna look at me. She's on welfare, the state got a lien on my house, I don't have a job, my back's killin' me—I mean, Christ, look around. C'mon, Balzic, please forget for a second, you know, who we both are. Just listen to what I'm tryin' to tell you, okay—"

"What have I been doin'? What am I doin' here if I ain't listenin' to you, huh? Tell me."

"Well every once in a while you act you like you gotta

170

threaten me, like if I don't get to the point, I'm in a lotta trouble—"

"If you don't give me something that makes sense, something I can explain to my bosses, who in case you don't know are the mayor and the chairman of the safety committee on city council—see, all it takes is a coupla phone calls to them about what I'm doin' here, what you're doin' here and then my ass is in the pan, get it? I got a lot of discretion about who gets arrested, who gets charged, I mean, at this moment, I'm the guy who's gonna decide whether you're dischargin' a gun inside city limits, which is worth thirty days and a fine, or whether you're committin' a felony with a gun, which is five years. So what I'm tellin' you is, you better make me understand this, whatever's eatin' you, because your explanation's worth about, lemme see—"

"Fifty-nine months," Myushkin interrupted him.

"—right, plus fines, plus costs. In other words, talk ain't cheap here."

"Okay okay okay. So what's different about what you do and what the libraries do. Okay, here it is. The libraries, they buy my books, then—and this very important, man—without ever once askin' my permission, without ever once askin' if I minded, without ever once sendin' me a thank-you note— they buy copies of my books and then they give 'em away to every intellectual welfare bum who walks in off the street—"

"Every what kind of bum? Huh?"

"Intellectual welfare bum. You know, Buckley and his brothers have been bitchin' about welfare bums for years now. That's how that two-bit ham Reagan got to be governor of California, that's how he got to be president, man, bitchin' about this nigger welfare queen, you know, the one with the nine kids by nine different guys, and she used to drive down to the welfare office in her white Caddy convertible—"

"You're startin' to ramble again, forget about Reagan, get back to you and the libraries."

171

"I'm not ramblin' goddamnit! I'm makin' my point! Reagan and Buckley and those guys have been ridin' around in the first-class seats for years, man, because of this nigger welfare queen they dreamed up, man, 'cause she never existed. Reporters been lookin' for her for years, and nobody's ever found her yet, but the public bought it, man, the public, the people who think they're gettin' ripped off by the bums on welfare, they bought that story!"

"You tellin' me there ain't no bums on welfare?"

"What I'm tryin' to tell you is there is a whole different class of bums who don't think they're bums at all! That's what I'm tryin' to tell you! Intellectual welfare bums. People with jobs, ladies with blue hair that just came outta the beauty parlors, man, they go in the library and come out with their arms fulla books, man, includin' mine! And I'm tellin' ya, they're takin' my property for their public use without the first goddamn thought of compensatin' me, never mind fairly, I'm tellin' ya, they don't even think of this when it comes to the Fifth Amendment—THEY NEVER THOUGHT OF IT ONCE IN THEIR ENTIRE FUCKING LIVES, that's what I'm tellin' ya for crissake! I mean, you tell me what it is—"

"What what is? When?"

"Oh man, come on! If the people who don't work but should be workin', according to Reagan and Bush and their buddies, if they're gettin' money and food stamps for nothin', then what's the difference when people walk into libraries and come out loaded with books, man? What's the difference? They're both gettin' somethin' for nothin' for crissake."

"But the libraries bought the books. They paid for 'em!"

"They paid for 'em ONCE! And that's the problem. They get 'em for fifty, sixty percent off retail, man. And when they buy 'em three hundred, four hundred at a time, they get 'em for cheaper'n that and my royalty goes down. I'm supposed to get ten percent of retail, man, but not when libraries buy 'em by the hundreds, hey, my royalties go way down, like half. But once, man! Once, they pay for 'em! The rest of the time, all the time they're givin' 'em away, I get nothin' for that! NOTHIN'! They can give 'em away until they fall apart, man, give 'em away once a week the first year, man, every two weeks every year after, until they fuck-ing fall apart, then they tape 'em up, and throw 'em on a table and sell 'em for a dime. And I don't get another goddamn penny outta that! You understand?"

Balzic sighed and shook his head. "I'm sorry. Maybe I'm stupid, I don't claim to be the smartest guy in the world, but so far you still haven't explained to me how this is any different from me buyin' the book and givin' it to my wife when I'm done with it."

Myushkin hung his head and took several deep breaths. "My wife tells me, a hundred times she's told me I don't know how to explain this to people. She says all I do is alienate people, all I do is rant and rave and make a general pain in the ass outta myself. It's so frustrating. No shit. I think I've explained it perfectly, like now to you, and you look at me and you say, you know, you still don't get it—"

"Well I don't! So maybe your wife's right. 'Cause so far I still don't see what your bitch is. And don't be bringin' Reagan or that other guy, that Buckley, into it. Stick with me, I'm tellin' ya, right here, right now, explain it to me."

"It's taxes, man. It's taxes that make it different. And forget who pays your salary. Do you know—listen to this—do you know you can buy a copy of my book, and when you're done and your wife's done with it, you two can take it down the library and donate it to the library, and they'll give you a statement of a charitable deduction, and you can write that off on your taxes, man, you know that?"

"So? I can do that with clothes and the Good Will too. Or furniture and the Salvation Army, so what?"

"The so what is writers ain't allowed to do that, man. The

173

IRS Code forbids it. You didn't write the book, you can do it. I wrote the book, I can't do it."

"Oh please, what, there's injustice in the IRS Code? Taxes ain't fair? No shit, Myushkin, gimme a break."

"Okay, so listen to this. My own income taxes, federal, state, and local—I mean when I was makin' enough money to have to pay taxes, my own tax dollars are used to maintain libraries."

"So are mine, so what, so are everybody's, so what?"

"Hey you ain't the writer, I am. It ain't you gettin' screwed every time one of my books leaves that building, it's me."

"Not that I understand how you're gettin' screwed, 'cause you still haven't explained that so I can understand it yet—"

"It's a public building, for crissake. It's supported by taxes for crissake. Including mine for crissake. I don't even get a tax break for donatin' one of my own books for crissake. But there are a whole lot of people in this country, man, you ever hear of tax-exempt foundations? Tax-exempt foundations, their whole reason for bein', man, is they make charitable contributions, you know? United Way? Ever heard of that? Huh? One of the organizations that gets money from United Way is the libraries—"

"So do the Boy Scouts. You pissed off at them too?"

Myushkin blew out another sigh. "You really ain't makin' this any easier, man—"

"You're the one's makin' it difficult, Mister Myushkin, by takin' every goddamn detour there is—"

"Look. What you think are detours are, uh, uh, they're how these things are all connected, you know? I mean one's tied in with the other and I got to explain them all in order for you to see what my bitch is—"

"Well do it!"

"Well when people give money to United Way and things

174

like that, you know, it means they don't have to pay taxes on the amount they gave, you know?"

"I know already, I know."

"Well through that charitable tax dodge, there are people who make a career outta givin' money away so they can avoid payin' any taxes at all. That's the whole purpose of those foundations. You think they'd exist if they didn't get the tax dodge? You kiddin' me? How do you think this savings and loan thing got nuts, huh? 'Cause the sonsabitches changed the tax laws on the interest on borrowing, man, that's how. I mean, you do see how the S'n'L's went into the toilet, don't ya?"

"Oh god, Myushkin, you gonna get into that now too?"

"Of course I'm gonna get into that. 'Cause it's exactly my point. Whenever those bastards on the Ways and Means Committee change the tax laws, man, some things go kaflooey, battaboom. They took away the deduction on home mortgage interest and they gave it to the guys doin' the takeovers, man, the leveraged buyouts. They changed two parts of the IRS code, and within no time at all, man, the money is goin' where the tax dodge is, don't you get it? That's what people with money do, man, they try to keep it, you know?"

"And this affected you personally, right?"

"Balzic, Balzic, listen to me, please. The people who wanna keep their money the most, the ones with the most money, they set up these foundations, where their only purpose, the only goddamn thing they do, is they get up every morning and figure where they're gonna go party that day, and every month or so they sit down with their tax accountants and their tax attorneys, and what those guys've been doin' is sittin' around calculatin' exactly how much money the rich bastards have to give away to meet the requirements of the IRS Code for charitable gifts, man. And once they reach that point, whatever it is, where they meet the percentage of money they have to give away in order to maintain their tax-exempt status, that's when they stop givin', see? But if the fuckin' Ways and Means Committee took that dodge away from them, if they did to them what they did to the home mortgage deduction and what they did to the S'n'L's, you'd see money flyin' in a whole different direction is what I'm tryin' to tell you."

"Myushkin," Balzic said, sighing hard and long, "you probably know what you're talkin' about, but I'm here to tell you all you've done so far is confuse the hell outta me, I mean it."

"Listen, just listen some more, I promise I'll explain this, honest, so you can understand it, really. Tell me something, what's slavery? Huh? What is it?"

"Slavery is—aw shit, whatta you gonna say now, you're on some fuckin' plantation here now, is that it?"

"Balzic, you may not understand this just yet, but when I'm done, what you're gonna understand is tax-supported libraries are to writers in America what plantations were to slaves, that's exactly what I'm tryin' to tell you. They give my work away, *my work*. They don't give *their* work away. Hey, you wanna give your work away, fine. But don't be givin' my work away. They didn't ask my permission. They have never asked my permission. I published my first book twenty-one years ago, and I have never heard from a librarian anywhere, not from the Library of Congress, not from the Rocksburg Public Library, nobody who works for money—hear that part? They all get paid, man, every one of 'em, all those librarians. The director of Rocksburg Public Library, man, makes forty-some thousand bucks a year—for givin' away my work! They get paid to give my work away, but they can't even find the time to send me a thank-you note."

"Myushkin, they're giving away something they bought," Balzic said slowly. "You hear what I said? They're giving

176

away something they bought—which is what you said I can do—"

"Balzic, Balzic, listen! Not gettin' paid for your work when other people profit from it is slavery, man. The only other words for it are involuntary servitude. The Thirteenth Amendment outlawed slavery except as a form of punishment for people convicted of crimes, remember? You listen to me. The library buys one copy of my book, I get one royalty from it. If it's a really big library system like Los Angeles or New York, they buy two hundred, maybe three hundred copies at a time, I get the equivalent of a hundred and fifty royalties. You know why? 'Cause in my contracts with publishers, every time they sell in bulk, the royalty they gave me on page one they take away on page three, understand? But let's just stick with one book. The libraries put that book on the fast track, which means it gets circulated fifty-two times in the first year. Fifty-two different people read my work, man. They got the benefits of my education, my experience, my effort, the product of my labor, in other words. All I got was one royalty. The next year they put it out twenty-six times a year. Seventy-eight readers in two years, all gettin' the benefits of my education, experience, and effort, all gettin' the result of the sweat off my brain and what do I get, huh? I still only get one royalty. Now you add that up—well, wait, first you gotta know that libraries buy most of my books. If the first printing is five thousand copies, the libraries buy forty-five hundred of 'em. You multiply each one of my nine books by seventy-eight circulations times forty-five hundred copies, man, what do you get? Huh?"

"What, I'm supposed to do this in my head?" Balzic said. "You kiddin' me?"

"Never mind. When you multiply nine times forty-five hundred you get forty thousand five hundred. I'm estimatin' now 'cause I really don't know how many times I didn't get a full royalty from library sales, man, but say I got three

177

thousand royalties for those forty-five hundred sales. Now multiply forty thousand five hundred times seventy-eight circulations. I'll tell you what you get. You get three million one hundred and fifty-nine thousand circulations, that's what you get. Three million circulations, and that's stoppin' each one after two years. One of my book's been in public libraries for twenty years. Mull that over, Balzic. Three million people got the benefit of my education, my experience, my labor. And I got about three thousand royalties. That's what the librarians and the goddamn politicians, the bastards who write the tax laws think is 'just compensation.' Remember that, huh? 'Nor shall private property be taken for private use without just compensation,' remember? The Fifth Amendment?"

"Yeah yeah yeah, I'm startin' to get your point, Myushkin, but you're forgettin' one very important thing here. You're thinkin' if it wasn't for libraries, people would be buyin' your books—"

"Oh bullshit I never said that—"

"Well hell, that's what you're implyin' and don't say you ain't."

"Balzic, number one, I never said that, and number two, whether people buy 'em or not doesn't change a goddamn thing that happens in libraries. What happens in libraries happens no matter whether anybody buys my books in bookstores, no matter what anybody does anywhere else. But as long as we're talkin' about this, tell me somethin'. Whatta you think ol' Lee Iachokea, that bullshit artist who runs Chrysler? You know the one I'm talkin' about, huh?"

Balzic nodded. "Who doesn't? He's on TV every time you turn it on."

"Yeah, well he's another bum, another moocher. He fucks up his company somethin' fierce, he goes runnin' to the government, please, Uncle Sugar, gimme gimme, you gotta guarantee all these loans I need or Chrysler's gonna go in

178

the toilet. Jesus Christ, these bottom-liners kill me, all the time bitchin' about the government, but when they're about to go under 'cause they don't know what the hell they're doin', the place they finally get to is Congress, man, they're on their knees with their hands out, oh please please please, Uncle Sugar, you gotta help me save my company. All these people are gonna lose their jobs. Bullshit. So whatta you think he'd be sayin', if down the block from every Chrysler dealership in America, you know, within a coupla miles, instead of libraries, there were these carbraries, huh? Where if you had a carbrary card, you could walk in there and these people, who were gettin' paid themselves, you know, they were on salary too, and you could walk in there and flash your carbrary card, and they would lend you a brand-new Chrysler, man, to drive around for a week for free—and just down the street from where some other guy was tryin' to sell Chryslers. Where do you think ol' Iachokea would be spendin' his days and nights, huh? In Congress, that's where. Until he greased enough palms to get Congress to put a stop to that shit, you kiddin' me?"

"Then we go right back to the same thing I just said. You think, you're implyin' that people would be buyin' your books instead of gettin' 'em outta libraries."

"No man that is not what I am implying. I was just tryin' to make an analogy, that's all, with cars and books. Book publishing is the only business in America where the guys tryin' to sell the books are in direct competition with people who are givin' 'em away for crissake! And the people who are givin' 'em away are doin' it with tax money they collect from everybody—including writers! And and and they do it, they give 'em away with taxes they collected from everybody except the people who have so much money they don't pay any taxes, man. People who give money to libraries as a charitable contribution to avoid payin' taxes, goddamnit! Now you tell me that's fair. Tell me! I wanna hear you say

it, Balzic. I wanna hear you say that's what the Fifth Amendment means by 'just compensation.' C'mon, say it."

"So you wanna burn down all the libraries and shoot all
the librarians, is that it?"

Myushkin's eyes turned once again to slits. For the first
time, he pointed the revolver at Balzic and cocked it. He
wobbled to his feet, grimacing from the pain in his back, and
took a step, then another toward Balzic until the barrel of
the pistol was a foot from Balzic's chest. "In all the time I've
been talkin' here, I have never once said a word about burnin'
anything down or shootin' anybody. I don't know whether
you're just bein' cute or what, but you say somethin' that
dumb again, you try to twist what I'm sayin' again, I will
shoot you, you hear what I just said? Huh? Yes or no, you
hear me?"

"I hear you," Balzic said as calmly as he could. "I hear you
very clearly."

"I don't care what people think of me, man. Only my
wife and my kid, they're the only ones whose opinion of me
matters. But don't fuckin' twist my words. Don't take my
words and turn them into somethin' I didn't say. Never do
that."

"I won't do it," Balzic said. "I won't do it again."

"Did I ever say anything about burnin' libraries down? Yes
or no?"

"No you did not. It was an assumption on my part."

"Did I ever say anything about shootin' any librarians?
Huh?"

"No you did not. I was makin' a joke. It was stupid. I should
not have done that. I won't do it again."

Myushkin lowered the pistol to his side. He stepped backward until his legs bumped against the chair, and then he
eased himself down onto it, grunting and hissing with pain.

"If the truth be known, man, I'm all for libraries. Some of
the happiest times of my childhood, man, I spent in libraries

180

with my mother. Don't ever even think, Balzic, not for a second, that I wanna do anything to hurt libraries. Or librarians. They're just part of a system, you know, it was here before they were born, they're just tryin' to make a livin', just like me, just like everybody else, just tryin' to get paid for what they do. And most of 'em, they do good work, man. They care for the knowledge, and they try to get it out. It's just most of 'em have never given any thought to the consequences of what they do, not where it applies to writers. But even if they did, you know, even if they did think about it, there's nothin' they could do by themselves to change it. I mean, shit, they couldn't do any more than I've been tryin' to do. Write to the goddamn Congress, to the Ways and Means bastards, to those bastards on the judiciary committees, subcommittees on copyrights and trademarks and patents."

Balzic cleared his throat. Outwardly he was very calm; inwardly he was boiling. His pulses were hammering in his ears. His fingers got very cold. Surging up through his gut from his scrotum to his chest was a storm of fury and fear. That pistol a foot from his chest changed everything for him. Until that moment, he had been trying to understand what Myushkin was complaining about. After that moment, all he was thinking about was how to get the pistol away from Myushkin and how to get him into custody while faking interest in what he was talking about.

"Is that what all those letters, uh, in that box, that what they're about?" Balzic said evenly.

"Yeah, certainly, what else? I write and I write. They write back—when they understand what I'm bitchin' about, which is never—and they tell me they're gonna hold hearings, you know, but they never do. They revised the whole goddamn copyright law in '76 or '78 or somewhere around in there. All they were worried about was jukeboxes and composers and singers and musicians gettin' screwed outta royalties

181

from jukeboxes, you know. Which was right, they shoulda done that. That was fair, 'cause those people were gettin' screwed. And then they got all outta joint about copyin' machines and videocassettes, you know. Doctors copyin' stuff other doctors wrote in their medical journals, you know, and these poor fuckin' underpaid doctors, you know, they need all the relief they can get, so Congress takes care of their asses, but the bastards never once said a goddamn word about libraries. And they're still rasslin' with how to pay royalties on videotapes. Audiotapes too. I don't understand about libraries, I really don't. It's like libraries came down the mountain with Moses, you know? Thou shall not interfere with the way writers get screwed by tax-supported public libraries. I don't understand it."

Myushkin grew pensive for a long moment. Then he said, "You know, I could understand it if it was some white-bread bastard like Bush, you know? But the chairman of the House Ways and Means Committee, man, he's a goddamn hunky! Rostenkowski! Ros-ten-kow-ski for crissake! Nobody expects guys named Bush to understand involuntary servitude. But Rostenkowski?"

Balzic's eyebrows went up. "What, you remember all this other shit, you can't remember there were princes in Poland?"

Myushkin blushed and hung his head.

"So you don't know everything. So whatta you want from him, exactly."

"Tax credits! Christ, Balzic, didn't you hear anything I said? I mean really, what the fuck were you listenin' to?"

"I must be slippin'," Balzic said, trying not to let the slightest sarcasm slip into his tone, "but I really don't remember hearin' you say anything about, uh, any tax credits."

"Well Christ, just how do you think I want to change my life if I don't wanna burn down the goddamn libraries or shoot the librarians? How else? I mean, why do you think I was bitchin' about all the tax exonerations the goddamn state gave to Volkswagen, the same goddamn thing they're doin' now for Sony? Shit fire, I mean, if you're gonna write loopholes for the Japs and the Germans to jump through so they build their goddamn cars and TVs here, how about givin' some to me? Huh? Jesus H. Christ, I could use some tax exemptions my own self. Like for example, listen to me now, Balzic, 'cause this is where my wife used to say all the time this is where I fucked up. She used to tell me all the time, she'd say, 'You dummy, you do it all backwards. You tell 'em how you get screwed first and then when they're sick of listenin' to you, when you've pissed them all off with your rantin' and ravin', then,' she says, 'then you tell 'em what you want and by that time they're all deaf from hearin' you yell and shout and cuss.' I guess she's right. I probably am the wrongest guy in the world to be doin' this."

"Well, hell," Balzic said softly, "don't stop now. I mean, you've had me cooped up in this refrigerator this long, you owe it to yourself to tell me what you want."

"Tax credits! What I want is tax credits. I want a tax credit equal to the royalty I lose every time a book of mine goes out of the goddamn libraries, that's what I want! And if Rostenkowski and his white-bread bastard buddies can give 'em to all their pals, then they can goddamn well give 'em to me—and to every other writer in America."

"Tax credits? If you don't make enough money to pay taxes, I don't get it. What good're tax credits gonna do you?"

"Aw what're you talkin' about? C'mon, man, think! Christ, I can save 'em up for the years I don't do so good, you know? Hell, the bastards used to allow us to average our income over five years, you know, at least we got a break that way, then they took that away from us. Hell, the year they took that away, that was the best year I ever had from writin', I

183

made more than fifty grand from writin' that year, and by the time they got through with me, they cleaned me outta more than half of it."

"Half? C'mon, get serious."

"I am serious. First they got me on the taxes for that year, right? Then they got me on quarterly estimates for the whole next year, and and and don't forget—the estimates are based on the stupid-ass supposition you're gonna make the same money the next year you made last year. So for the first year I got nailed almost the highest rate 'cause I was also still workin' at Volkswagen, and then I got nailed on the quarterly estimates, man. So I'm tellin' ya, out of that fifty-four thousand I think it was, I got to keep like thirty-one thousand, no shit. Yeah. And all the while, the libraries are givin' my work away and I'm gettin' zippo for that. Nothin'."

Balzic shook his head sympathetically, or what he hoped would appear to be a sympathetic shaking.

"Listen, Balzic, I could also sell 'em to other writers, you know? If my books are goin' good this year and I got a lotta tax credits, then I could sell 'em—or I could give 'em away to other writers, the ones whose books weren't doin' so good, you know? Jesus Christ, corporations do it all the time, man. They got these books full of schedules of depreciations and losses—they're all just different words for dodges, man, and when it's more to their benefit to sell the dodge to somebody else instead of takin' it themselves, hell, that's what they do. But see, that's bizzzzzz-ness, man. And bizzzzzz-ness, see, they hire these whores to go down to Congress, you know, and do what whores do."

"Whores?"

"Lobbyists. The actual whores come later, but really, same difference. Writers, see, I mean, if I had enough money to hire me a whore to go to Congress to do my talkin' for me, shit, I wouldn't be bitchin' now, would I? All I got money for is stationery and stamps. So they can jag me off forever, you know."

"Don't take this the wrong way," Balzic said, "but I think your wife is right. I think you really don't know how to explain this—"

"Okay, maybe she is. But listen to this. A guy I know from way back, he knows I write, he likes my books, he's all the time tellin' me to hurry up, you know, when am I gonna write another one, you know, he says nice stuff to me. So I saw him about six months ago, he was comin' out of the library. I was comin' out of the post office. He comes over to me, he says, 'Man, how come you're still here, I thought you'd be on the Riviera by now.' So after I tell him how long it's been since I had a square job, I ask him what he means. Me? On the Riviera? The one in Europe? So listen to what he says, Balzic. He says to me, these are his exact words, I'll never forget 'em. He says, 'Man, it used to be I could just walk in the library and take your books right out. Now,' he says, 'now, I gotta get on a waitin' list. I had to wait two months to get your last book.' And I look at him and I say, 'And you think that's why I should be on the Riviera? 'Cause you had to wait two months to get one of my books outta the library?' And he says, 'Yeah, man, you must be rollin' in it.' Honest to god, Balzic, that's what he said to me. And this is not a dumb guy either, he's been around, he's in business, politics, you know, he knows his way around city hall and the courthouse. And that's how little he understands about the library swindle, that's how little he thinks about it."

"So you didn't explain it to him?"

"Aw he had to go someplace. But listen to this one, I'll tell you another one, how little people understand the swindle, I swear to you this is true. I know this lady librarian, she was married for a couple years to a writer I knew. One day—I don't know how it happened, so don't ask—one day she found out that all their private conversations? He was writin' 'em down, turnin' 'em into stories—"

"He never told her he was doin' this?"

"No, nah, never said a word. So I don't remember how she found out, but when she did, man, she got so pissed she threw him out. I mean, she was supportin' him on her salary from the library, you know, and they're livin' on the dream that he's gonna one day turn into Stephen King or somebody and they're gonna move to Florida and lay around on the beach all day or somethin'. But anyway, she tells me about this, you know, she's lookin' for a friendly ear so she tells me the whole story, and she wants me to say what a rat I think the guy is, you know, takin' their most intimate conversations and turnin' 'em into his own stories. So I knew it ain't gonna do me any good to tell her, you know, what the hell you think writers write about? You know? I mean, here she is, a goddamn librarian, she doesn't know where real fiction comes from. So she's practically in tears tellin' me about this guy and I can see she thinks maybe she made a mistake tellin' me about this 'cause I ain't commiseratin' the way I'm supposed to, you know?

"But I can't help it, 'cause all I'm thinkin' about is, hey, sister, you're pissed off because your hubby's takin' your words and writin' down and tryin' to sell 'em, you know? I mean, I finally said to her, 'Hey. What exactly do you think you do to me every day, huh?' And she looks at me, you know, like I got two heads, and she doesn't have a clue. So I told her, I said, 'Look, you dump your husband, you throw him away 'cause he took your words and his—don't forget some of them were his words too, 'cause he was also writin' his part of the conversations down too—you dump him because you think he betrayed you and that betrayal, or what you think is a betrayal, that pisses you off so much you throw him away.' I said, 'But you don't see the slightest contradiction when some stranger walks up to you with one of my books in his hand, and you stamp it, give him a big smile, tell him to have a nice day—and away he goes with my work.' I told her, 'At least your old man was tryin' to sell your words, you know? You just give mine away. And to this day I never heard you once ask me, hey, do I mind?' You know what her response was? Huh? I swear to god, Balzic. She looked at me, this librarian, she looked at me and said, 'Writers. God, what did I ever see in writers?' "

Balzic had been listening, or trying to appear as though he'd been listening, but what he'd been doing was estimating distances and calculating reactions. Then, because Myushkin had stopped talking, he knew it was time for him to say something. "Uh, can we go back to the letters?"

"Huh? What?"

"The letters," Balzic said, "the letters you wrote to Congress. I wanna know about the letters."

"What about 'em?" Myushkin said disgustedly.

"What were they about? All this you've been tellin' me here, now?"

"Oh, man, of course everything I been tellin' you, sure, what do you think?"

"Well didn't they ever write back?"

"Sometimes, yeah. Not them. Their go-fers, their do-fers. Most of the time, no."

"Well what'd they say when they wrote?"

"What did they say," Myushkin said, scoffing noisily. "What do they say about anything if you didn't pay 'em somethin'? Lemme see, what did they say. 'Dear Mr. Myushkin, I want you to know that I share your concern about that very important concern which you shared with me. I know that all Americans believe as you do in the sanctity of private property, and I assure you I share your commitment to preserving the American way of life, liberty, and the pursuit of happiness. In regard to your special concern about your copyright protection about your very private property, I wish to point out to you that we will be holding hearings on that very issue in the very near future and I think I can speak for my colleagues on the Judiciary Committee when I say that we will be exploring that issue in all its ramifications and that issue will be fully explored and you will be fully explored and I will be fully explored and the whole fucking free world will be fully explored. Thank you very much for sharing your concern about exploring this issue with me. Very truly yours, Senator Claghorn Moneygrubber, Esquire, United States Senate Judiciary Committee, subcommittee on copyrights, patents, and trademarks.' "

"You never got one letter back from anybody that saw there was anything that was worth talkin' about in what you said?"

"C'mon, Balzic, I don't have to explain this to you, do I? You mean to tell me you don't know how Congress works, huh? The only reason those guys do something for free—I mean when there's no cash involved or the equivalent of cash, you know, plane tickets, hotel reservations, trips to Europe, Hong Kong, wherever—the only time they do something that doesn't involve cash is when it involves free advertisin', you know, when it's gonna look good on the highlight film which they drag out when they're runnin' for reelection. Mark Twain had it right, man. Congress is the closest thing we got to a criminal class in this country."

"So what you're tellin' me is, you guys, you writers, you don't have any lobbyists? Writers, Christ, they can't all be as broke as you are—"

"Yeah, writers got lobbyists, of course they do. They just don't think this is very important. Or they don't seem to. Every time they write to me, tryin' to get me to join up, this library thing is way down on their list. I don't know. My old lady's right. I'm the wrong guy to be talkin' about this, I get too emotional, too pissed off. Besides, Balzic, every one of those goddamn writers' clubs, man, they cost a lotta money

188

to join. Seventy-five, a hundred bucks a year dues. Who the hell can afford that? Hundred bucks dues? Hell, I've learned how to live for a month on a hundred bucks—not countin' rent. I shop around? Hey, I can get ten pounds of potatoes for under two bucks I shop around. You learn how to do these things, you get forced into it, believe me."

Myushkin leaned on the table and stood up again. He turned the pistol around, handle forward, and motioned for Balzic to come and take it. "Here, take this goddamn thing before I shoot myself. I'm done. You do what you have to do, I won't hold it against you. But tell me somethin', Balzic."

"What's that?" Balzic said, moving slowly, carefully toward Myushkin, and taking the pistol from him. He was still outwardly calm, but all the fury and fear he'd felt when Myushkin aimed the pistol at his chest was still there, still pounding away.

"You know any chiropractor owes you a favor, huh? I really need to get my back cracked, honest to god, I'm about to start bawlin' here."

"Really? Hurt that bad, huh? Where's it hurt? Down your legs or where?"

"All the way, top to bottom, my neck to my ass. The phrase 'up tight' have any meaning for you, Balzic? Huh?"

"I've heard it once or twice."

"I'll bet you have. So whatta you say, know a chiropractor who owes you one? I used to know a good one, but he retired."

"I'll have to think about that. Meantime, c'mon, you're gonna clean up the glass you broke. Then I got to get you in front of a magistrate."

"You're gonna make me clean up the glass? Christ, I can't be bendin' over."

"Well you don't think somebody else is gonna clean it up, do you?"

"Aw c'mon, Balzic, have a heart."

189

Balzic held the pistol up in Myushkin's face. "I lost my heart for you, you sonofabitch, when you pointed this at my heart."

"Huh?" Myushkin was genuinely surprised.

"What, you as dumb as those bastards in Congress and the White House, huh? The ones you're bitchin' about? That's what they used to talk about durin' Vietnam, remember? Huh? All that bullshit about winnin' over their hearts and minds? Remember? How many times did we hear that, huh? And all the time they were tryin' to do it with napalm and Bouncin' Betties and Agent Orange. And they didn't understand why it didn't work. Just like you don't understand it now. Christ, you oughta see your face. You put a gun in my chest and you think what you're doin' is showin' me the rightness of your cause, the depth of your convictions. But, buddy boy, all you showed me is you had a gun and I didn't, and for a long coupla seconds there my life wasn't my own. It was yours, it was in your hands, and now look at you. You got this stupid-ass expression on your face, like, 'What happened? What's wrong with him? What'd I do? I didn't do nothin'.' C'mon, get your ass outside, you're gonna clean up the glass—every goddamn piece."

"Awwwwww man, shit, I thought you were understandin' what I was tryin' to say. Why you gotta turn on me like this?"

"I told ya why," Balzic growled, holding the pistol up in front of Myushkin's face again. "This is why. And I got some good advice for you, for when you get out of the slam. And you're goin' in the slam, mister, I guarantee that. When I get you in front of a magistrate I'm gonna charge you with every weapons offense in Title Eighteen, includin' unlawful restraint, you know? That's just a hop, skip and a slide away from takin' a hostage. And you did it all with a gun. Automatic five in Pennsylvania, hear that? You're good at numbers. That's three hundred and sixty-five times five. How many's that make, huh? You'll have lotsa days to write to

190

Congress, won'tcha, huh? C'mon. Outside. You got a garbage can out there, huh?"

"Yeah I got a garbage can," Myushkin said, hanging his head and sighing. "Jeez, man, I thought I explained it right. I thought you were gettin' it. I thought, hey, finally, I explained it so somebody could understand it. Sheeeeez. You weren't listenin' at all."

"Not after you stuck this in my chest I wasn't," Balzic said. "C'mon, let's go. Outside."

"Hey, Balzic, I'm sorry, man, honest to god I am, you know? I shouldn't've done that, I know I shouldn't have, but you were twistin' my words around. My words are what I am. I know how easy it is to confuse people, you know, by writin' sloppy, by not thinkin' things out, but you were twistin' my words around, puttin' words in my mouth, that's why I took the heat there and got all macho crazy'n shit. But lockin' me up ain't gonna do either of us any good, Balzic—"

"It's gonna give me a whole lotta pleasure," Balzic snapped. "C'mon, cut the bullshit. Outside I'm tellin' ya."

"Balzic, wait a minute wait a minute. It's all gonna just get worse here in this country. I mean, this fuckin' war, this isn't about America, man, and freedom from some new Hitler. This is about the fuckin' multinationals, man, the companies run by the bottom-liners. They got no nationality. Their only nationality is money. The bottom-liners are takin' over, man, and you're their pistolero, you're their gunslinger, whether you want to be or not. Don't you ever think about any of this stuff?"

"More than you know, mister. More than you know. But when somebody sticks a gun in my chest I stop thinking about what he's saying. My ears don't work when somebody's got a gun in my chest. Let's go. Outside. And when you get out? Huh? My advice to you is go find your wife and ask her how to do this. 'Cause she's right. You don't know how."

*   *   *

191

The next day Balzic was getting his ears trashed by Councilman Figulli about the miracles, wonders, and joys of father-
ing a daughter who exceeded his every paternal expectation.
It was late in the afternoon. The day was blustery, gloomy,
ashen, first snowy, then rainy, just the opposite of Figulli's
face as he harangued Balzic with one familial anecdote after
another until Balzic could stand it no more and escaped by
pretending that he had to relieve himself. Fortunately, Figulli
didn't follow him into the john.

When Balzic came out of the men's room and started
through the lifting door in the counter into the duty room,
Mo Valcanas, looking as ashen and somber as the day, was
waiting for him.

"Panagios, how goes it?"

"We need to talk," Valcanas said.

"Whoa. 'We need to talk.' No hello, hiya doin', go to hell,
how's the missus. 'We need to talk'?"

"I'm not a happy man, Mario. Let's go back in your office,
shall we?"

"Ouuu, 'shall we.' Man, you must be unhappy. I know it
wasn't anything I did, so what's the problem?" Balzic lead
him into his office and closed the door behind them. They
both sat, Balzic sprawling in his chair, Valcanas easing stiffly
onto his.

"Unfortunately," Valcanas said, "it was something you
did."

"You're kiddin'. You're not kiddin'. I did somethin' to you?
C'mon, I haven't seen you, hell, since last week. I couldn't've
done somethin' to you—"

"Not to me personally, you haven't, but to a friend of
mine."

"A friend of—who the hell would that be? C'mon, Mo,
I—"

"I've asked you repeatedly to not call me that anymore—"

"Whoa, excuse me. Panagios. So. What gives?"

192

"You have Nick Myushkin locked up on fifty thousand dollars bail. If he sold everything he owned, if he received every account receivable owed to him in the world, he couldn't raise ten percent of ten percent of that and you know it. For shootin' bottles off a fence? In the Flats? Into the Indian Mound? Fifty grand? The man's indigent. He cleaned up all the glass, you saw to that. What the hell's goin' on, Mario?"

"He stuck a pistol in my chest, did he tell you that part?"

"Of course he told me that part. He didn't leave that out. He may write fiction but he's not a liar. So what's goin'—"

Balzic hunched forward over his desk. "What's goin' on is I don't let people stick guns in my chest and get away with it. Not him. Not anybody. I get daymares, you know? Iwo Fever? Remember? I put up a good front, or I try to, but I'm sixty-four goddamn years old now and I have never gotten over havin' all those guns pointed at me on Iwo when I was eighteen. That's what's goin' on, Panagios. I may walk tough and talk tough and look tough, but most of the time I'm, uh, I'm scared. And every once in a while I'm scared almost shitless . . . why you think I drink every day? Huh? There hasn't been a day in my life, not since I came back from Iwo that I haven't put alcohol in me."

Valcanas was still sitting stiffly, his back not touching the chair, listening patiently, never taking his eyes off Balzic's eyes. After a long moment, he said softly, evenly, "Mario, when I was eleven years old, my sister drowned, did I ever tell you that? There isn't a day go by that I can't hear her voice calling me to help her. I have daymares too. And I've had them longer than you've had yours. I'm older than you are. But today is not yesterday, and I'm not eleven anymore and you're not eighteen anymore. We're responsible people. Like it or not, we're responsible for what we do now, you and I. And you have an indigent locked up on charges that cannot be justified—"

193

"He had that goddamn pistol a foot from my heart—"

"Of that I have his word as well as yours. But—and this is an important but—there are no other witnesses to that. But there are other witnesses to his actions before you came, and to his actions while you two were outside before you took him away. No one saw him threaten you in any way. I've spent most of the last hour taking statements from those witnesses."

Balzic leaned farther forward and put his fist on his desk. "I was a goddamn witness to what he did, and I have spent a lifetime training myself to observe and remember the details of unusual incidents and occurrences. You're, uh, you're stepping on a lotta years here, my friend."

Valcanas nodded. "Believe me, Mario, I'm very aware of that. But I think you've overstepped yourself here with Myushkin. He's in a bind in several ways. But so am I. Because you're my friend, but so is he. And while it is doubtlessly true that he acted stupidly, rashly, thoughtlessly, recklessly, foolishly, idiotically even, he still doesn't deserve to sit in that stopped-up latrine we call a jail for a hundred and eighty days waiting for trial because you've taken personal offense—"

"Personal of-FENSE! The man stuck a piece in my chest and told me that if I said something he didn't like he'd shoot me! That's assault. That's assault with a prohibited offensive weapon—for which he did not have a license. That's terroristic threats. That's reckless endangerment. That's unlawful restraint. And that's real close to takin' a hostage—"

"He discharged a firearm within city limits, that much is indisputable. There are witnesses to that. That's a violation of a city ordinance. If you want to stretch a point, you can kick it to a violation of a game law of discharging a weapon too close to a domicile, I forget what the distance is, but even that's stretching a point. And, Mario, you know as well as I do the man was not threatening. Except for the several seconds you say he pointed the pistol at your chest, he did not otherwise threaten you when you first encountered him at the scene, and he obeyed your orders. He surrendered the weapon voluntarily. You didn't even have to ask him to do that, am I correct so far?"

"Technically, yeah."

Valcanas licked his upper teeth and then his lips. He cleared his throat. "Excuse me, Mario, but technically is what we're both talking about. Actually—and you also know this as well as I do—my office is lined from ceiling to floor around three walls with books full of technically's. Nothing but." He paused again for a long moment. "Mario, I've known Myushkin since at least '67. I've seen him through fat times and skinny times, mostly skinny, but they've never been skinnier than they are now. In what is almost no time at all, he's lost his regular means of employment, then his wife, then his house. And now, pretty much on his own advice and encouragement, his son is in harm's way. He also believes, and I think with considerable justification, that he's being cheated by the laws of his own country out of the profits of his labors. I'm not going to sit here and tell you that I'd be willing to argue that case for him, but that's only because I don't feel qualified to argue copyright law. I mean, it's not something that comes up very often around here. Never, in my experience."

"So what's your point, Panagios? That .22 had a mind of its own? He was just holding it, right? It was aiming itself, right? And it came from a, from a, what the fuck's the word they're all tossin' around on TV these days? Oh. Yeah. Dys-func-tion-al. That's it. The .22 came from a dysfunctional factory. Nobody loved it there when it was gettin' built, nobody respected it, it didn't have any fuck-ing-self-es-teem. So it decided it was gonna fuck-ing assert itself. Yeah, right. When it saw my chest that's when it decided to get up on its hind legs and say, 'Yeah, this is me, I'm little. I ain't a .357, I'm only a .22. But I'm loaded. And I'm proud. And I can

195

kill you just as fuck-ing dead as a .357.' Right in my fuck-ing chest, it decided to say that."

Valcanas sat impassively throughout Balzic's tirade. Occasionally he licked his lips, but mostly he waited until Balzic was out of breath and red in the face and sliding back in his chair, loosening his tie and collar.

"Mario, I'm in a bind here. I can't think of a worse one. I've been put in between two friends. Correction. I've put myself in between two friends. If I had any brains I'd turn around and leave you both to stew in your own pot. But the truth is, and I don't say this carelessly, the truth is, I don't want to see you make a fool of yourself. Correction. Ignore that. I don't . . ." Valcanas paused again and let out a long sigh. "Mario, I don't want to have this thing go to trial. I want this thing to end in front of a magistrate . . . for everybody's sake. I mean that. You're making a mountain out of—"

"Panagios, stop right there. Stop right there, my friend. Don't you dare say the rest of that—"

Valcanas held up his left hand. His eyes were closed. He bit his lower lip. "Mario, this is a molehill. You're taking it very personally—"

"That was my fuck-ing chest! The same one you see right here. Me. Mine. this one. Open your eyes and look."

"Mario . . ." Again Valcanas paused. His eyes were still closed. he chewed on his lower lip again. "Mario, you don't know how it . . . how it disturbs me to say what I'm about to say. And the only way I can justify saying it is by saying that I have been your friend for a long long time and I don't want this thing to go to its conclusion in a trial. Honest to god, Mario, you have to believe me."

"What. What are you gonna say. Come on, what?"

"Mario, I realize that what I'm about to say is the unfriendliest thing I've ever said to you, but I appeal to your sense of fairness, to your honor, to your ability to hold two opposing ideas in your head at the same time."

Balzic screwed up his face. "Hey. This is me. Quit pussy-footin' around. You got somethin' on me you think I forgot about or somethin'? You think you can trade here? Huh? For this fuck Myushkin? He's your friend, fine. But he ain't my friend. He was never my friend—"

"Mario, if it goes to trial, if you let it go to trial, the only way I can defend him when there was only one witness is, as you very well know . . . for crissake, Mario, do I have to say it?"

Balzic hunched forward again. He put both hands on his desk. "Yeah you're gonna have to say it. 'Cause I don't know what the fuck you're talkin' about."

Valcanas folded his hands and dropped them into his lap. He leaned his head forward until his chin was almost on his chest, then squeezed his eyes shut. "Mario, if I say what you're apparently trying to make me say, I'm going to lose a friend. I'm asking you, please, charge him with firing the damn gun inside city limits, charge him with breach of the peace, vandalism, only forget about the rest, please."

"Shit, Greek, you got my nose wide open here. I mean, I got to hear this. What d'you think you got on me that would make me even hesitate about this?"

Valcanas breathed in heavily through his nose, his lips pursed tight. "Mario. Have it your way. You don't give me a choice. It is practically common knowledge that you suborned perjury in a homicide case—"

"I what? What did you say?"

Valcanas sighed heavily again. "If we go to trial and you're the only witness against him, the only way I can defeat your testimony is to defeat you . . . to discredit you. And I can do it. I can do it because, as much as I know you would hate me forever, I think you've grossly overreacted—for reasons that are perfectly understandable I'll grant you that—but I think your overreaction is motivated by feelings of vengeance out of particular spite for my client. And in a trial I will be

197

believed . . . because the witness you suborned is still very much alive and can be subpoenaed . . . and you will be disgraced . . . and I will have lost a friend."

Balzic felt his jaw going slack and his mouth dropping open. He slumped back in his chair. He didn't have to think long. He knew exactly what Valcanas was talking about. "Soup. Soup Scalzo."

Valcanas nodded.

"Awwww man. Awwww man. Panagios. You would do that? To me? To save this fuck Myushkin?"

"He's written nine novels, Mario. Which have been translated into eight languages. He's much praised all over the world. Really. I've seen some of his reviews. They're very complimentary. He's also a friend with whom I discuss things I discuss with very few other people else in this town, and while he's just some fuck to you—"

"Just some fuck with a gun, don't forget that little detail."

"—yes, but this writer, this friend, was only witnessed discharging this gun inside city limits, for which he should serve thirty days and go on about his business. If you, uh, if you should change your mind about him, well . . . what's the harm? Really."

Balzic mulled that question over a long moment. "How am I supposed to answer that? What's the harm. The harm is . . . ah, shit, you know what the harm is. I'm gettin' soft is what the harm is. A guy sticks a gun in my chest and I charge him with violatin' a fuckin' city ordinance? Shit. Why don't I just rent a goddamn billboard and paint the sign myself. 'Welcome to Rocksburg. Do whatever you want. Nothin' will happen. The chief cop's always been chicken. Only now it shows.' How much of a wimp message you want me to send— what's the harm, Christ. You kiddin' me? Panagios, Jesus, man, I'm sixty-four. I need every weapon I can get. My rep's one of my weapons, maybe my best weapon. You take my rep away, hell, what's left?"

Valcanas opened his eyes and sat up again and folded his hands.

"Mario, you're talking—and please forgive my choice of words here—but you're talking like an amateur. Which rep do you value more? Being able to stare down a punk? Or collecting your pension with, uh, an only slightly muddy conscience that your reputation for truth and veracity is well-known and well deserved?"

" 'Only slightly muddy'? As I recall *suborning the witness*, I did it because I was tryin' to save a priest's ass, remember? Who was dyin' of cancer. And five or six old ladies, remember? And if I hadn't done it, if I hadn't got ol' Soup to say he'd seen a murder he hadn't seen, what would've happened, you tell me."

"Your motive then was, what the hell," Valcanas said, shrugging mightily, "your motive may have been pure, Mario, I'm not going to question your motive, my god, but the fact that you suborned a witness does not cease to exist because it is ignored. Aldous Huxley said that. 'A fact does not cease to exist because it is ignored.' I've used that line dozens of times in trial. Somehow it never carried the same weight it does now. Or maybe I never felt crummy using it until now. But the facts are these, my friend: you solicited a convicted felon, you coached him in a lie, which he told under oath and which is part of the record of the Conemaugh County Court of Common Pleas, and which to avoid going to prison now himself, he will, I assure you, if I subpoena him . . . uh, Mario, I assure you he will reveal that lie and your part in it. He's only human. Just like us."

Balzic shook his head and laughed disgustedly. "I make up a lie to make sure that a priest and a bunch of old ladies don't get busted for riggin' a lottery. I make up a lie to make sure that fat prick Tullio Manditti does some time for beatin' some sucker to death with a baseball bat, which if I hadn't made up, the fat prick would've walked. What was this, huh—

199

fifteen years ago? Sixteen? And now, some sonofabitch who makes up lies for money, he sticks a gun in my chest, a little goddamn stinky .22 fuck-ing caliber, and because of him, this prick who tells lies for money, you walk in with a fuck-ing howitzer—Jesus Christ I can't remember when I didn't know you, you know that? I've known you longer than I've known my wife for crissake. And there you sit with a fuck-ing howitzer pointed at my chest . . . Jesus. How'd it come to this."

"Mario. I'm appealing to you—believe me, I'm as aware of how long we've been friends as you are. But right now, it's your, uh, your intransigence, it's your obstinance about this that puts the gun in my hands, that, believe me, I don't want to be holding—"

Balzic smiled in spite of himself. He canted his head and squited at Valcanas. "Oh that was a really sweet turnaround, Panagios. My obstinance? You turned that around on me real fast, didn't ya, Mo? Mo! MO!"

Valcanas winced each time Balzic said the nickname he detested.

Balzic leaned back in his chair and screwed up his face. "Oh fuck," he said after thinking for what seemed to him a day and a night. "Have it your way. Dischargin' a firearm within city limits. What the fuck. I'm too old for this shit."

Valcanas stood and extended his hand. "I owe you yet another one."

"Yeah yeah, right." Balzic reached up and took Valcanas's hand lightly in the fingers and pumped it listlessly.

"You'll call the magistrate?"

Balzic nodded. "Yeah. I'll call him. Then your lyin' friend can—you tell that sonofabitch he ever comes near me again. . . . aw listen to me . . . aw go on, get outta here."

Valcanas paused at the door. "I will remind him about discretion and valor. I will remind him of the purgatory nature of apology. I promise you. Thank you, Mario."

"You're welcome. I think."

*　　*　　*

In the weeks that followed, Balzic heard nothing about the whole business with Myushkin until he was beginning to think that maybe nobody except District Justice Tony Aldonelli had noticed the wild disparity in charges from one day to the next. Aldonelli's eyebrows had gone up and down and his face had twisted first left, then right, and he'd shaken his head, not side to side exactly, but in a kind of figure eight, and finally he'd said, "I hope nobody, uh, how do I want to say this? I hope nobody wants me to explain this, uh, because if they do, I'm not even gonna try. I'm gonna call you." Balzic had just chewed the inside of his cheek and muttered something about dropping the charges, that was all. "Charges get dropped all the time, what's the big deal here? If somebody wants to know, then, well, you tell 'em I, uh, I, uh, overreacted."

"Oh." That was all Aldonelli had said. One little syllable, one little sound hardly distinguishable from a grunt, but the sound came out of a mouth formed in a shape that was pointed at his chest.

The *Rocksburg Gazette* had printed a two-paragraph story near the classified ads the morning after it happened that a shooting had reportedly taken place in the Flats but there had been only one arrest and no injuries. Nobody had been named, and the story concluded with the standard cliché for such things: "Police are continuing their investigation."

Then somehow Councilman Figulli got wind of it and cornered Balzic in the parking lot behind city hall one dreary, drizzly morning in the middle of February when the sky was spitting water one minute and ice the next.

"Hey, Mario," Figulli said, stamping about, leaning, shrugging, weaving first one way, then the other, his body going twenty miles an hour even when he wasn't going anywhere, "what's this I hear about some guy in the Flats shootin' off a

201

gun, bustin' bottles or something. One day he's shootin' bottles, the next day it's practically attempted homicide, then
the next day it's back to shootin' bottles again. You know
anything about that?"

You little prick, Balzic thought, do I know anything about
that. Bastard. Can't keep your nose closed for ten minutes.
"Yeah, I heard about that."

Oh God, I didn't say that. "I *heard* about it." God almighty,
why didn't I say something really stupid.

"You *heard* about it? That ain't what I heard," said Figulli,
getting the wrinkles of a grin around his lips that showed
Balzic how much fun he was going to have with this.

"I, uh, look," Balzic said, his stomach bubbling queasily.
The message from his gut told him there was only one way
to handle this. "I, uh, I fucked up. I got into a situation and
I did somethin' real stupid. I took it personally. I lost my
temper, I couldn't understand how anybody could be doin'
somethin' that stupid, you know, and, uh, then he said somethin' and then I said somethin', and then he said somethin'
back, and, uh, what can I say? I got real unprofessional. I
took the heat. I threw my professional weight around, I
wanted to show this guy who he was fuckin' with. The next
day, after, uh, after I'd had a chance to sleep on it, I realized,
hey, I made a big boo-boo. There was no point makin' this
guy suffer just 'cause I'm gettin' old and I wanna show this
guy I can still get a hard-on. So I went back to the magistrate
and charged him the way I shoulda charged him in the first
place. You wanna put it in my record that I showed real bad
judgment, hey, you're the chairman of the safety committee,
that's your prerogative."

Every word came out of his throat as though it were a
barbed fishhook, but when Balzic saw the grin wrinkles dis-
solving on Figulli's face, he knew that humbling himself had
been the right move. Taking Figulli's fun away was worth
every word.

"Oh," Figulli said. "Okay, nah, I don't think that'll be necessary, you know. What the hell, we all make mistakes. I'm glad you told me this though, see, 'cause when somebody asks me, now, see, I got an answer for 'em. This way somebody says to me, Hey, what the hell's goin' on down there, see now I can come right back at 'em. That's the way it gotta be. Not too many guys woulda took it, uh, like you did . . . here, you know. Like you did just now."

Balzic almost felt like scuffing his shoe on the macadam and giving Figulli at least one "Aw shucks," but he said instead, "Hey, listen, Councilman, I got to go down that truck stop on I-79. State police fire marshal just asked me to go down there 'cause somebody just torched a truck and he's in court and can't get away so I'm gonna go down there and see what's goin' down. You know, Councilman, somebody's got to come up with some more money around here or we're gonna end up like Braddock or Ambridge or some of those places. You know, I think you oughta go down to Harrisburg and tell those clowns we can't do all this stuff they want us to do and not give us any money to do it with. Somebody oughta do it. I think you're the guy."

"You really think that, Balzic? Huh? Me? You think I should go down there and tell 'em what's, huh?"

"Hey," Balzic said, throwing his hands wide, "who's closer to this problem than you are? If not you, who? They gotta stop listenin' to the 'experts,' you know. They need to hear the real facts from somebody who's gotta deal with the problem day to day. Somebody said once, 'Facts do not cease to exist because they are ignored.' "

"Hey, I like that one. Facts don't cease to exist because you ignore 'em. Yeah. That's a good one." Figulli was still nodding his head and muttering and rubbing his mouth and jabbing the air with his index finger when Balzic got into his cruiser and drove out of the parking lot and headed south on Main Street toward the truck stop on I-79.

"If not you, who?" Balzic said aloud to himself. "Is that what I said. You who. Youwho, youwho . . . you fuckin' jaboney. Oh god, I sincerely hope nobody's listenin' to any of this . . . but if they are I hope they ain't takin'notes . . ."

Ten minutes later he saw the black smoke, wispy and high, and then flattening out like an anvil.

Two minutes later, he turned off I-79 South into the vast parking lot of Truck Stop 79 and found tractor-trailers parked everywhere, but not in the configurations where they might normally be found. It was as though they had all been driven as far away from something as fast as they could and then were stopped. Many of their driver-side doors were still open. Truckers and mechanics, looking somber and gnarly and surly, milled in clusters and knots. Cooks and waitresses, shivering in short sleeves, the men with their hands deep in their pockets, the women clutching sweaters at their throats, kept turning and looking back toward the far corner of the lot where black smoke was still curling up.

Balzic followed the line of cars with bumper stickers identifying the drivers as volunteer firemen. Then he came upon the cars with municipal license plates, vehicles from the County Emergency Management Agency and its Hazardous Materials Team. Then he came upon the fire trucks and volunteer firemen from at least half-a-dozen different municipalities including Rocksburg and Westfield and Kennedy townships, many of them already rolling hoses and recovering their gear. Of the only two police cars he could see, one was from the incorporated village of Daviston, where the truck stop was located, and the other was from the Pennsylvania State Police, but he didn't see either officer. He rolled down his window, and the smell of burnt rubber and plastic and paint and diesel fuel stung him so hard his head jerked backward and his eyes immediately filled with tears. He called out to a cluster of truckers, most of them in cowboy hats and boots and jeans and down-filled vests and flannel shirts: "You boys tell me where the state cop is?"

They said nothing, but two or three waved for him to keep going the direction he was headed.

He drove on, wiping his eyes, easing his way around and between the fire trucks, careful to avoid firemen who were yelling at him to watch it and take it easy, all of which he was doing as best he could, given the confusion outside his cruiser and the burning in his eyes and sinuses.

He spotted Rocksburg Fire Chief Eddie Sitko at the same moment somebody was shouting at him and waving to tell him to pull over, there was an ambulance coming through. He saw the flashing lights and got one short blast on the siren to pull out of the way, and he managed to get the front end of his cruiser into a wedge of space between a fire truck from Westfield Township and a pickup truck. He got out and immediately shook his head in reaction to the fumes and blew out his breath and covered his mouth and nose with his handkerchief.

He hurried toward Sitko, stumbling at least once over a hose, still clutching the hanky over his face. When he was about a dozen yards from Sitko, another fire truck came at him and Balzic ducked aside and waited until it passed before again making his way toward Sitko who was talking with the state police trooper. Beyond them was the burned-out cab of a tractor, blackened, blistered, glistening, dripping rainbow-colored water as firemen continued to douse it and the trac-tor-trailers parked on either side of it. What stopped Balzic was the blanket on the macadam. It had that terrible shape Balzic had seen too many times, a still, rumpled mound. But this one was small. And that smallness looked especially out of place among these largest of road and emergency vehicles.

Balzic came up to Sitko as the young state police trooper was saying ". . . so did any of them give you their names?"

"Huh?" Sitko said. "What the fuck would they be tellin' me that for? I was trying' to find out what the fuck happened, I wasn't takin' no goddamn poll, what the fuck'samatter with you, ain't you ever done this before? Huh?"

"Just take it easy, Chief—"

Balzic got out his ID case and thrust himself into the conversation by holding it up so the now flustered state trooper could see it. "What's goin' on, Sitko?"

"Huh? What the fuck you think's goin' on, we're havin' a wienie roast—oh, it's you," Sitko said, glancing at Balzic and wiping his nose with the back of his hand and coughing and spitting.

"This one's right up your fuckin' alley, Balzic. You ain't gonna believe this shit. This little girl, no shit, she's carrying a kid on her hip, comes waltzin' through the lot here, and she puts the kid down, takes this bottle outta her bag, it's a fuckin' Molotov cocktail, yeah, no shit, and she walks straight back to this truck. And two, three guys are standin' there like assholes, you know, just watchin' her, I don't know what the fuck they thought was goin' on, maybe they thought it was the Fourth of July or somefuckin'thing, and she walks right up to this truck, opens the fuckin' door, crawls up on it, you know, takes her a while to do this, you know, one of the guys said she was so small she was like half a midget, she opens the fuckin' door, stands there, I guess she was tryin' to light the goddamn thing, who knows exactly, you know, we probably ain't never gonna find out. But I guess the kid started followin' her or somethin' and she turned around and was wavin' and hollerin' at the kid to get back, you know, get back get back, and the next thing, ga-boom! She's standing on the runnin' board, with the door like half-open I guess, and ga-boom, she's goes flyin' headfirst, her back's on fire, and she lands on top of the kid, and the kid goes backwards into the wheel of the truck on the right there. These two, three guys, the ones that was watchin' her, the ones that first seen her?

206

They run over and take their vests and jackets off and you know, they get the fire out on her, but they, uh, they dragged her a long way away and one of 'em grabbed the kid and carried it, you know, to where you see it. And she's dead. The kid. I guess when the other one landed on her, she just drove the back of her head right into a wheel nut, you know. Christ, she couldn't be more'n three or four. Makes you sick, no shit."

Balzic's head was spinning as Sitko was talking. "Uh, uh, so what happened to the other one, the big one, was she in that ambulance? Or what?"

"No no nah, shit, they took her away in a chopper 'bout ten minutes ago. That was the trucker that just went. He had a fuckin' heart attack. He was standin' there tellin' me, you know, poor sonofabitch, he was standin' there tellin' me all he was doin' was takin' a dump inside, the next thing he knows there's a fire out here, he figures it's a dumpster or somethin', he don't even come outside to check it out for like another fifteen, twenty minutes. So when he finally comes out, when it finally comes to him it's his rig, he comes over to me, he's goin' nuts, you know, then he sees the kid, and next thing you know, he's hyperventilatin', you know, starts grabbin' at his chest, and boom, down he goes.

"I'm tellin' ya, Balzic, people're gettin' fuckin' nuttier and nuttier, I'm not shittin' ya. Poor bastard said one minute he's in there takin' a dump, the next minute he's out here watchin' his life go up in smoke. Then he sees that little girl gettin' covered up, boom, grabs his chest, down he goes. Ya know, I could've stayed home, watched this shit on TV over in Iraq, I don't have to come out and watch this shit, kids gettin' killed for crissake. Them fuckin' Arabs, that's one thing. This shit here, this is somethin' else."

Sitko wheeled around at the approach of yet another fire truck from yet another fire company. He waved his arms and hollered, "Hey, get that fuckin' truck outta here. We don't need that sonofabitch, who da fuck called them? You gotta turn them fuckin' monitors on once in a while, you know? You can't hear nothin' if you don't turn the fuckin' monitors on!"

Balzic nodded for the state trooper to follow him and led him away from Sitko's bellowing. They stopped by the small, still mound on the macadam. Balzic bent down and lifted the blanket until the child was exposed. His stomach turned into a stew of revulsion and he gagged as his throat filled with sour saliva. He gently replaced the blanket, his hand clutching the hanky to his mouth. When he turned back to the trooper, he coughed and cleared his throat for a what seemed a minute before he could speak. "Gimme a minute here, I'll be okay."

The trooper nodded and said. "I don't know if I'm cut out for this. I thought I'd be doing good work, you know? But I didn't know good work meant this . . . man. You ever see anything like this?"

"Depends what you mean by this. You mean this little girl?"

"Yeah," the trooper said, his face pinched in bewilderment and pain. "God she can't be three years old. What would possess somebody to do that?"

Balzic didn't answer because he had other things on his mind. Pointing to the burned-out tractor, he said, "D'you run this number through BMV yet?"

"Not yet. I, uh, I'm really not keeping up, uh, I'm way behind here. I haven't talked to any of the guys who pulled them away. I got tied up with the owner, after he went down, I was so busy giving him CPR, I'm just way behind. I would appreciate any help you can give me, uh, who are you again?"

Balzic identified himself again and said, "First thing, run that truck's numbers through the BMV. Get a next of kin on him and make sure they know what's goin' on. And tell me as soon as you know, 'cause I know a little somethin' about this mess and I'm wonderin' if it's anybody I know. What'd the guy look like?"

"I didn't really look at him. Somebody just said he went

down, I think it was that fire chief we were just talking to. God he's a madman, isn't he?"

Balzic shrugged, "That's just him. Just the way he is. So what about the driver? D'you get any look at him at all or were you too busy with the CPR? Like how old was he?"

"I honestly couldn't tell you. I never saw him until somebody said he was down—"

"Okay, that's all right. Listen, you go do what I said about puttin' the numbers on the truck through BMV and I'll talk to the guys who saw it. After that, you get your camera—"

"Camera? I don't have a camera."

"Well then, shit, call somebody who does. Get somebody out here to get this on film. Man, this is a mess. Nobody's gonna remember everything we're lookin' at. And don't let anybody move those trucks on either side until you get the pictures, you hear?"

Balzic turned and started to try to find Eddie Sitko again to see if he knew where the three truckers were who pulled the woman and the child away from the truck, but Sitko was raising hell with somebody else. Balzic turned back to the state trooper who was just getting into his cruiser and shouted at him, "Did anybody call the coroner? Call the coroner. Get him out here. We can't leave that little . . . we can't leave . . . we can't. Get the coroner out here, do that first, okay?"

Balzic took another look at the rumpled blanket. He turned away fast because he was starting to swallow many times, and he broke into a trot and headed for the restaurant. After much confusion he found the truckers and got them into a booth in the back of the restaurant, as far away from the front door as he could. For the next hour he interviewed them, making notes as fast as he could to get as much as they could remember onto paper. He began to wonder why he didn't do what his wife had been telling him to do for years: get one of those pocket tape recorders so he wouldn't have to bother writing in the frenzy of the moment.

It was the usual slow going, getting all their names, addresses, phone numbers, employers' addresses and numbers. One trucker was from Ohio, another from Indiana, the third from Michigan, all passing through to New Jersey and then to New York. Going over the details of where they were when they first saw the woman carrying the kid on her hip was the easiest part. She hadn't said a word to anybody. They didn't know the trucker whose truck she'd torched. It happened in just a few seconds. One second they were making their separate ways toward the restaurant and they happened to fall in together to allow her to pass, and they all sort of stopped and looked at each other, wondering who she was and what she was doing. There wasn't anything unusual about truckers bringing their wives or girlfriends along, any more than it was unusual to see women behind the wheel these days. But it was unusual to see a woman with a kid that small; they all agreed that was what had made them notice her. And it was no time at all, just a matter of seconds really, between when they'd first noticed her and when they saw her put the kid down and take the bottle out of the bag she had slung over her other shoulder, no more than two or three seconds. It was as though she didn't give a damn if anybody saw her. It was the driver from Ohio who'd lagged behind to watch her and it was he who'd called the others back to take a look at what she was doing. They disagreed about how much time had passed between when they'd first spotted her and when the explosion sent her flying away from the cab onto the little girl. The trucker from Ohio said twenty seconds, the one from Indiana said thirty, the one from Michigan said he was sorry but after the explosion he couldn't think about time.

Balzic thanked them all and told them they'd be hearing from many different people, the county coroner, the state police fire marshal, and the district attorney for sure, and many attorneys after that. He advised them to put their memories in writing as best they could and to get their written memories notarized at their first opportunity because memory fades fast and time does tricks with it and they were going to be answering the same questions repeatedly until they were sick of the whole business—not to mention how angry they were going to be the first time they had to take off work to testify and found out what the word *continuance* meant.

Balzic shook hands with them, wished them good luck, and went out to look at the burned-out tractor. He had been intensely curious from the moment Eddie Sitko told him what had happened to see what was painted on the doors of the truck—if anything could still be made out. When he finally got back to the truck—he had taken the longest way around way to avoid having to look again at the blanket on the macadam—all he found was blackened, blistered paint. He couldn't make out one word of whatever had been painted or fixed to the doors, but when he went around to the front of the truck to look at the license plate again, he was baffled because it did not have a Pennsylvania plate on it. It had a West Virginia plate. He would have sworn it had a Pennsylvania plate when he'd first looked at it, not that it made any difference to anybody but him, but it was just another needle to him that he was getting too old for this.

He located the state police trooper and asked him what progress he'd made.

"Well, I got a make on the truck from West Virginia. It belongs to an independent named, uh, John Randolph Bohmer, age fifty-one, address—"

"Wait wait, what'd you say his name was? Bohmer?"

"That's what they said, B-o-h-m-e-r, John Randolph, age 51, Martinsburg RD4, West Virginia. Why?"

"How'd they pronounce it? D'you have any trouble understandin' them, huh?"

"Yeah, as a matter of fact I did. I thought they were saying, Boomer or Boomah. But I figure that's just the way they talk."

211

"They take him to Conemaugh General, do you know? D'you hear anybody say where they were goin'?"

"Well that's the closest one, isn't it? I assume that's where they were taking him, but I didn't ask, so I don't know."

"What about the woman, the torch? Where'd they take her, you know?"

"Probably Pittsburgh. What's the one with the burn unit? Montefiore?"

"That's one of 'em," Balzic said absently, thinking wildly about this John Randolph Bohmer. Eddie Sitko had said the guy was inside when it happened, in the john. Oh hell, Balzic thought, I won't get anywhere speculating about this from what Sitko said. Balzic turned his attention to the state trooper again and said, "Well you got everything pretty much under control here? Huh?"

"Good god no. All I've done so far is find out who the truck belonged to and, lemme think, yeah, I got the coroner, he's on his way, or one of his deputies is, and I found a trooper with a camera on patrol on the turnpike, so he ought to be showing up any minute now. Other than that I'm, uh, I'm still way behind—"

"You're doin' just fine, you're not behind. Hell, kid, you were givin' first aid to one of the victims, you can't do every-goddamnthing at once. Can't give CPR and do a license check at the same time. You ain't Supertrooper. You're doin' fine, don't worry about it. Next thing you wanna do is get some-body in West Virginia to find a next of kin for the trucker, understand? Then you secure the area here, get that trooper with the camera to get as much on film as he can, 'cause there's gonna be lawyers askin' questions about this for years and years, believe me. Now listen, I interviewed the three best witnesses we got so far, those truckers that pulled them outta there? So try to talk to anybody else maybe saw it, okay? If you wanna talk to those three guys, go 'head, but remember you don't have to do it today. Then later on, we'll

212

trade notes, okay? Uh, d'you say they took the trucker to Conemaugh General or do I just think you said that?"

"I think we were both speculating about where he was."

"Well, you're gonna have to know so you can tell the next of kin where he is. Listen, I'm gonna head back in, and I'll find out where he is on the way, and I'll call your dispatcher and you can find out from him. I'll talk to Bohmer if it's possible, maybe talk to the torch if that's possible, so when you get squared away here, you give me a call or I'll call you, okay? We'll see what we got then, okay?"

The trooper looked more than a little frazzled, so Balzic patted him on the shoulder and nodded and winked and said, "You're doin' fine, kid. You'll be all right. You know what you're doin' and you're doin' it and that's all anybody can do, you hear me?"

"I hear you, I'm just having a little trouble believing you."

"You're doin' good I'm tellin' ya. Oh, hell, I almost forgot. Gimme your card. I won't know who to ask for."

The trooper fumbled around until he found his wallet and drew a card out and handed it over. Balzic patted him on the shoulder again and said, "Fire chief's a real pain in the ass, but he does know what he's doin'. You got any problem with people tryin' to move trucks before you're ready, you go to him. Just don't let him bully you, that's all. He loves to bully people. See ya around, kid."

Balzic hustled to his cruiser and wove his way out of the huge lot and back onto the highway into Rocksburg. On the way he called to confirm that John Randolph Bohmer had indeed been taken to Conemaugh General Hospital, and Balzic relayed that information to the Troop A state police dispatcher to pass it on to the trooper he'd just left, one William J. Houser. Then Balzic got his own dispatcher to patch him through to Montefiore Hospital's burn unit to confirm whether the torch had been admitted there and what her condition was. He was told that someone matching all the particulars had been flown in by medical helicopter, but there was no word on her condition at that time.

He parked in the visitors lot behind Conemaugh General, thinking that he could make a pretty good guess what had happened between Bohmer and this woman, but he still wanted to hear it from Bohmer's own mouth, if that was possible.

He made his way through the tunnel from the parking garage to the main hospital and then up to the third floor where the cardiac intensive care unit was. He went into the nurses' station with his ID up by his face and asked for the head nurse. There were three nurses working, two seated and writing, and one standing, arms folded, watching EKG monitors on the wall above windows looking into the ward where the patients were. One of the seated women pointed with the back of her pen over her shoulder at the nurse with her arms crossed.

She nodded when Balzic asked her if she was the supervisor. He hadn't recognized any of the nurses. It struck him that they seemed to be too young to have this much responsibility, especially this head nurse, who looked to be barely out of her twenties.

She peered at his ID case and then studied his face for a moment. "What can I do for you," she said.

"I'm here to talk to John Bohmer. He was just brought in a little while ago. Age fifty-something, Caucasian."

She nodded and pointed to the bed farthest from where they were standing. When Balzic asked her what his condition was, she said that he'd been sedated by the EMTs during transport, he appeared to be resting comfortably, and that his EKG appeared to her to be normal.

"A doctor seen him yet?"

"Not yet. One's on the way. Should've been here."

"Well, what I wanna know is, did, uh, did he really have a heart attack?"

214

"That's something you'll have to ask the doctor."

"Yeah yeah I know that, but what I'm askin' is, uh, your, professional opinion, you know, 'cause I wanna know how hard I can lean on this guy. And since the doctor's not here yet—"

"My professional opinion is I can't answer that question. And before you say anything else about how you promise not to tell anybody I told you anything, uh, my divorce just came final last month, and I was married to a cop, so, uh, I know how cops are, okay? Nothing personal, but you have your job to do and I have mine to do, and you want to keep yours, and I really really really have to keep mine because I have two little girls at home, okay?"

"So, uh, okay, but off the record, did this guy have a heart attack or what?"

She shook her head and laughed and looked at the floor. When she looked at him, she was chewing the inside of her lower lip and smiling. "You guys . . . it must be genetic, really. All I can tell you is what I've already said: he was sedated by the EMTs on his way in here. His EKG looks normal to me. He appears to be resting comfortably. I cannot say what his condition is other than that. You want to talk to him, you get five minutes. Is there anything else?"

"No. Yeah. Did you or anybody take any blood from this guy?"

"Certainly."

"Got enough to give some to the coroner?"

She shook her head and laughed quietly in disbelief. "Where have you been, Mister Po-liceman? You want me to give that man's blood to the coroner? On your say-so? You want the coroner to get some of that man's blood, you go find a doctor to write me an authorization. What, you want a drug or alcohol analysis?"

"Nah. Well, maybe. You're ahead of me here. I was thinkin' about somethin' else."

"Well, whatever you're thinking about, I can't authorize any analysis of a patient's fluids that do not specifically pertain to work done in this unit. Otherwise, my rule of life is M-D-W-P-A-P, medical doctor with paper and pen. You find a doctor to put it in writing—"

"Okay okay okay," he said, "but just between us girls, you know, did he have a heart attack or not?"

"It *is* genetic, isn't it? You guys just don't quit. Well, I don't know about you, but I haven't been a girl for some time now, so you can save all that stuff for somebody else. There were more than a hundred applicants for this job and they gave it to me and I'm not going to do anything to blow it, okay? You get five minutes with the patient, just like everybody else. How you do your job is up to you."

Balzic scratched his cheek and nodded and thanked her and tiptoed into the ward and over to Bohmer's bedside. The first thing that struck Balzic about Bohmer was how much he looked like somebody else. Balzic didn't have to think long to remember who that was. Farley Gruenwald. Same long, angular face, same gray beard, same black hair streaking with gray.

Balzic tapped Bohmer on the shoulder and waited.

Bohmer turned his head toward Balzic and opened his eyes dreamily. He opened his mouth wide and stretched it and licked his lips and screwed up his face. "Water," he said. "Gimme some water."

Balzic looked at the head nurse on the other side of the window and made a motion of drinking and pointed at Bohmer. She nodded and pointed back at a pitcher and glass on the stand beside Bohmer's bed. Then she spread her thumb and index finger about an inch apart.

Balzic put an inch of water in the glass, which already had a flexible straw in it, and held it up to Bohmer's mouth.

When Bohmer finished drinking, he said, "You the doc?"

"No. I'm a cop." Balzic replaced the glass and got out his ID case. "You John Randolph Bohmer?"

"A cop, huh? You here 'bout my rig? What's left of it."

"Yes and no. You are John Randolph Bohmer, correct?"

"Yeah, that's me. Who're you again?"

Balzic held his ID case about a foot from Bohmer's face.

"Ain't no use holdin' that thing up there. I done lost my glasses somewheres. Don't know what the hell happened to 'em. Jus' tell me who y'are. A cop you said. That's good enough. I won't remember yo' name anyways."

Balzic pocketed his ID case and said, "How ya feel? You up to answerin' some questions?"

"How do I feel. I feel like shit, that's how I feel. I got pains in my chest, my arms feel like I can't even lift 'em up, I'm dizzier'n hell, I got heartburn so bad I musta swallered a whole horseradish. On toppa all that I'm feelin' real dopey. They gimme somethin' I don't know what. How you think I feel?"

"Well, aside from lookin' a little woozy, you look okay. Your color's real good. Your lips ain't blue, your fingertips neither. I'm no heart specialist, but I've been around enough heart attacks to make a guess that you don't look like one, for what that's worth."

"Ain't worth nothin' atall to me. Millions of people been around trucks on the highway all they goddamn lives, you think they'd know if something was wrong with my transmission jus' from lookin' at my paint job?"

"No. I'm sure they wouldn't. Anyway . . . let me move on here. How do you think this happened?"

"How do I think what happened?"

"Your truck. How do you think that happened?"

"Now how the hell would I know how it happened? I was takin' a crap. I come outta the john, some ol' boy says, 'Hey, looka there, somethin's on fire, somethin's aburnin',' and I

217

goes awalkin' over to the front window and looks out like everybody else in that damn place, we was all gawkin' at it. But I was in the back, they was like two or three deep there, couldn't see nothin' but smoke, so I went over and ordered me a cuppa coffee, picked up a menu there, some guy comes aracin' in hollerin' like crazy, 'Move your trucks, move your trucks.' So I go out there figurin' it's some dumpster on fire or somethin', hell, you know, they wanted us to move our rigs so the fire trucks could get to it. Last thing in the world I'm thinkin' is, it's my rig. So I go walkin' back, I ain't even in no hurry or nothin'. I mean I seen the smoke, but my rig was way back damn near the end of the lot, and the angle I was comin' from, it jus' didn't look to me anyways like it was somethin' I oughta be worried about. It took me awhile to get back there, trucks was goin' everywhichaway, you know? Some of them guys haulin' chemicals was just aflyin' outta there, you know?"

"So you had no idea about this woman?"

"I had no idea about—huh? This woman? What woman?"

Balzic's mind came to an abrupt stop. Did this guy not know how that fire got started? Was that possible? It became sharply clear to Balzic that he'd made several assumptions, driving to hospital. You ever going to learn? he groused to himself. Never assume anything. When are you going to wise up?

"You don't know how the fire got started? You didn't talk to anybody? You don't remember talkin' to a fire chief?"

"Yeah, sure, I mean, no, I wasn't talkin' to somebody. Somebody was talkin' at me, some fireman, I don't know who. I don't remember what he said. All I remember is comin' around this trailer, the back end of it, and it was gettin' real warm, I could feel the heat real fast, and I was smellin' all that shit burnin', and, man-oh-man, I said hoooo-leeee shit that's my rig . . . and I just couldn't move, it was like my feet got stuck in this big gob of chewin' gum god done spit out. I just could not make a move. Only goddamn thing I could see was my license plate, all the rest was fire and smoke."

"You don't remember anything that fire chief said, the fireman you were talkin' to?"

"Not a damn word. I jus' remember my feet wouldn't work. I could not make 'em move. I was jus' standin' there, lookin' at about a hunert thousand dollars' worth of tractor and trailer goin' to hell right in front of my eyes . . . and that ain't sayin' a thing 'bout what was in the trailer. Shoot. It was fulla mighty fine furniture, I got no idea what that was worth, I mean, everything's insured, I don't mean to say it wasn't . . . I got insurance upta my armpits, but shit, this is hassle city. And then . . ."

"And then what?"

"Then I seen that little girl, that little chil', on the ground, and, man-oh-man, and the next thing I remember is I was on my back, and some guy had his hands in my face, uh, he was afixin' a, a thing for oxygen up in my nose. Did I have a heart attack, do you know?"

"They wouldn't tell me. But for what it's worth, the head nurse says your EKG looks normal to her."

"My what?"

"EKG, the thing that measures your heartbeat and charts it, that thing hangin' on the wall over there above that guy's bed, can you see that? That box with the green circle and those lines goin' across and up and down? The thing that's hooked up to those wires on your chest."

"Uh, without my glasses, I can't see a damn thing. I got wires on my chest? I didn't know that."

"Well, you do, and that's what it's for and that's what it is. When you find your glasses, you'll see what it looks like."

"And she said what again? Mine was normal?"

"Yeah. She also said the doc was on his way. Uh, Mr. Bohmer, you got any next of kin? Anybody you want to know where you are?"

"Anybody I want to know where I'm at, is that what you said?"

"Yes. You want me to call somebody for you?"

Bohmer shook his head. "I'm sure none of my ex-wives wants to know where I'm at."

"How many of those do you have?"

"Three."

"How 'bout your parents? They—"

"Passed on."

"Brothers, sisters, anybody?"

"Got a brother in Moundsville. Killed his wife and shot her boyfriend, so I don't reckon he'll be comin' 'round. Got 'nother brother in California, but I ain't seen him in twenty years. Ain't talked to him neither. He's a jealous prick."

"Anybody? Children? Sons, daughters?"

Bohmer closed his eyes and appeared to drift off. He slowly brought his left hand up, the one that didn't have an intravenous tube in it, and wiped the corners of his mouth. "Gawd-damn, my mouth's dry . . . must be what they give me that's doin' it."

"No kids, huh?"

"Can I have some more water?"

Balzic turned and made all the water and drinking motions he'd made earlier to the head nurse. She responded by holding up her wristwatch and tapping it twice with her index finger.

Balzic turned back to Bohmer. "The nurse'll get you some water in a second here, Mr. Bohmer. I didn't hear what you said, you got any kids or not?"

"Just one. Daughter."

"You give me her name and address I'll get in touch with her, if you want."

The head nurse came squishing up on the tile floor in her white running shoes and said, "I'm sorry, Chief, but your five minutes was up about a minute ago."

"Water," Bohmer said. "Please?"

She poured about an inch of water into his glass and directed the flexible straw into his mouth. He drank it all and put his head back down, the effort of raising up and drinking causing him to let out an involuntary belch. Then he broke wind, loudly.

"My my," the nurse said, "you're practically a one-man hurricane, aren't you."

"I'm practically a what?" Bohmer said, turning his eyes toward the nurse. Then suddenly his eyes were closed and within seconds he was snoring.

"Shit," Balzic grumbled. He held up his hands at the nurse and said, "I'm goin', I'm goin'."

He waited for her inside the nurses' station. When she came in, he said, "Listen, do me a favor, okay, please? He's got a daughter. Find out what her name is and her address, please? Okay? And then call the Rocksburg Police Department and give that information to whoever answers the phone and tell 'em it's for me, okay? Will you do that please? It's important."

She nodded and made a note of it and showed it to the other nurses. Then she tacked it up on a bulletin board on the wall next to the door.

Balzic thanked her and left the CICU and took the stairs to the basement where the pathology labs were. He was looking for Coroner Wallace Grimes, but when he got there Grimes was nowhere to be found and none of the lab techs knew where he was. They had not seen him leave.

Balzic went into Grimes's office and sat at his desk and found a legal tablet and printed this note: "Doc, I need a favor. The little girl you're bringing in from the truck stop, would you please make a comparison of her blood with the

221

blood from a guy in CICU, John Randolph Bohmer. Head nurse in CICU said they took blood from him but she couldn't send you any of it on my say-so, she needed a request from an M.D. I forgot to get her name. I'm slipping. Mario Balzic. P.S. I'm looking for a paternity match."

* * *

In the days that followed, Balzic found himself chasing after people who were either never where they said they were going to be or who would not talk to him about the things he wanted to talk about if he did find them. It started with an old friend of his in the Pittsburgh Police Department, a lieutenant on the homicide squad named John Martinovich. Because one administrative thing after another kept popping up, Balzic could not get away to Pittsburgh to interview the torch in Montefiore Hospital, so he called Martinovich and asked if he could find a half-hour to interview her. Martinovich agreed, but then Balzic couldn't find him again.

If Martinovich was on duty, he couldn't talk because he was talking to his boss or to a witness or to somebody else and couldn't be interrupted. If he wasn't in the office, he was on his way to some other place and nobody who answered the phone could say where that was or when he'd be back.

The nursing supervisor in Montefiore Hospital's burn unit kept insisting that the torch wasn't talking to anybody so it wouldn't matter if she had seen this Lieutenant Martinovich, he wouldn't have been able to get any information out of that woman either. The woman was simply not responding to human communication, didn't Balzic understand the words?

"You mean she doesn't talk to anybody? You tellin' me she doesn't even ask for water or ice or somethin', to go to the john?"

"That's exactly what I'm telling you," the nursing supervisor said. "And this is what I've said to you at least three times

222

now, if she is able to speak—and I do not know that she is or isn't—she isn't speaking, am I making myself clear?"

Balzic said he guessed she was, but when he hung up he wished he could hear that from Martinovich.

The same thing was happening with Trooper Houser. He had either just left for someplace or was on his way back, or was expected back in a half-hour at the latest. But when the half-hour had passed, so had Houser, going in another direction.

The one person Balzic did not want to see, Nick Myushkin, kept showing up every place Balzic was. Myushkin, saying he was just following the advice of his attorney and was just trying to make amends, seemed to materialize out of thin air and was leaving a trail of apologies. He came into city hall twice, but Balzic happened to spot him first both times and managed to duck out a door opposite the one Myushkin was coming in. In Muscotti's, Balzic left a full glass of chablis and a couple of bucks in bills and change on the bar when he came up from the john one day and Myushkin was just sitting down on the stool next to where Balzic's drink and money were. Balzic never looked back; he turned and beat it out the front door.

Myushkin even showed up at his house one night, but Balzic made his wife answer the door after he'd seen who it was. Ruth had been indoctrinated to never let anyone in who couldn't produce legitimate ID, a driver's license at the very least. Since Myushkin prided himself on being a fugitive from capitalism, as he'd put it, he'd let his license lapse and had stopped carrying his wallet anyway, as a matter of principle.

"What principle is that?" Ruth asked him, with Balzic standing out of sight in the dining room and peeking around the corner.

"The principle that when authority wants to know who you are if they arrest you, they have to work to find out," Myushkin said. "The only honorable course of action for a citizen in America today, ma'am, is to not make it easy for government to govern. By refusing to carry a wallet, I'm not allowing myself to be tempted to cooperate with the law in my own identification if they want to harass me."

Ruth thought for a moment and then said, "And why do you want to see my husband, did you say? You're following the advice of your lawyer who told you to apologize, is that what you said?"

"Yes, ma'am."

"You're here to tell my husband you're sorry because he's a cop and you did something wrong, is that it?"

"Yes, ma'am."

"But you—let me see if I've got this right—you don't carry a wallet because you believe as a matter of principle you shouldn't do anything to help the law, or the authorities, if you should get arrested, is that what you said?"

"Or harassed, yes, ma'am. I know it's a contradiction. But I'm used to that. My whole life's pretty much a contradiction."

"Uh-ha. Well," Ruth said, "I'm sorry, but my husband's still not at home. He should've been here by now, I thought he'd be here ten minutes ago at least, but he isn't, so, uh. . . ."

"I understand, ma'am. I do. Just tell him I was here and I want him to know that I'm sorry for pointin' a gun at him. I was pretty nuts that day. And I'm really hopin' he doesn't hold it against me."

"You have a trial coming up soon, don't you?" Ruth said.

"Yes, ma'am, I do. Well, no. A magistrate's hearing, uh, I guess is what it is."

"Uh-ha. I see. Well, he's still not here, but I'll tell him you were here and what you said, I will."

Myushkin gave a little nod of his head and a slight tilt from his waist, a sort of apologetic bow that had Ruth shaking her head when she closed the door and came away from it. She

turned back to face Balzic and said, "See, this is another
thing, in this new partnership we have, I'm not going to do
that anymore. I know I did it for years and years—my god
you trained me to never let anybody in—and I just did it
again right now—"

"Did what?" Balzic said.

"Did what? What do you mean 'Did what?' You were standing right there, hiding in the dining room. How can you even
say those words, 'did what,' my god. I'm not going to do that
anymore, Mario, I promised myself I am not. I used to think
it was a really good thing I did for you, I used to take pride
in it, being a buffer for you against the world. It made me feel
really important—used to make me feel really important."

"Hey, you would've had to answer the door no matter
whether I was here or not—"

"That's not the point! And you know that's not the point.
I don't get paid to be a cop. You get paid to be a cop. I don't
get paid at all. By anybody. I wait around here until you
hand me your check."

"Right, exactly, that's what I do, I hand you the check. I
don't keep the check and give you, like, uh, what's-his-face—
hell like any number of what's-his-faces. Christ, I know lotsa
guys never give their wives their pay. They give 'em house
money, here here here, here's twenty bucks, go to the Giant
Eagle—"

"Twenty bucks? What's twenty bucks supposed to buy?
What? Groceries for a week?"

"Okay, fifty, a hundred. The amount ain't the point. Most
guys I know, they give their wives house money, the money
they think she has to have to run the house on. The rest of
the money they keep. I mean they sure as hell don't do what
I do—what I've been doin' as long as we been married, you
know, come home, just hand you the check and never think
nothin' about it."

"You're forgetting the time, what was it? Ten years ago? Twelve? When you thought you could do it better than me? When we got into all trouble with the IRS, remember?"

Balzic pulled his head back and scrunched up his face. "Trouble with the IRS? What trouble with the IRS?"

"Oh my god, what trouble with the IRS? When you screwed up our tax return so bad we had to get Mo Valcanas to go with us to Pittsburgh and he had to explain that you weren't used to doing the taxes and there was no attempt on your part to commit fraud, *that* trouble with the IRS. Talk about selective memory—"

"Oh. Okay, okay. I remember now. So, uh, I screwed up that time. So we got it all straightened out—"

"Mo Valcanas got it straightened out or we would have paid about seventeen hundred dollars penalty and interest."

"So," Balzic shrugged, "so you, uh, started takin' care of the money again. So I'm not so good at it. But what's this stuff about you're a buffer between me and the world, I mean, I don't get that, just 'cause you answer the door for me once in a while, I mean—"

"How about all the times I answer the phone and take a look at you and you're goin', no no, you're not here, you're wavin' your hands like a baby bird or something, and how many times have I stood there and lied through my teeth and said you weren't here and you're standing right there in front of me—"

"I do it for you too."

"Oh yeah? When? Name me one time you ever answered the phone and it was somebody I didn't want to talk to, c'mon, c'mon, name me one time. I wanna hear this, boy, is this gonna be good."

"Okay, so not that many people call you that you don't wanna talk to—"

"Not that many people call me?! Honest to god, Mario, I'm in here praying that people are going to call me. Name me one person I ever in the whole time we've been married that I ever said to you I don't want to speak to that person, tell me, please, I have to hear this, I have to know who this person is."

"Okay, so I can't think of anybody right now, but that doesn't mean if you needed me to do it I wouldn't do it for you. What kind of a rat would I be if I wouldn't lie for you on the phone."

"Oh honest to god, Mario, the only thing that's missing here is a little turned-down lip, you know, stick your lower lip out, why don't you, and look at the floor, honest to god."

"You still would've had to answer the door if I wasn't here is all I know—"

Ruth poked herself in the chest with all her fingers. "Mario, was that me at the door or was that me in the dining room, peekin' around the corner? Who was that in there? And who went to the door first and looked out and said, 'Oh shit not him again,' who was that? And who said to me, 'Hey, Ruthie, you wanna answer the door for me, please, I ain't here, okay?' Who was that said that? Was that me?"

"But yeah yeah yeah I know what you're sayin', I hear ya, but what I'm sayin' is if you would've been here by yourself—"

"Oh Mario stop! My god! It's bad enough I have to look at television every day and listen to those, god, I have to look at all those trucks burned out and blown to bits all over the desert in Kuwait and those bodies, they try not to show us the bodies, d'you know that? But they show us the trucks and the jeeps and the tanks all blown up and we're supposed to think there were no soldiers in there. You know, like they were just out there in the desert, those trucks and tanks, just drivin' around by themselves. Honest to god, these guys from the Pentagon and the Defense Department and the president, they want us to believe they're just blowin' up machines and tanks and trucks and buildings and there's nobody in them. There's no young men or no women or children or old people. God I'm sick of these lies! Every day, day after day, they keep showin' us these pictures, and the only time they show us any people is when they show these guys been surrendering, what kind of boobies do they take us for?

"My god, it's bad enough when they do it, I mean Bush, this guy's been telling us we're going to liberate Kuwait, liberate Kuwait, my god, Mario, do you know that in some of those places over there they cut the clitorises off little girls so they can't get any pleasure from sex when they grow up? You think the Jews are bad when it comes to women? My god, the Lubavitchers, when they have sex they put a sheet between them, the men don't even touch the women when they're making love, they have a hole in the sheet! They pray every day, 'Oh thank you, God, for not making me a woman'! But they think the Moslems are scum! And when it comes to women, those Arabs, Mario, can you imagine if you lived in such a place we had to cut the clitoris off Marie? Off Emily? Can you imagine that?"

Balzic started to move slowly toward her. "Ruth, Jesus, Ruthie, all I did was ask you to get rid of the guy for me, that's all—"

"You don't understand! You're not listening to me! I've been doing this for you as long as we've been married. I used to save dimes for you so you'd always have dimes for the pay phones. Now I save quarters. I answer the phone for you, I answer the door, I lie for you and . . . and . . . I have no money. I don't make any money. If something happened to you, what . . . what would happen to me? And those bastards in Washington, they want us to think there's nobody underneath those goddamn smart bombs when they explode. Smart bombs. My god, my god . . ."

Balzic had been moving closer to her, his arms out, ready to put them around her, but she held up her hands and backed away from him.

"I don't know what it is," she said, "it's a whole bunch of things all at once. But I don't want you to tell me anymore that you're not here. There's something about those words, they just really scare me now. It's looking at you and hearing you say those words, 'No no, I'm not here,' and you're whispering them, and sometimes all I can see is your lips moving, I can't even hear you whispering, and I can't do that anymore, Mar, honest. I don't know who actually is holding the knife when they cut those little girls, when they cut their clitorises off, maybe it's women who do the actual cutting, you know? But it's men who made the decision. And if the women do it to their daughters, it's just 'cause they're trying to please the men.

"Just like it's men now, here, on the TV every day, every night. Men drop the bombs, men tell us the bombs are smart, men decide to show us only the pictures that don't have bodies in them. I'm really disgusted with it. And I'm disgusted with myself for thinking I have to tell people you're not here . . . 'cause what I feel like is, what I've felt like for years and years, Mar, and please don't be mad at me for saying this, but it's the truth. For years and years, you *weren't* here, and the person who was here isn't here anymore and I miss her so much. God I can't tell you how much I miss her."

Balzic was going to say that he missed his mother too, but he had the sense to keep quiet. He let his arms fall to his sides and waited.

"It's not just me, Mar. It isn't, really. All the women in my group—"

"Your group? What group?"

"At the community college. Where I go every week, I've told you about that. Don't you remember? Please god say you remember."

"Oh. Yeah, sure of course I remember. I just never heard you, you know, uh, call it 'my group' before, that's all."

229

She shrugged. "What else am I supposed to call it? The women I go talk to every Wednesday. I . . . we were talking last time about how Rocksburg used to be. This one woman, she's sixty, she was talking about how when the whistles blew and the shifts were changing, if you were dumb enough to be on the wrong street at the right time, if you were in a car, you just had to wait, you just had to sit there, you couldn't move because the men were all over the street and you'd be stuck there for ten minutes until they were gone. She was talking about the intersection under the bridge, you know? When the Pressed Steel Car Company and Continental Can and the Wheel and Axle and the P and LE railroad were all changing shifts, remember? God, she says sometimes she drives down there at four o'clock just to try to remember what it looked like and . . . and she just started to cry. Her father and her uncles and her brothers and all her cousins, she says she doesn't know where half of them are anymore, the ones from her generation. She knows where her brothers are, I mean. She says there's not one of them making today what he was making twenty years ago. One of her brothers, she said, used to make seven something an hour at Continental in 1960, and now he's in North Carolina making about seven and a quarter an hour, thirty-some years later. And her husband's dead and she's living on a widow's pension from Social Security. All the years he worked for J and L, her husband, for about five or six years there, they were in bankruptcy and they weren't paying anybody's pension, and they said they didn't have to. And then the Supreme Court finally said they had to pay, but they still won't answer her letters. All of his pension that they wouldn't pay him because they were in bankruptcy, she figures she has something coming, they shouldn't just be allowed to keep that, and they won't even answer her letters. What's she supposed to do, Mar? She can't get welfare because she won't let the state put a lien on her house. She says she can't do that to him, her

230

husband, he worked so hard to pay for the house. Did you hear what I said, Mario? The man's dead, and she's alive, but she won't let the state put a lien on the house to get welfare for herself out of loyalty to him—did you hear that?"

Balzic shook his head and shrugged feebly. "I heard, I heard. But I don't know what she's supposed to do," he said. "But, uh, I won't make you answer the door for me anymore. When I'm here. Or the phone either. I promise."

"Oh god I don't mind doin' that. I'm used to it. It's just . . . sometimes I start feeling real sorry for all the women, I mean, is there a greater insult really in America than some guy sayin', 'Oh, that's woman's work,' is there, really? I mean, it's sickening when you think about it. Men put us down and they won't pay us, but when there's something they don't wanna do, who has to do it? It's not just me. Not us here, you and me.

"I hear these women and that's all they say, how they've done all this work all their lives and men think it's just shit housework, woman's work, women ought to be glad to do it, what else do they have to think about, and then they keep the women hanging on the ends of their strings, here, here's fifty bucks for the house, like you said, or when the company decides to go into bankruptcy, and if your husband dies in the meantime, while it's taking years to go through the courts, then to hell with you, lady, your husband's dead and you don't have any money to hire a lawyer to get what should've been paid to him, so what? So take a hike, go to the end of the line. And then this goddamn country can't take care of its own and we're over there in the desert blowing people to bits and pretending the only things we're killing are buildings and trucks, no people. Our bombs are smart, they're so smart when they see the people, the women and children, they just veer off and go find an empty building. What a crock. Why do we keep putting these people—these *men* in Congress? In the White House?"

"You want me to answer that? I can't even tell you who elected Eddie Sitko fire chief. His cronies, his worshippers, the guys who think the fire department wouldn't exist if he wasn't around to run it, who knows? Every time they have an election, he's the only guy runnin' for chief, that's all I know. But for us, here I'm talkin' about, I mean it what I said. I'll answer the door myself from now on. The phone too. And I'm sorry I made you do it before."

Ruth had turned away from him, but now she turned back, her eyes glistening with tears. "You know what that woman said? She said—my god it sent such a chill through me—she said, 'I'm here, but nobody sees me. Don't anybody try to tell me ghosts don't exist. 'Cause when I try to tell these men what I have to live like, that's exactly how I feel. Like a ghost. How am I supposed to know I'm not a ghost?' And every woman there, there was such a gasp, you should have heard it, 'cause everybody knew exactly what she was talking about."

Balzic's mind flashed to the image of Farley Gruenwald, full of beer and amphetamines, racing on his Harley across a deserted campground in the middle of the night, doing wheelies with his light off to prove he was alive. Balzic didn't know what to say to Ruth. The only thing he did know was that he should not say a word about Farley Gruenwald.

"Could I, uh, would it be all right if I hugged you?" he said after a long moment in which he was very uncomfortable.

"Yes," she said. "I'd like that. I always like it when you hug me."

While they were hugging, swaying slightly, Ruth leaned her head back and said, "Aren't you glad I taught you to hug? Huh? And aren't you glad I taught you to say those words?"

"What words?"

"What words, listen to him. 'Would it be all right if I hugged you,' those words. You think you thought them up all by yourself?"

"You mean I didn't?"

"Oh god," she said. "You're incorrigible. Okay, okay. You can think you thought them up all on your own. All I want to tell you now, Buster, is you'll never know how they saved your buns tonight. 'Cause I could see in your eyes, I could see the wheels turnin', you were gettin' ready to tell me about some man."

"You mean because of that woman thinkin' she was a ghost or somethin'?"

"Uh-ha." She leaned her head back farther and said, "Now I can't wait to hear this, how you were never ever goin' to tell me anything like that. Go 'head. Say it."

"Ruthie, I know I told you this before and you never believe me, but it's the truth—"

"Yeah yeah yeah, there ain't a man in the world scares you half as much as I do, blah blah blah blah."

"Aw shit, Ruthie—"

"Don't you 'Aw shit Ruthie' me. It's time you gave that old baloney a rest, you know? I mean, there was a time when I'd fall for lines like that—'There's not a man in the world scares me as much as you'—god I melted the first time I heard that, but you aren't the guy you were then and I'm not the girl, so it's time you thought up somethin' new, big boy. Somethin' to fit now. And don't stop huggin' me while you're thinkin' either. You have to learn how to think while you're huggin'. Us women've been doing it for centuries. It's time you learned."

Balzic couldn't do anything but shake his head.

*   *   *

Balzic kept calling the pathology labs in Conemaugh General, hoping to find Coroner Wallace Grimes in his office. This time, about the tenth time he'd tried, he got Grimes, who answered on the first ring.

"It's me, Doc, Balzic, what's the word on, uh—"

233

"Yes," Grimes said.

"Yes? You got a paternity match?"

"Yes. Anything else?"

"Guess I caught you at a bad time—"

"Yes."

"Well wait a minute, Doc, I mean I know you're in a rush there, but, uh, this paternity match, which way's it go?"

"Beg your pardon?"

"Well what I mean is, is the girl that died, is she his daughter for sure?"

"You asked me to determine whether the man was the father of the child. I just said he was. Was I supposed to determine something else?"

"Uh, no no. I'm thinkin' about something which I guess there's no way you could figure out unless—"

"Mario, I'm extremely pressed for time here—"

"Yeah right right, thanks, good-bye."

Grimes hung up without so much as a grunt.

So, Balzic thought, John Randolph Bohmer was the father of the little girl on the macadam, the little girl who'd been wrapped around her mother's leg in the middle of the road in Edna No. 3, the little girl with all the fingers of one hand in her mouth at once, the little girl named Coo. So why was this information so unsatisfactory, so much of a grimy, grubby, godforgotten letdown? Because that's what it was, Balzic thought. Exactly that. But it was also because he had a pile of messy questions that wouldn't go away: What was the child's mother to John Bohmer? Was she one of his three wives? Was she some waif he picked up in some truck stop, a one-hour stand in the back of his cab? She was eaten up with revenge about something, but what? And what if she was Bohmer's daughter? And what the hell did any of this have to do with Farley Gruenwald, outside of the peculiar fact that Gruenwald happened to bear a strong resemblance to Bohmer?

Balzic picked up the phone again and called the cardiac

intensive care unit of the hospital. He was hoping he was calling at the right time of day to get the right shift of nurses because even as he was punching the buttons he was mentally kicking himself because once again he'd let somebody get away without getting a name. He couldn't remember the name of the head nurse he'd talked to when he'd gone to see Bohmer. It was becoming more and more evident to him that he was slipping.

"Cardiac intensive care," a voice said wearily when his call was transferred from the main operator.

He identified himself and then stammered around before finally getting the words out: "Does the head nurse on your shift remember talking to me about a patient named Bohmer? John Randolph Bohmer?" God, what a question. What a way of broadcasting what an over-the-hill jerk you were turning into.

"That's me, and yes I do remember talking to you."

"Uh, what is your name? So I don't have to continue to make an ass out of myself?"

"Well, since you're a cop and since my ex-husband was— is—a cop, I really don't mind if you feel you have to make a whatever out of yourself. I need all the laughs I can get." She paused long enough to let Balzic twist on that one, and then she said, "My name is Trudy Zemkowiak. Unfortunately. Unfortunately 'cause I don't have the money to buy my own name back. Which was Wilson."

"Uh-ha. Well," Balzic said, clearing his throat, "I see. Well look, remember when I asked you about that Bohmer fella's relatives, you know?"

"I remember."

"Well, has anybody turned up? Anybody called or visited or written a get-well card or anything?"

"Not that I know of. My note's still on the corkboard here. Nothing's written on it that I can see. Nope."

"And he hasn't asked you to call anybody for him or—"

"He certainly hasn't asked me."

"Well have you asked him about it? Did you just go out and say to him, you know, 'Hey, Mister Bohmer, can I call somebody for you?' Did you do that?"

"Of course I have. You asked me to, didn't you?"

"Yes yes I know I did—"

"Well I did. Several times. And so have the other nurses. And he doesn't want us to call anybody. Not his daughter or his wife—"

"He said he had three wives. Three wives, one daughter, that's what he told me."

"Yes, but it doesn't seem to matter how many of which he's got. He doesn't want me or anybody else to call anybody. Believe me, if he'd asked me I would've done it. And I would remember that I'd done it. You satisfied now, Chief?"

"Man-oh-man, you really didn't like your old man, didya?"

"Is there anything else?"

"No no. But thanks for your help. I appreciate it."

She too hung up without so much as a grunt.

Balzic put all that into the pot and stirred it around. And stirred it some more. And every time he dipped the spoon in and brought it out for a taste, it was the same grimy, grubby, godforgotten letdown.

He called Lieutenant Martinovich again and this time caught him in.

"Your torch ain't talkin', Mario. Little girl wouldn't say a word. I mean, if I was in her condition I don't know how much I'd feel like talkin' either, but the fact is—and it doesn't matter how many ways I say this—she ain't sayin' nothing' to nobody about nothin'."

"If you were in her condition, huh? What kind of condition is that, anybody tell you? Like how long's she gonna be in there?"

"Oh man, she's burned bad. All over her back and down both arms clear to her elbows and down to the top of her

236

butt. Her hair's gone off the back of her head clear up to her ears. She's a mess. Really. The doc I talked to was talkin' like months and months, and he said she wasn't helpin' herself at all. It was his opinion she'd given up. He was not very optimistic. He said if she doesn't start to perk up, you know, like real soon, it's gonna be all she wrote. How the hell'd that happen anyway?"

Balzic summed it up for Martinovich.

"Well ain't that the shit, huh? Every time you think you heard it all, you find out you haven't. So, uh, Mario, what's your pleasure? You want me to check in on her every week or so or what? I'm not sayin' I'm gonna have the time, but if I do, you know, just say it and I'll do it."

"No, nah, hey, thanks, you've done enough. I heard from the nursing supervisor down there she wasn't talkin', I just wanted to hear it from a cop. Now I've heard it."

"So whatta you think?"

"I don't know what to think. The guy whose truck she torched ain't talkin' either. All I know for sure is he was the father of the little girl. But what he was to the torch, hell, it's all speculation. I mean, if she lives and she decides she still doesn't wanna talk, what's anybody gonna do to make her? State cops'll prosecute her, but, hell, that's so far down the road, I mean if they know what you know and I'm sure they will if they don't already—and so they get a conviction, so what? I mean, this little girl calls 911 one day and they sic me on her, and she tells me this crazy story, not a goddamn word of it is true, and six, seven months later, her little daughter's dead, she's almost dead, and a guy's in a cardiac unit, hell, I don't know what kinda shape he's in, except that he ain't talkin', so you tell me."

Martinovich grunted. "It just struck me," he said. "Remember that little girl on TV, testifying about how those babies were gettin' tossed outta their incubators over there in Kuwait, remember that?"

"No," Balzic said. "I must've missed that."

"Yeah yeah, this little girl, testifyin' in Congress, claimin' she was a nurse or somethin', a volunteer or somethin' in this hospital over in Kuwait and these Iraqi soldiers come bustin' in and, you know, she said they just started tearin' wires outta the walls, unpluggin' the incubators and tossin' the babies on the floor and all that hideous shit, you know? I remember watchin' her and thinkin', man, is that chick tellin' the truth or what?"

"I'd think I'd remember that if I'd seen it," Balzic said.

"Well, I saw it. And right after that, man, the ol' U.S. of A. was on the march, and all the while I had this bad bad feeling, you know? Like I sure wish somebody coulda come up with some corroborating testimony on that, you know?" Martinovich snorted a laugh. "Like it makes any difference what kinda evidence I want, sheeesh, who am I shittin'? Hey, I'm just another clump of the great unwashed out here, Mario. Guys like you and me, they send us when they need somebody to pick up the pieces and mop the floors. Speakin' of which, I gotta get goin'. So you don't want me to check on this girl again, right?"

"No, believe me, you don't have to waste Pittsburgh gas for me if she's in the condition she's in. I'll just keep checkin' myself. Thanks anyway, John, I'll see ya around maybe."

Balzic dropped the phone into the cradle and leaned back in his chair and thought, Like it's gonna make a difference to me, whether I ever know what the hell was going on between this woman and Bohmer. Not gonna change a damn thing. I could know everything and that little girl'd still be dead, that truck'd still be burned up, and the woman that caused it all'd still be in a burn unit.

Balzic needed a drink, a glass, a big glass half-full of some big healthy live wine, red, something the winemakers kept for themselves, and if he couldn't have that, then something they would give to their best friends, and if he couldn't have that, then something they would sell to their best customers, and if he couldn't have that, then something a smart, shrewd dago would buy for himself and keep in the back room of his saloon for occasions such as this when the world stunk with grimy grubby godforgotten retribution gone haywire.

Balzic walked to Muscotti's in the rain, a chilling drizzle suited perfectly to his temper, making his thirst for the wine all the more compelling, and it was the thought of the wine that he kept using to expel the picture of the rumpled blanket on the macadam in Truck Stop 79.

After he'd parked on a stool near the kitchen, he tried for some minutes to convince Vinnie that he wasn't there to drink the stuff Vinnie was hustling to strangers.

"Strangers, huh?" Vinnie said. "Only fuckin' strangers come in here is from the new—you hear what I'm sayin'? Huh? The new improved Liquor Control Board, whateverthefuck they're callin' them state cops they got now doin' graft instead of the regular ol' grafters we was all used to and didn't have to fuck around with, you know what I'm sayin', huh? Christ almighty, do you love me, honey, of course, darling, yes, but will you love me in the morning, why certainly, sweet thing, you know I'm gonna love you in the morning, yeah, fuck all that. We already done all that with them old grafter bastards, now we gotta go through a new romance with these new grafter bastards. And oh, what kills me, listen to this, what kills me is they get so fuck-ing indignant, like, what? Are you trying to offer me a bribe? No you stupid prick, I'm tryin' to give you this money 'cause I forgot to give it to your mother last night, you fuckin' asshole."

Given his sour depression, Balzic sat through Vinnie's oration with amazing patience. "So you got any good stuff back there or not? I mean I'm convinced I shouldn't've ever said the word *strangers*. I promise I'll never say it again."

"Hey," Vinnie said, pursing his lips and drumming his

fingers on the bar, "I think maybe I can do something nice for you."

Balzic reached out and snatched Vinnie's wrist. "Don't make it personal, okay? Let's keep it strictly commercial, okay? You got the wine, I got the money, I don't want no favors, okay?"

"You don't want no favors," Vinnie said, pulling his arm away indignantly, "then you can just drink the bar stuff. You want the other stuff, I gotta do a B and E in the boss's cabinet. Easy for you to say you don't want no favors. Huh. So now what's it gonna be, darling, you gonna respect me in the morning or what."

"Get him the good stuff for crissake," came a voice over Balzic's shoulder.

Oh no, Balzic thought, not him again, Jesus Christ almighty.

Myushkin plopped down on the stool beside Balzic. "Go'on, Vinnie, don't be lookin' at me that way, I got money. Look. Look at this. This is what you get for detailin' a man's Cadillac, seventy-five beanies, U.S. currency. I could go for some of the good stuff myownself."

"Seventy-five bucks," Vinnie said. "Shit, you can't afford the good stuff."

Myushkin stuck his chin across the bar. "And you ain't ever poured anything that cost seventy-five bucks a bottle, not in this life you haven't, you can save that bullshit for your girlfriends. Just go on back and get the good stuff, go on, I owe this man several drinks. And don't worry, there's more where this came from. Guy was so happy when he saw what I'd done to his filthy ol' Caddy, he's gonna let me do his old lady's Caddy and his brother-in-law's Caddy too. I'm tellin' ya, I may have finally found my profession. I made as much doin' this car as a shrink makes, just took me four hours instead of one."

Vinnie rolled his eyes and headed for the back room, shaking his head and muttering.

240

Myushkin coughed and cleared his throat and lowered his voice. "I know I been makin' a pain in the ass outta myself, you know, chasin' you around, but, Balzic, honest, that's what Mo told me to do. I'm just followin' his advice, that's all. Please don't, uh, please don't run away again, okay? I feel shitty enough. I mean, I had to get really drunk to go to your house. Really, man. And your wife? Man, she's great. Must be somethin' to have a woman lie for you like that. Really. I mean she never blinked, looked me dead in the eye, drunk as I was, I mean, shit, your cruiser was right there in the driveway. I had to walk right past it. But she never hesitated, man. There's about a half a billion guys wish they had what you had right there."

Balzic squirmed around on the stool until he was almost facing Myushkin. "You wanna apologize to me, you apologize to me. You leave my wife out of it, understand?"

"Yeah, sure. Absolutely."

"Then say what the fuck's on your mind and get it over with. 'Cause I don't want you followin' me around no more, understand?"

"Yeah, absolutely I understand. Uh, I want to apologize for pointin' that pistol at you, I mean it. That was a really stupid thing to do. I got no excuse. I'm sorry, I'm—"

"Okay okay okay that's enough. You said it, I heard it, now I don't wanna hear any more about it. And never come to my house again, you got that?"

Myushkin nodded several times. "Yeah. I got it."

Balzic swiveled around on his stool and stared absently at the back bar. "So, uh, so how's your back? Must be okay you're detailin' cars, gotta crawl around like a monkey and all that."

"Hey, my back's pretty good lately. Mo set me up with a chiropractor, he does his thing on my back, I autographed a couple of first editions for him. He's happy, I'm happy. Somebody told him how much some of my first editions are goin' for in California and New York, so, uh, we worked out

241

a deal. I go to him about once a month, and so far all it's cost me is three autographs. Ain't this America? Huh?"

Vinnie came out of the back room with a bottle of Gattinara, holding it down by his leg. He stopped in front of Balzic and pushed out his lower lip with his tongue and lifted and lowered his eyebrows and nodded several small quick nods, as though to say, Well, what do you think of this? When Balzic didn't respond to his faces, Vinnie leaned forward from his waist and growled, "So?"

Balzic shrugged. "So? You want a standing ovation or what? Open it. Give it some air for crissake. Needs at least a half-hour. So what's gonna happen in the meantime? Gimme some water—never mind, I'll get the water myself."

Vinnie sighed disgustedly. "Man, if you ain't a piece awork. Dom better not come in here is all I know. He sees me pourin' this for you, he's gonna shit. All over me, y'understand? And you're givin' me lip." He turned away and found a corkscrew. In moments, he'd peeled the lead and removed the cork and set the bottle on the back bar among others to make it less conspicuous.

"So I guess you think you're gonna have some too," Vinnie said to Myushkin.

"Hell no. Gallo Hearty Burgundy's good enough for me. Good enough for anybody, really, that's not bad, I'm tellin' you. Best five-dollar burgundy you can buy in this state."

"Yeah, you're right," Balzic said. "Lotta people turn up their nose when you say Gallo. But you're right about that wine. As a matter of fact, I think I'll have some of that while I'm waitin'."

Vinnie shook his head and muttered, "Gallo Hearty Burgundy, man, if youse two ain't somethin'." He poured two glasses full of the Gallo and leaned across the bar and said in his most sarcastic voice, "I certainly hope youns two don't ruin your taste buds with this while you're waitin' for the good stuff."

"I ain't gonna ruin anything," Myushkin said. "This is good stuff."

"Yeah it is," Balzic said.

"Oh what, you girlfriends now? Cheezus. This one comes in here, says I'm sorry, ou ou I'm sorry. How's come you never apologized to me, ya prick? Huh? Ya ruined my pants, I ain't heard nothin' outta ya yet."

"Hey, Vinnie, I'm sorry, okay? I'm sorry I ruined your pants. You sorry you busted my hand?"

"I didn't bust your hand, ya prick, you did that yourself—"

"Hey! Ho! Whoa! Wait a goddamn minute. Just stop right there, the both of you."

"Tell him!"

"I'm tellin' you both, knock it off."

"Yeah, right right, that's the way it goes," Vinnie said under his breath and hustling down the bar to wait on a couple of students from the community college.

Balzic turned to Myushkin. "You're never gonna learn, are you?"

"Learn what? What do I need to learn?"

"When to shut your mouth. You're an agitator."

"Hey, Mo told me I was supposed to apologize, and I did that. I should've apologized, because what I did wasn't real smart. But I'm never gonna learn what you think I oughta learn. 'Cause when people try to shit on me, I ain't never gonna shut up. 'Cause it's not just me, you know? I speak for a lotta people who don't know how to speak. I mean I hope you understand that, but I don't care if you don't. I'm not gonna go out and buy another gun, and I should've never pointed that one at you, but as long as I'm alive I'm gonna talk and I'm gonna write. 'Cause all my life I've been watchin' rich white pricks think they can shit on anybody who doesn't belong to their club. But they can never seem to remember that they're the ones who make up the rules for who gets in and who don't. You know the guys I'm talkin' about, and

243

don't say you don't. They come in every flavor, but in this country they're mostly white-bread bastards."

"You're shovelin' sand against the tide."

"Yeah, you're right, you're right, I am, but that doesn't mean I'm gonna throw my shovel away. Hey, Mo told me you like the blues. He said you play the harp, is that right?"

"I try. I been tryin' for a coupla years. I'm not any good at it. It's hard."

"You like the blues, really? No shit?"

"Yeah, some of 'em. Not all. Who likes all of everything?"

"Yeah? Well, I'm no musician, but I got somethin' here I wrote last week. Here, listen to this. You wanna hear this? Don't worry, I ain't gonna sing it, I'm just gonna read it. It's a blues. I wish I could write music, man, I'd love to be able to sing this."

Balzic took a long drink of the Gallo and shrugged. He knew he wasn't going to get out of it, Myushkin was too intense about this, whatever it was. Myushkin was too intense about everything.

Myushkin unfolded a sheet of yellow lined paper. He took a sip of his wine, cleared his throat, and shifted around. "Uh, this probably doesn't really fit the blues structure, you know, so, uh, well, lemme just read it."

"Go ahead."

"Uh, The Bottom-Liner Blues. Copyright 1992 Nicholas Matthew Myushkin.

> *Oh I ain't got no money*
> *'Cause I ain't got no job*
> *Company's been sold*
> *To the multinationals*
> *And I got the bottom-liner blues*
>
> *I used to carry some clout*
> *Used to like to dance'n shout*

244

BOTTOM LINER BLUES

Company's been sold
To the multinationals
And I got the bottom-liner blues

All my savings're gone
My unemployment too
Company's been sold
To the multinationals
And I got the bottom-liner blues

Boss had his day in bankruptcy court
Then he got leveraged out
Company's been sold
To the multinationals
And I got the bottom-liner blues

Yeah the company's been sold
To the men with no faces
To the men with no flags
'Cept when the locals go nuts
In those overseas places
Then we're all 'sposed to sign up
For the Purple Heart Club
'Cause the company's been sold
And bought and sold again
And I got the bottom-liner blues

So say g'mornin' to food stamps
Say hello to welfare
'Cause the company's been sold
Oh yes, the company's been sold
And I got the body-baggin'
Physical rehabbin'
Employment retrainin'
Attitude adjustin'
Bottom-liner blues

245

*Yes I do, I got those
Ol' bottom-liner blues."*

Balzic took another long drink of his Gallo. He drained his glass and coughed and stood up suddenly. "Excuse me," he said and bolted for the john downstairs. When he got downstairs he struggled to get into the one single stall. He was gasping and pulling at his tie, and the waves of fear, chest-pounding, throat-constricting, sternum-stabbing fear rolled over him, the Iwo Fever back in all its gruesome glory. Balzic looked at his right hand and it was doubled in a fist and then it was opening as though it belonged on somebody else's arm, and there, in the palm of his hand, as plain as plain could ever be, two dog tags, wrapped with tape so they wouldn't clink, and they were soaked in blood, but he could see through the tape, and the name was vivid and huge, the letters were spilling out over the edges of his hand, huge, blood-red letters spurting out, and the letters said "Winoski, Edward F." and there was a slashing hole where the serial number and the initials for blood type and religion should have been and then there were the letters "USMC" and Balzic fell to his knees sobbing, his shoulders shaking, "Eddie Eddie Eddie Jesus Christ Eddie god don't die Eddie don't die please god don't die Eddie oh god. . . ."

Somebody was trying to open the door to the stall, but Balzic's back was against it.

"Hey Balzic, you okay? You all right, man, you need some help?" It was Myushkin.

"Yeah yeah, I'm okay, lemme alone," he said through his sobbing.

"Well whatta you doin', man, Christ I could hear you cryin' clear upstairs."

"Hey, Mario," Vinnie said, "what the fuck's goin' on, you okay, Jesus, you scared the shit outta me, all that screamin'. You want a ambulance or what?"

246

"No nah I don't need no ambulance, Jesus Christ, just let me alone, okay? I'm okay I'm tellin ya. I just remembered somethin', that's all." He struggled to his feet and turned around and his eyes were so clouded with tears all he could see was fuzz. He couldn't tell for a few seconds which was Myushkin and which was Vinnie.

"You remembered somethin'! Musta been some fuckin' memory," Vinnie said. "You sure you're okay now, huh? I don't wanna leave you down here if you ain't—"

"I'm tellin' ya I'm all right," Balzic lied. "Go on, go upstairs, they'll be stealin' you blind up there."

"Oh shit," Vinnie said, turning and taking the steps two at a time.

Myushkin shrugged uncomfortably and coughed and said, "Hey, I didn't pretend it was the greatest blues ever written, you know, but I didn't think it was that bad—"

Balazic looked at him and said, "You're a pain in the ass, you know that? Just shut up for once in your life. Just shut up."

"Uh, so, right, I'll shut up."

Balzic looked at him. "What? I need to send you a telegram. Get the fuck outta here."

"Hey, look, I'm just tryin' to help you out, you know? Jesus Christ, you're screamin' 'Eddie Eddie Eddie Eddie,' and I come down here and you're in the crapper here on your knees, you know? I mean, I don't know what your problem is, but Christ, the last thing that happened was I was readin' somethin' I wrote, you know? I mean I gotta feel like, what the fuck did I do, you know?"

"You didn't do nothin', just get lost, okay?"

"Okay okay okay, I'm gettin' lost, Jesus," Myushkin said, backing away with his hands up.

"No. Hold it. Wait a second. It was some of the things you said, and I don't wanna repeat 'em, but . . . uh, it just brought somethin' back I haven't been, uh, I haven't thought about,

247

Jesus, I haven't been able to think of for forty, forty-five years, whatever. And you said those things and I all of a sudden thought I was gonna be sick and I came down here and . . . plain as day, right here in my hand . . . I had his dog tags in my hand, I had 'em right there in my hand. And I saw his name, this kid I went all through boot camp with and we bunked together, he was on the top rack and I was on the bottom, and he was from the Northside, and all the way across the Pacific we used to play gin and bullshit about what we were gonna do and, uh, there we were on Iwo and he was on the beach, on that fucking black shit, and one second he was right behind me and the next second . . . the top of his head . . . Jesus Christ, the top of his head was gone, and when he fell, his fucking dog tags, I couldn't even try to catch him, he went down that fast, he just dropped like a stone, and I fell down . . . I don't know why I fell down, and his fucking dog tags, somehow they were in my hand. . . ."

Balzic covered his face with his hands and once again began to sob. He sobbed and sobbed until his whole face hurt and his throat and his chest, and when he finally quit, he said, "He was my friend . . . and for forty-five fucking years I couldn't remember his name . . . and then we were up there drinkin' wine and you were, uh, you were talkin' about the blues and the Purple Heart Club and all those overseas places and it just fuckin' all came back to me. His name was Winoski. Jesus Christ I drink wine every goddamn day of my life. . . ."

"Hey, you stay here, okay?" Myushkin said. "I'll be right back."

He was back in a moment, carrying the Gattinara and two clean glasses. He gave one to Balzic and then filled them both. "Here," he said, holding his glass aloft. "Here's to why you drink wine every day."

Balzic sobbed again, twice, then shook his head hard. "Take it easy, man, okay? Take it easy, I gotta stop cryin' here, I mean, my whole fuckin' body hurts. So don't say anything for a while, okay? Please?"

"Sure. You got it. Silence. For once in my life."

They drank the bottle, the 1987 Gattinara, thanks to the talented hands of Vinnie, in silence, in the men's room in the basement of Dom Muscotti's saloon. When they finally went upstairs, Dom Muscotti was waiting for them. He was scowling. But when he saw Balzic and looked at the empty bottle in Myushkin's hand, Muscotti took the empty from Myushkin and disappeared into the back room. When he returned, he had another bottle of Gattinara. And the four of them drank that, Balzic, Myushkin, Vinnie, and Dom.

"I hear you're cleanin' cars now," Muscotti said after they had passed a long time in silence.

Myushkin looked at Muscotti. "Yeah. That's what I'm doin' for money now."

"Well, you keep drinkin' this stuff, you better hope there's lotsa dirt out there."

Vinnie howled. "Man, are we in Rocksburg or not? That's Rocksburg's nickname, for crissake. Dirt."

"Not anymore it isn't," Myushkin said. "This place is as clean as Pittsburgh. You don't get dirty cars the way you used to. You want real Pittsburgh dirt you ain't gonna get it from a bunch of bureaucrats shufflin' data bases."

"Shufflin' what? Data what?"

"Papers, Vinnie, shufflin' papers. Only now they do it inside computers. Same difference. Computers is just a new piece of machinery to get depreciated on the corporate tax schedules, that's all."

"He writes songs too," Balzic said, hoisting his glass aloft. "Here's to your blues. I hope you find somebody can put it to music."

"Hey, me too," Myushkin said. "I ain't gonna hold my breath, but I'll drink to that. Why not."

249

"I hope so too," Muscotti said. "'Cause these two bottles gonna cost you everything you made today."

Myushkin looked at Balzic, and Balzic looked back. "You can't win," Balzic said.

Myushkin got his seventy-five dollars out and put it on the bar in front of Muscotti, who pushed it toward Vinnie.

"Hey, lotsa dirt out there. May not be real dirt, but what the hell. The goddamn Steelers and Pirates been playin' on phony dirt ever since they tore down Forbes Field. And you know what they put in there, Balzic, huh? Right about where the left field bleachers used to be?"

Balzic frowned and tried to remember.

"A goddamn library," Myushkin said. "That's where the University of Pittsburgh put their goddamn Hillman Library."

Until that moment, Balzic thought it was going to be a long time before he had a good laugh again, but there he was, laughing in spite of himself. "You're relentless," he said to Myushkin. "I mean it, you are relentless. He's relentless. I mean it, the sonofabitch is relentless."

"Got to be."

U.D. SELLERS LIBRARY, UPPER DARBY, PA
ADMY M   1993
Constantine, Bottom liner blues /

3 9845 0605 3954 4

ept

d

M

Constantine   207226

Bottom liner blues

UPPER DARBY TOWNSHIP &

SELLERS MEMORIAL FREE

PUBLIC LIBRARY